# CROSSING BORDERS AND GENERATIONS

*One Man's Journey To Search For His*

*Ukrainian, Greek, And*

*Bulgarian Roots*

## Kiril Kirstoff

# Dedication

As my final statement, I would like to clarify that, though this story is fiction, it is, in no way, a fairy tale. Those of my readers looking for a history or travel book could go to the history section in their local library, where they will find one very authentic history of Bulgaria.

All characters' names have been changed to protect my loved ones' privacy. A few of them are no longer among the living–and I hope if they are looking down from the "balcony of heaven," they wouldn't mind.

The events depicted in this story are inspired by personal struggles and triumphs. Though the events in the story may not be actual, the lessons it imparts are profoundly accurate. I attribute all credit, first and foremost, to Our Father in Heaven - GOD. Without his boundless and everlasting gifts and love, I wouldn't have the ability to pen this book, nor would I have the substance to nourish my body and mind, granting me the strength to conceive it.

I would also like to send my love to my wife, Vessy.

No amount of book dedications, flowers, or romantic nights could ever make up for what you have given me. The most I can do is love you as long as I live.

Secondarily, I extend my heartfelt gratitude to my grandfather, Georgiy, the patriarch and progenitor of the

Kakhovskiy family. Additionally, I am indebted to my parents — Hristo and Ruska — who showered me with love, patience, and unwavering support, making countless sacrifices that paved the way for my journey.

Third, I owe a debt of gratitude to my in-laws, Kolyo and Paraskeva Stoychevi, whose inspiration and encouragement have sustained me during the most challenging moments of my life.

Finally, but by no means least, I want to express my deepest gratitude to my children. Kris, your ideas have been invaluable to shaping this story, and I cannot fathom what it would be like without your input. Thank you, Nina and Julie—you've made me stronger and fulfilled my "American Dream" beyond anything I could have envisioned. You three are the shining lights of my life. I love you and will always be here for you to the moon and back.

To my family in the future, which I cannot yet thank: I hope that this book brings you both guidance and pride.

# Foreword

"CROSSING BORDERS and GENERATIONS" and "AFTERLIFE STORIES MY GRANDPA TOLD ME" narrate an unexpected voyage bridging Heaven and Earth, unveiling our lost family history.

The narratives traverse our physical and spiritual borders, spanning generations, cultures, and ideologies, interweaving tales of emigration and international exploration.

"CROSSING BORDERS and GENERATIONS" is a historical fiction memoir in which names, characters, places, and incidents are products of the author's imagination or used fictitiously. Any resemblance to actual events, locales, or persons, living or dead, is entirely coincidental.

A Testimony of Faithfulness to God, this memoir chronicles the family history spanning four generations across the Old and New World. It's dedicated to the memory of Captain Georgiy Kakhovskiy, the author's great-grandfather, who migrated from Kakhovka, Ukraine, in the Russian Empire to Ljubimetz, Bulgaria, in the Balkans in 1878. Following his ancestor's footsteps, George embarked on his journey to America in 1952, precisely 460 years after discovering the New World.

"CROSSING BORDERS and GENERATIONS" marks an astounding, stunning, and awe-inspiring narrative..."

Angel Kolev, the President of the Bulgarian Writers League in America, commends the work for its profound exploration of heritage and migration.

*"For the dreamers and do-gooders. For the weirdos, outsiders. For the curious ones who have the guts to be different and adventurous_ This historical fiction story of an immigrant is for you."*

Kiril Kristoff

Who are you? For the Bulgarians, you are an American, yet for the Americans, you are an immigrant with Bulgarian roots. Sometimes, you linger as the passenger aboard the original flight from Paris to New York, from the old airport 70 years ago. Yes, the outset was daunting. George encountered numerous closed doors in Sofia but stood resolute, recognizing that yielding to fear and retreating home would equate to defeat.

He couldn't come back. He committed treason. If he wanted to succeed, he had to burn the bridges to his past to escape.

He had to believe in the future.

Today, we read tales of talented Bulgarian writers. For the immigrant's reality, the battle for survival is "pearls in the mud." Real and miserable!

George always believed that to craft something beautiful, something authentic, he needed to use the ink of blood from his wounds. He had to sit in front of his computer and sense that he was metaphorically bleeding. Only when the final word had passed, and pain and anguish had become a shared experience in his life, could his writing be a genuine success.

America was an "enigma" to our generation, a life mystery we couldn't quite explain but had to navigate in our unique ways. After the fall of 1989 and the collapse of the wall, many Bulgarians resembled hungry sharks, confined in the Communist-Controlled aquarium, suddenly set loose into the treacherous and untamed ocean. Each person had to find their own way of coping. In my personal experience, unless you had someone to guide you from the start, life as an immigrant was a tragedy. You were thrust into one ordeal after another. Overall, one had to endure several painful phases of adaptation:

*The emotional pain from being separated from your parents, your siblings and close friends, and your country.*

The uncertainty is due to starting a life abroad, literally from scratch.

The painful sorrow is because of missing everything you knew before and being rejected for everything you tried before you were finally adopted.

This book represents the life of six generations, highlighting family members who are steadfast in identifying themselves as good 'Bulgarians,' particularly Ukrainians. George hails from a Russian noble family rooted in Kakhovka, Ukraine. Within this historical narrative of two brothers, Georgiy Kakhovskiy emerges as a figure determined to uphold family traditions while remaining loyal to the Russian czar, symbolizing the grand empire that influenced a nation as small as Bulgaria and defeated the triumphed over the fading Ottoman Empire in the Balkans.

Remarkably, Captain Georgiy, the protector of his Christian brethren, settled his family in the shadow of the two mightiest empires, straddling the borders between Bulgaria, Greece, and Turkey. This decision starkly contrasted with his brother, Vasiliy Kakhovskiy, who harbored revolutionary fervor, actively engaging in the tumultuous events of the October Russian Revolution in 1917. Vasiliy emerged as a staunch Bolshevik leader and Stalin's red commissar in the USSR, playing a pivotal role in shaping Socialism in Bulgaria following the conclusion of World War II in September of 1944. The family name was altered to Kakhovskiy to embrace their new identity, reflecting a desire to assimilate more seamlessly into Bulgarian culture. However, Georgiy Kakhovskiy was among the "lost generation," forced to emigrate from Bulgaria during the communist regime's grip. He ultimately sought refuge in America in 1948, where he adopted George Kakhovskiy.

Like a boomerang, the next generations in his grandson will return to Socialism, a value he always tried to escape.

One day, he returned to his birth country after the fall of the Berlin Wall, where he unearthed the missing fragments of his ancestors' generational history. These revelations he shares with his grandson, Alex, against the backdrop of peculiar changes sweeping through America following its 2020 US Elections.

I firmly believe that my story is a compelling narrative, chronicling the unique struggles that I've overcome in pursuit of a brighter future. It is a testament to the true essence of bravery, sacrifice, perseverance, determination, and, perhaps most importantly, love. For many, this tale will offer newfound perspectives as I guide them beyond their comfort zones. For others, it may guide them to steer their lives and personal paths toward improvement.

I anticipate and hope my readers will be from all walks of life. Regardless of one's origin or purpose, I am sure this story can tell—or contribute to—a universal truth.

More than anything, I hope this book makes readers think more critically about their freedom, specifically. I know that at least one reader will understand that, though they, as humans, are entitled to freedom, it is still a great privilege they've been given to live under it and that such a thing is— in no way— free.

# Introduction

*Crossing Borders and Generations: One Man's Journey to Search for His Ukrainian, Greek, and Bulgarian Roots* is Kiril Kristoff's memoirs, spanning historical fiction, time travel, afterlife exploration, and the immigrant experience, are woven from the fabric of his own memories. The book delves into the intricate tale of the Kakhovskiy family, focusing on their trials and triumphs as immigrants in Brighton Beach, New York, and the City of Chicago.

This narrative is a timeless tale of an immigrant grandfather finding his place in Brighton Beach, New York. While it may appear short and straightforward, its significance extends far beyond that moment. Delving into the journey of George's family to America, the story explores the sacrifices and challenges they faced, ultimately shaping the trajectory of their family history—for better or for worse.

The story begins with George and his unwavering faith in his grandfather, Georgiy, and the revered military icon of Saint George. George shares with his grandson the profound significance of the icon and its storied history just before embarking on an otherworldly journey triggered by a harrowing car accident.

As they battle for survival in a coma, both George and Alex are granted a unique opportunity to journey through their family's history, as well as George's own. Throughout this extraordinary experience, George guides Alex, unraveling the significance of each moment and its profound implications. Alex gains insight into the challenges, conflicts, and triumphs that shaped George and his lineage, paving the way for Alex's present existence. From a younger, newly immigrated George, Alex learns the true meaning of perseverance and diligence with an open heart.

# Prologue

The roads in this story originate from a fiery place on our beautiful planet—a point shrouded in darkness yet illuminated throughout the centuries. Positioned at a picturesque crossroad, this point witnessed the ebb and flow of war and peace. It became a thoroughfare for countless souls during great migrations, saturating its soil with their blood.

Civilizations flourished and perished on these lands. Here, the fires of once-invincible armies were extinguished. Mountains echoed under the hooves of mounted knights bearing a cross on their chests in the name of their faith.

Legends of Thracians and Ancient Greece rustle through the mountains and forests. The muffled sound of galley oars slicing through the waves reverberates in the deep, black night.

I will recount the tale of this fiery place, shaken by centuries of human tragedies that have seeped into the soil. I will narrate the story of a land ablaze with the flames of unwavering hope.

Amidst such grandeur, I will divulge something seemingly insignificant: the fate of a humble family and their struggle for survival.

I will recount the destiny of a young boy armed only with hope.

I will unveil the unparalleled cruelty of an ideology cloaked in the guise of utopia: a communist tyranny that stifled individual thought and tarnished human fulfillment.

I will narrate a story that demands true strength to unearth from the ashes of history.

Having reached an age where I can document the tales of those with the power of will—the power to carve their own destiny and defend it—I am compelled to share this narrative.

"The longest journey is the journey inwards. Of he who has chosen his destiny and embarked upon his quest for the source of his being."

"The American Dream" is a phrase often used to encapsulate the essence of this great nation.

Though the interpretation may vary, the core remains unchanged. It embodies a land of freedom, life, liberty, and the pursuit of happiness! A life dedicated to freedom and liberation from the world's misfortunes.

This is an extraordinary tale of how a Bulgarian-American immigrant family's heritage exemplifies the American dream's ideals. It explores the bond between a grandfather and his grandson and the conflicting ideologies of his great-grandfather and brother, spanning a century of tumultuous events.

At the heart of this narrative lies an unexpected journey that leads the elderly George and his grandson back to their motherland.

At eighteen, George immigrated to New York City in the United States, leaving behind his home, family, friends, language, culture, and ideals.

George encountered numerous challenges in his quest for self-discovery in this new capitalist world. However, in 1989, following the fall of the Berlin Wall, both grandfather and grandson freely returned to George's homeland.

# Table of Contents

# Chapter 1:

# Why Tennis?

"Why did it have to be tennis?" George pondered, poring over maps for his grandson's upcoming tennis competition the next day, seated in his office. Alex, his grandson, had offered to set him up with a digital map app on his phone, claiming it would be more convenient than the "old-school" maps George preferred. But George deemed himself too old for such technology. Traditional maps had guided him through the old country and all the way to America, and he believed they would suffice for his needs in the autumn years of his life.

The trip had been sprung on him at the last minute, or so it felt to his aging mind. Nicolay, his son, had called two days ago, asking George if he could drive Alex to a tennis competition. Nicky had become engrossed in a work project and no longer had enough time in his schedule for the trip. George scoffed at the idea.

"What a foolish boy," he thought. "Never keeping track of his time. His American mind never learned that time is his most precious gift!"

Despite Nicky approaching middle age, George always saw his son as a young child needing old-world discipline.

Of course, George agreed to the trip. After all, he had nothing better to do the next day, and spending time with Alex seemed like a good idea. He loved his grandson, but as Alex grew into a full-fledged teenager, resembling more and more a man, he appeared to George like a strange, alien creature from a different world and time.

"Bah," George muttered aloud. He hadn't come this far and endured so much in America to lose his progeny to changing cultures and generational norms. If necessary, he'd bridge the gap with Alex even if it meant driving back to the Old Country.

Still, he couldn't shake his disbelief at the idea of tennis. In Eastern Europe, back in his day, that was considered a woman's sport. But times had changed, and George had to adapt.

Having mapped out what appeared to be a successful route, George folded the map neatly and set it down on his desk. With nothing else to do, he glanced around his office.

George's so-called "office" was a small garage filled with tools he had used as a handyman. It served as his sanctuary from the female company. Above his desk hung a haphazard collection of Bulgarian, Russian, and Greek native folk souvenirs.

They were surrounded by old family photographs, postcards stamped from Italy, France, Moscow, and Kyiv, and landscape pictures of the Black Sea Riviera and Balkan Mountains. George's first American passport was at the heart of this collection, encased in a reasonably priced yet dignified polished wood frame. He displayed it on the page adorned with the most stamps and visas from the various countries he had visited. Notably, the US entry asylum visa is prominently featured on the document's front page, proudly showcased in his office.

On the left wall of his office hung a map of the world, adorned with red flags marking the countries he dreamt of visiting with his grandson. Adjacent to it was a bucket list and travel-themed art décor.

*"Well! I haven't been everywhere, but it's on my list,"*

George would say. He had activities to cross off his bucket list this year.

His eyes continued to wander. On the wall to his right were photographed from Trieste of him and Mia before their wedding in Italy. The two were engaged before George was cleared to arrive in New York City, and they had to break off their engagement.

Trieste was renowned for its refugee asylum center, located directly on the border between Italy and Yugoslavia. This center provided refuge to those fleeing from Communism in Eastern Europe.

"Though, had Trieste been part of Italy then?"

He rubbed his chin. Was it still Austria? Or Yugoslav? Or an independent city-state before being absorbed into Italy? The city seemed to change hands more frequently than the village whore.

But regardless of its tumultuous history, there he stood with Mia by his side. He wore a simple but elegant brown suit, all he could afford aside from the true centerpiece of the picture—the beautiful and intricate white dress adorning Mia. Though the dress was stunning, Mia had skillfully altered it after purchasing it from the Italian "Salvation Army" thrift stores. The two of them stood arm in arm, the glistening waters of the Adriatic providing the backdrop. It was a scene worthy of the most luxurious settings, with the "Savoia Excelsior Palace Trieste" looming behind them.

On the left side of his office wall, he displayed a map of the world marked with flags indicating the countries he hoped to visit one day with his grandson. Adjacent to this map were several framed photographs of their grandchildren, with a mix of infant and childhood snapshots, though most were now in their teens.

Born in 1932, George considered himself part of the great "lost generation" that emerged from the communist era. He also identified with the "silent, traditionalist" generation, which followed the "greatest generation" in the West and preceded the "baby boomers."

On his wall were pictures of The Godfather Paradox and photos of Al Pacino and Robert De Niro in the first two Godfather films, which stand as two of the greatest films ever. The movie introduced iconic lines into American vocabulary, such as "I'm gonna make him an offer that he can't refuse."

The name "Silent Generation" is believed to originate from this generation's perceived silence. In other words, they came of age during the McCarthyism era, a time of hardship when it was often deemed wiser to remain silent.

Despite being labeled the Silent Generation due to their lack of public protest, they have allowed their accomplishments to speak for themselves.

Next to those pictures were a few more framed photographs of their grandchildren, mostly in their teens, along with some infant and childhood photos. Among them was a picture of George and Maria, his Italian wife whom he had met on Brighton Beach in Brooklyn's "Little Russia" (though George preferred "Little Odessa"). Adjacent to it was another framed image from a few years later, capturing the whole extended family gathered in Chicago. Maria, Nicky, Margarita, Alexander, Mary, Ellen, George Jr., and George stood in a close, familiar circle, with the Sears Tower towering above the city skyline behind them.

Notably, there was a beautiful photo of George's son, Nicky, and his wife, Margarita, in front of La Louvre from their younger days, before Alex's time. The most luxurious frame held a photo of George standing proudly in front of his newly opened shop, "Nicky's Auto Repair," the first shop he had opened on Coney Island Avenue in Brighton Beach.

Adjacent to the photos was a picture of him and Maria standing beside the Sears Tower. Did they call it something else now? The Willis Tower, perhaps? George frowned. Damn, Americans are constantly changing the names of their famous buildings. No wonder Alex and his American friends knew next to nothing about geography.

Turning his attention to his desk, George felt somewhat nervous about the next day's trip. He heard Maria's voice in the morning: "George, dear. Be careful; tomorrow is Friday the 13th." Maria was somewhat superstitious about such "unlucky days," though George couldn't reasonably determine why. Sure, the trip bore the risk of awkwardness between him and his grandson, who undoubtedly thought his old grandpa wasn't "cool" or whatever. But George had endured far worse than awkward silences between generations. So why was he nervous? Unable to find an answer, George cleaned his desk, finding his papers a bit more messy than he'd wanted.

He had learned long ago, during a youth in another world, that order was sometimes all one could carry through chaos. Gathering a few random papers, he began organizing them to be filed into the old cabinets across from his desk. As he moved the papers, he uncovered an old notebook stashed on the far-left side of his desk, almost at risk of falling. Without hesitation, George grabbed it and held it in his right hand, examining it closely before opening it.

Inside, he discovered an old Russian army bronze icon of St.

George the Conqueror, adorned with the initials "GK" engraved in the Cyrillic alphabet—the very same icon he had inherited from his grandfather and namesake, Captain Georgiy Kakhovskiy.

In his treasury box, George found a 400-year-old single silver ruble and an antique 1880 silver coin (20 kopeks) from Emperor Alexander II, a gift from his grandfather. These were valuable relics, his key to the front door of his house on "Tsar Liberator" street, which he had taken before escaping the border. The magic of a child's imagination led him to believe that each time he turned the key in times of need, something new would happen the next day. Between the icon of St. George and the silver ruble, it was a combination that unlocked a doorway to magical opportunities for him. He believed his grandpa and Saint George would always watch over him.

These relics were tangible connections to the past and the world he had come from, cherished by elders in the Old Country who believed St. George was their guardian. Was his own grandfather now sitting alongside his saintly namesake in heaven, looking down on him?

George rubbed his chin and gazed out the small window of his office, running his other hand across the St. George icon. In the back of his mind, a thought lingered—a notion that his grandfather, upon passing into the next life, had created a spiritual portal, leaving his soldier icon behind as a point of faith for those like

George to maintain their connection to the past. He had clutched that icon when he miraculously escaped to the other side of the Maritsa River on the Bulgarian-Greek border, and he had held onto it through countless hardships in his new life in the USA.

What if this icon was indeed a connection to the spiritual realm, gifted by his grandfather and a long-dead saint who watched over him? And if so, what did George have to pass on to Alex?

"As if Alex even needs the luck of the kind I had to call on, George thought, though he immediately felt guilt over allowing it into his head."

George carefully placed the icon and the notebook back on his desk, taking extra care this time, and continued surveying the room. He had ensured that his office was adorned with links to the past more than any other room in his house.

The reason for this, he wasn't entirely sure, though he believed it might have something to do with a need for deeper motivation in this setting. It was as if he needed constant reminders of where he had come from and why he needed to keep pushing forward into the future.

The walls were pictures of Nicky and Margarita, newly wedded at the "Le Tour Eiffel" in Paris and later at Lake Vevey in the Swiss Alps. Views from Sofia, Istanbul, London, Paris, Jerusalem, Israel, and finally, New York City adorned the walls, forming a crude timeline. Closer to his desk were more modern

1980s photos showcasing Monaco, Nice, the French Riviera, the Alps of Northern Italy, Southern France, Switzerland, Croatia, and Slovenia. Photographs of his grandchildren, around the ages of ten and eleven, were also prominently displayed, some showing the children sitting next to a visibly older George.

Shaking off the nostalgia, George reminded himself to focus on the present. He needed to plan his road trip for the next day. Thankful that he could still drive at his age, he hoped it would give him something to talk about with his grandson—something other than tennis.

The following day, George arrived at Nicky's house early. It was a winter day, with roads still bearing the remnants of snow and ice. Stepping out of the car to greet Alex, George noticed the abnormal gait in his grandson's walk. At sixteen, Alex had injured his right knee while escaping through the Bulgarian-Greek border. Though George had learned to deal with the discomfort in his younger years, as he grew older, the pain became unbearable. Refusing the orthopedic surgeon's recommendation for a total knee replacement, George saw his injured knee as a souvenir from the old world—a reminder of his hardships. With Alex and his mother trailing behind, they proceeded to the car.

"You're sure you can drive in this, George?" his daughter-in-law asked while bringing young Alex's things to George's car.

It was rare for George to be addressed by his American name

– George – reminiscent of George Washington. Most of the time, his beloved wife Maria referred to him by his title in the motherland: Georgiy. Though imperfectly, she understood the immigrant's struggle, having shared much of it by his side.

George waved his hand dismissively. "I'm from Eastern Europe, remember," he said with a laugh. "Compared to the winters I've lived through, we might as well be in the Caribbean now."

Alex's mother hugged her son while Nicky spent a few minutes fitting Alex's tennis gear into the trunk of George's small car.

"Dear Lord, George thought to himself. How much luggage does a boy need for a tennis competition?"

Within an hour, the two cruised along the interstate, with Alex occupying the passenger seat next to George. As George had anticipated, an awkward silence settled between them. Alex spent most of the drive engrossed in his phone, his fingers dancing across the screen in a flurry of activity. Meanwhile, George focused on the road ahead, stealing occasional glances at the young man beside him, feeling a paternal urge to ensure his well-being.

After a while, it seemed Alex grew weary of whatever had captured his attention on his phone. He sat the device on his lap, sighed, and gazed out the passenger-side window. Taking this as an opportune moment to break the silence, George cleared his throat and initiated a conversation.

"So," George began. "I am looking forward to seeing you play tennis tomorrow." This was a lie, though George thought God would forgive him. "I'm sorry I have missed your past matches, but I am excited to see what you have in store for me on the… court."

George thought that was the correct term. Next to him, Alex cringed slightly, though George couldn't be sure if that was due to an incorrect term or just a reflexive reaction to the lingering traces of an Old World accent in his grandfather's voice.

The boy shrugged. "I'm not that good," he mumbled. "Probably won't win."

"But you're trying," his grandfather said. "To stand tall, even in defeat, is the real triumph."

Alex shrugged once more, remaining silent. Again, the car fell silent, and George focused on the road ahead. The interstate was unusually quiet, with few other vehicles in sight, likely due to the perceived "bad" weather that had deterred most potential drivers.

George chuckled to himself. "Hmm! Silly Americans. If only they could see a real Russian winter."

"Hey, Grampa, what's that?" Alex asked next to him. George moved his eyes toward where his grandson had gestured.

Hanging from the rearview mirror was the same icon George had discovered in his notebook the day before. He couldn't quite explain why he had decided to bring it along on the trip and display it so prominently. Perhaps he had hoped it would prompt a meaningful conversation between himself and his grandson. If that was his intention, then it seemed the icon was fulfilling its purpose. George silently offered a prayer of gratitude.

"That's St. George," George said. "Not your grandfather, but the original George. He was a Roman soldier and guard of Emperor Diocletian. In those days, Diocletian persecuted Christians in the Roman Empire. But George converted to Christianity, and as a result, he was martyred." Alex did not look particularly thrilled to be given a history lesson.

"Some legends also say that he slew a dragon. Anyway, that icon was given to me by my grandfather, Captain Georgiy Kakhovskiy, during his service with the Russian army."

"Lotta George's," Alex responded carelessly.

"Well, it's a lucky name, as your grandfather can attest. But anyway, my grandfather believed that the icon gave him a direct connection to God and kept him safe during his army days. I've tried to carry that on."

Next to him, Alex shrugged again. "I only know one god and that's me."

George pursed his lips, searching for a new angle to steer the conversation. Meanwhile, as he drove, he tuned the radio to a classical music channel playing Tchaikovsky's Nutcracker.

"You know," he started, "I questioned everything, too, at your age. When I was sixteen, my grandpa gave me a Bible, which was illegal in the Communist state. It was his original Ukrainian copy. I read it and found myself searching for answers within its pages."

"Look out, Grandpa!"

Alex's sudden shout jolted George out of his thoughts, momentarily forgetting he was behind the wheel. His aching legs refused to respond swiftly, hindering his ability to hit the brakes. As he turned to look through the windshield, he noticed a car sliding on the icy road, hurtling towards them in the oncoming lane. Despite his efforts to react, the impending collision felt inevitable.

With a surge of panic, George grasped the wheel tightly and attempted to stomp on the brake pedal, but it was too late. In the blink of an eye, the car thundered with the force of the impact. The windshield shattered, the hood crumpled, and the St. George icon hanging from the rearview mirror vanished from sight amidst the chaos as darkness enveloped everything.

# Chapter 2:
## Circumstances Beyond Control

George knew he was in the air but had no idea where or how he was floating. Everything George encountered seemed connected to him, to live inside of him. Fortunately, however, he appeared to be embedded in everything.

He was floating; he was sure of that, though where and how he was floating, he didn't know. It was a profound feeling within George; all beings and life seemed to be connected to him, within him. But just as well, it seemed he was within all things.

George stopped breathing, but he was aware of that; George was aware of everything he was doing, so he kept breathing after a second, but the breathing seemed to blur everything, so he stopped again.

Despite ceasing to breathe, George felt fine; it resolved itself effortlessly. The world around him was not engulfed in darkness; instead, it was characterized by a murky ambiance punctuated by indistinct, irregularly dispersed lights. It wasn't entirely dark but enshrouded in a hazy atmosphere, with lights manifesting in erratic patterns.

The kind of lights that dance and merge behind one's eyelids just before falling into sleep. He didn't know if he still had a body, but if he did, it was weightless.

Alex went back to his last moment of thought in the car. He leaned against the car window and watched the scenic landscape and views.

Alex kept pondering: "I am so happy and grateful to be in a warm car. Tomorrow, I'll have a tennis match with the famous Brooklyn-Russian player in the same age group. I close my eyes to enjoy the divine music."

George thought, "My grandson has had his first taste of competitive sport – and he loves it at 17!" The number one sport in the world! Alex was chubby and 6'2". Tall, but not fat. So, his father signed him in to play after meeting National tennis player Gregor Dimitrov In the district of Haskovo, Bulgaria.

After this game, if he wins, Alexander should be moving up in the ranking list. He was in 66th place in the Junior National Boys' Championships in the USA! The Bulgarian tennis player Grigor Dimitrov, born at the beginning of the 1990s, was his idol.

Highest ranking - Top # No. 3 (20 November 2017), making him the highest-ranked Bulgarian player in history. This year, Grisho, from the district of Haskovo, Bulgaria, climbed to the...top of the world ......Fuhgeddaboudit!

What then happened interrupted George's peaceful contemplation–A car crash! The car was driving perfectly fine. In another moment, the vehicle was disemboweled.

The collision's aftermath destroyed the car and reduced it to a metal skeleton. Its once-intact body was now torn apart, with shattered glass strewn both inside and outside of the vehicle. The metal framework was contorted and twisted, making it unrecognizable. If there had been any passengers in the car, they would have been unidentifiable due to the deployment of the airbags.

George squeezed whatever served as Alex's hand in this strange state of existence. However, once he gazed down, he could see himself dead, but he could hear Tchaikovsky, his favorite composer. "The Song of the Lark" was playing faintly; he could listen to the light trills come out as though they were being played right before him. The song seemed to speak briefly and tell George, "Everything's going to be all right." He could also hear the sounds of the ambulances coming. He could listen to Tchaikovsky on the car's radio when he gazed down from the top.

"Grandpa?" The voice seemed to come from everywhere at once, echoing softly in George's ears. It was Alex. Despite the chaos around him, George's paternal instinct surged at the faint trace of fear in his grandson's voice. He felt Alex's presence beside him and sensed the distance that separated them.

Either they were dead, and the oaths of the fathers are eternal, or else he retained his grandfatherly instincts in whatever body he had left.

"Yes, Alex?" George heard himself say in a soft, calming voice. He wasn't sure if he moved his mouth or if any air came streaming out of his lungs (or, really, if he even had lungs anymore), but his voice resonated through their strange space.

"Where—where are we?" Alex asked from somewhere and nowhere.

Everything was so perfect!

"What the heck happened? Bozhe moi! Goodness Gracious!"

Upon witnessing the accident, the first driver promptly stopped and reported it via 911. Subsequently, the dispatcher dispatched the first ambulance crew, which rushed to the hospital.

George tried to open his eyes, thinking his vision was impaired or blurred from an injury, though he wasn't sure if they even were closed to begin with. Still, the strange, dancing colors and lights around his vision looked like they were merging into something solid. Or, at least, something with enough form and depth to mimic something solid.

The lights solidified until George could see the paramedics swarming him and his grandson. One young man in the swarm said, "There's no pulse! He's dead." They continued CPR and defibrillation until a face of ever-so-slight relief overcame every single person around them. Of course, neither George nor his grandson was conscious yet, but they were alive.

They were unconscious or alive! Probably, they were comatose. Who knows what is going on?

"Hurry Up!" I called the dispatcher on the radio, "Bring them to Lutheran Medical, Level One trauma center!" Someone cries.

They were pronounced dead before they arrived at the hospital!

First responders arrived at the accident scene fast!

Both victims were entrapped in the front seats.

"Use your spreader and clutter for car removal extrication!" screamed the approaching firefighter.

"Well, Alex," George said. His voice seemed to stream directly from his mind to Alex's. George didn't know if others were sharing this strange space with them or if they could hear him. Or if that line of communication was exclusive to just grandfather and grandson. "I admit that I am not sure where we are. But we're together, at least," George thought. George had a feeling, in some distant sense, that Alex was close to him, be it in body or soul.

But somewhat together.

"What–what happened?" Alex asked. He still sounded somewhat frightened, but George could pick up a slight easing in his voice as if he had succeeded in his grandfatherly duty of calming his grandson's nerves. George felt himself smile, though whether that was in body or mind, he didn't know.

"What the heck happened?" he still wanders.

"We were driving," Alex continued. "We were talking; I remember that. You – you showed me something. On the dashboard..."

"Sveti Georgiy Pobedonosets—St. George the Victorious," George said suddenly.

"Yes," Alex said. "I remember that. The icon. And then...then..."

"St George," George repeated, "This is his doing."

George envisioned Alex's hand gradually drifting towards his own. He reached for it with whatever hand or body part he possessed.

"Yes, my boy, this is Saint George's doing."

"What do you mean?" Alex asked.

"I always thought that the St. George medal, given to me by my grandfather, had forged some path to the spiritual world. The old Saint must have come through for us!" In front of him and all around, George witnessed the lights persistently merging and solidifying, gradually forming into tangible structures. They appeared to be transforming into buildings, stark against the gray light of a winter's day.

The winter sun of the old country, George thought. He felt Alex's hand touch him, and he grasped it gently. "Are, are we dead?!"

Alex stammered.

"I don't know," George said. Then, "Are you afraid, Sasha?"

Alex was silent for a few seconds. "I – I don't know. It's weird." "If I had to guess," George said. "I would lean toward us not being dead. At the very least, not quite ready to pass into eternity just yet."

"Why?" Alex asked.

George experienced a mix of fear and happiness; his arthritic right knee, a reminder of the 1948 border injury, was now free of pain. He felt as if he were on top of the world, able to bend and jump with the agility of a sixteen-year-old—much like Alex, who was in peak physical condition.

"I think we have something to see," George said. "Look, do you see ahead of us?"

In front of him, the lights blended and merged into a more complete scene. It was a city marked by dark, red-brick buildings and gray clouds. Byzantine architecture's recognizable spires and domes define the familiar facades of Christian Orthodox Churches. He saw gentle snow falling from the gray clouds above, caught in a soft sea breeze and thrown into twirling dances and spins in the soft, frosty air.

Yeah, the worm-fresh air of the Aegean Sea.

In Sofia, the winter was bitterly cold, influenced by the

presence of Vitosha Mountain.

"What the heck just happened?" Alex repeated in wonder.

"I – I see it," Alex said. "What is this place? Where are we?" "This is Bulgaria," George said. Though he hadn't seen the landscape in decades, his memory came pouring back with the speed and force of a flash flood.

"Bulgaria?" Alex said.

"Yes," George replied, "The great city of Sofia. The second oldest capital of Europe, next to Athens, Greece.

The motto of the capital of Bulgaria, Sofia, is "ever-growing, never aging."

Before him stood a grand church building, distinguished by its gray brick construction and expansive Byzantine domes. These architectural elements rose and melded together, creating a singular and almost mystical structure.

"Sveta Nedelya Church," he thought.

In the background, he observed the recognizable, snow-capped peak of Vitosha Mountain rising from the horizon, barely visible against the backdrop of gray clouds.

On 16 April 1925, Inside the church, in this bloody Easter, six hundred souls had gathered for the funeral service of a general who had been assassinated two days earlier by a Communist terrorist.

Remember 9/11 in New York City? Terrorist acts that I will never forget!

The assassination had been merely a pretext for the actual attack, which targeted the government of Tsar Boris III. However, he wouldn't be present at the funeral.

George remembers that his parents had always been religious during the atheistic regime. His mother stood her ground when a young Komsomol guard working as an undercover secret agent stopped her on the street at Easter / Vemik Den in Sofia and demanded:

"Excuse me, comrade, citizen, where are you carrying this beeswax candle?" "To church," she said.

"We commend you to put it out," the undercover communist member gangster said. 'Is it illegal to carry a church candle or go to church?' It's not just illegal. It's punishable for refusal like this; you can end up in the wrong place, prison, or lose your job.

Suddenly, the loud gong of Alexander Nevsky Cathedral's festive church bells, all hundred tons of them, resonated through the air. Before George stood the glittering Hotel Sofia while the former King's Palace loomed across him. Between them lay an empty space, once occupied by the mausoleum of the Great Leader Georgi Dimitrov, which was later destroyed after the fall of the Berlin Wall.

Three generations of bewildered school kids passed through the marble catacomb. They gazed at the mustachioed wax mummy lying inside, the "Great Leader" of the Bulgarian Communist Party.

"Remember, today we should arrive in Canada; we will be late. Today is my tennis tournament!" We should be in Montreal, Canada, by now.

Why are we in Bulgaria?" Alex asked. "Is this some heaven? Or Hell?

Despite everything, George felt himself a chuckle, though with what lungs he didn't know. "My boy, Bulgaria can be more heaven-than-hell and hell-than-heaven, sometimes both simultaneously!" George started.

"That – that doesn't make any sense," Alex said.

"Neither does Bulgaria," George said. "But this is where I spent much of my youth, back when it was still controlled by the communists. I was around your age back then. Of course, I had more to worry about than tennis matches."

"But why are we here?" Alex asked. His voice still held a degree of feat, but George thought he could also pick up something else there. A degree of wonderment and adventure. George and Alex were together in spirit, but they were also in the hospital emergency room simultaneously.

They found themselves unable to communicate with their family members. Still, they could see their bodies lying on hospital beds connected to life support systems. Despite their desperate attempts to attract attention, nobody in the bustling emergency room seemed to notice them. Doctors and nurses hurried in and out, focused solely on their assigned patients.

George couldn't comprehend why the nurses were neglecting their duties. He was taken aback to see other patients in their beds, seemingly unnoticed by the medical staff. Frustration and confusion gnawed at him. What kind of hospital allowed such negligence? What was happening?

Perhaps, he speculated, they had been relocated to the basement floor for MRI tests, and their beds were being prepared for new patients. As a nurse drew blood from his arm, George felt nothing at all. Was he still dreaming, or was something else at play?

These questions lingered as they found themselves flitting between moments in time. George observed his wife, Maria, seated next to their daughter-in-law, Margarita, attempting to console her amidst tears and blame directed at her husband, Nicky. Why hadn't he taken a day off to accompany their son to the tennis tournament?

As Maria clasped George's hand and offered prayers for his recovery, he and Alex remained unable to communicate with their loved ones. It was as though they existed in a separate dimension, isolated from the world around them.

"Grandma, I see dead people!"

Little Georgie was able to see grandfather George and his brother.

When someone dies, especially a close family member, little Georgie (five years old) doesn't know how to cope and process this great tragedy.

If you combine a child's imaginative tendency with knowledge of close relatives, I would be surprised if they didn't "see a ghost."

Margarita was thinking about calling their Orthodox priest, Father Valeriy.

Suddenly, Little Georgie said, turning to his father:

"Daddy, Grandpa George wanted me to tell you that he and Sasha are doing fine. Don't you worry!"

"Oh, how much he loved his grandpa," said Grandma Maria while hugging him and crying!

George felt the same sense of adventure and excitement on his first trip to Manhattan, his new home in America. As George put it, "afterlife" is "even more real than real," "I crossed over," and "I am finally home."

Alex came close to his mommy and stretched his arm to touch his mother's right shoulder. His arm was like a knife in a yogurt passing through the inside of her body. She didn't even react.

Alex stopped to be surprised anymore.

"Mom, don't worry, we are okay."

Alex tried to touch and hug her again, but the burst of her vivid memory of her son hit her like a heavy stone.

Alex reached out to take her right hand, but she bent and put her arms like a scared child between her knees and started to cry, "Oh my God, what happened? "Spasi, Gospodi Pomilui!" ("Lord, save us and have mercy on us")

"God, please help my boy and bring him back to safety!" Alex looked into his eyes, touching her forehead. Her pale, devastated wax face was motionless from that moment of tragedy, and just by the thought that it was over with her son, she would not see him again.

Margarita and Alex felt a strong urge to communicate despite being physically close yet separated by the vast expanse of different worlds. They were overwhelmed by the events of that morning, grappling with the inexplicable circumstances that had led them to this surreal and disorienting reality.

What the heck just happened? Bozhe Moi!

Is this a bad joke?

Someone was trying to separate them!

"I cannot explain what is happening, but I love you, Mom; I love you forever!"

The telepathic connection between two loving souls remained intact; the mere thought of Alex brought Margarita to tears as she mourned the loss of her beloved son. Despite the pain of separation, they found solace in believing they would soon be reunited in heaven.

Observing this human tragedy from the perspective of their guide from the afterlife, Captain Georgiy made several attempts to gently but firmly remind them of their schedule to follow. He commended them softly, emphasizing that they would return on unique paths. However, Alex and George remained fixated on their family, unable to tear themselves away from Maria, Margarita, and the rest of their grieving loved ones.

Captain Georgiy gave his last command to them and stopped to repeat himself, "It's time to go, boys; we have work to do. It's not your time yet. Let's go!"

At this point, the wrestler, George, gave up the fight deep inside. He understood that he needed to complete some unfinished business that his grandpa had for him.

"Don't worry, boys, we will be back."

Suddenly, little Georgie saw his grandpa's face for the last time. He turned and talked to his mother, "Mom, look to your right;

I can see them, I can see them! They will be back!"

"They just pass next to your right side. They were trying to talk to you. I cannot see them anymore!" The mother burst out in tears again.

"It's over, my dear little!" She hugged him to distract him, but little Georgie screamed, "I can't see them again! Why can't I see them, dear?!" his mother sighed.

Maria stood next to Margarita and prayed, "Blessed are the pure in heart, for they will see God." She believes that her husband's soul is around. She thought and felt in her heart that there was life behind the veil.

Rita was on the edge of crying again. Maria was calming Georgie Jr.

"Please stop traumatizing, my son! He's too young to process this great tragedy!

Rita's pale face was like wax, and she was again on the edge of tears.

Maria slowly whispered into her ears, "Don't worry, he is still alive; Sasha will be okay."

Rita jumped and said that's enough.

"I don't believe in life after death! Do you know how much I loved Alex? I cannot live apart from him."

She couldn't believe that this was happening to her family. Margarita asked for her husband.

At this moment, Nicky, Alex's father, went and asked the minister for prayer in the Lutheran hospital Chapel on behalf of his loved ones for God to be merciful to their soul and save them.

Is this the illusion of death?

An enlightening or terrifying spiritual awakening? Is it possible to exist outside or inside of your body? Having abandoned the body.

Imagination or a dream? Can the Bible mean this when it says, "And God shall wipe away all tears from their eyes, and there shall be no more death, nor sorrow, nor crying, nor shall there be any more pain: for the former things are passed away"?

"Do I have hallucinations, or do I not?"

George's heaviness bore a resemblance to the weight of evil forces at work, akin to the presence of Satan and his fallen angels, their nefarious acts of evil manifesting in myriad forms within the spiritual realms surrounding him. Just then, amidst this ominous atmosphere, he heard a terrifying whisper in his ear.

Vasiliy's ghost is here!

Both were hearing the wicked demonic laughter of Vasiliy, "Ma Ha Ha Ha Ha!"

Muhahahaha!

"Gospodi Pomilui (Lord Have Mercy on us)," he whispered.

George recited "The Lord's Prayer."

"Our Father, who art in heaven, hallowed be thy Name; thy kingdom come; thy will be done on earth, as it is in heaven." And he finished with: "In the name of the Father, and of the Son, and of the Holy Spirit."

Like the Orthodox faith, George instinctively made the sign of the Holy Cross, seeking divine protection in the face of darkness.

He couldn't shake the feeling that St. George, the legendary dragon-slayer, would confront this ancient adversary: Vasiliy, the old snake. As he pondered the nature of this evil force and its master, questions swirled in his mind. Was this "Dracula" figure a vampire, akin to the bloodsucking lamia of folklore? And who was Vasiliy, the Bolshevik, perhaps embodying the red dracula, a symbol of oppression and evil?

No one in the family knew the old story of the two brothers, Kakhovskiy, leaving George to grapple with these shadowy figures' enigmatic identities and evil intentions.

His teacher, Karl Marx, the red Vampires and Grave Diggers of Capitalism, who once died.

"A Specter is haunting Europe – the specter of Communism." So argued Marx and Engels. In 1848, at the opening of their Communist Manifesto, The line certainly had its hour of glory.

They laid him to rest in an unholy grave, taking with him the evil he wrought upon this world. Yet, history remembers only the darkness that consumed him, much like the specter that haunted Shakespeare's legends and chronicles, from Hamlet to Marx.

In the annals of history, Vasiliy emerges as a demon whose hero, Vlad the Impaler, served as the bloodthirsty inspiration for Dracula. He is depicted as a cruel red ruler, a Bolshevik tyrant, and Joseph Stalin's trusted lieutenant in the Soviet Embassy in Sofia, Bulgaria. But where did the legends of his vampiric nature originate?

According to the tales passed down through generations, Vasiliy is a vampire who sold his soul to the devil for power and control. The indomitable Brothers Kakhovskiy and Captain Georgiy are depicted as fierce warriors locked in eternal battle against Vasiliy, the vampire who cursed his brother Georgiy over a century ago.

Once a mortal, Vasiliy transformed into the Red Demon, leading the Soviet demons as a military attaché and Soviet ambassador in Sofia, Bulgaria. Legend holds that Saint George, the red dragon slayer, symbolizes hope, foretelling the day Captain Georgiy will vanquish his brother Vasiliy, his relentless and fearsome spiritual foe, and deliver his descendants from darkness.

I firmly believe that one day, St. George will triumph over him, casting Vasiliy underfoot and restoring peace to our world.

Trust in God!

George always carried his military icon of St. George the Conqueror, a symbol of protection against the demonic forces represented by Dracula, also known as the Demon Vasiliy, to safeguard himself and his descendants.

The myth of Saint George slaying the dragon has roots in stories across Europe, depicting his valor and bravery in triumphing over evil through courage.

Despite an army of evil ghosts and demons surrounding them, George and Alex sensed something ominous was looming. They knew that the Demon Vasiliy must be nearby, orchestrating malevolent intentions.

Haunted by the whisperings of ghosts from his past, George was reminded of the enduring battle between light and darkness and the eternal struggle to overcome the forces of evil with divine protection.

George turned in prayer to St. George for protection after his car accident. What we say in Bulgarian is "Bozhe Moi!" Help us! Have mercy on us! If he needed help, he'd pray to any Saint he could think of.

George asked his distant grandfather: "Grandpa George, did you remember me?" as he saw him in the vision. "Your bones and flesh are in me; I am your grandson. It's never just the two of us!

A pleading plea for assistance: Please help me; save us!"

George said, "I must admit that I do not know for sure. But if I had to speculate, I'd say St. George has something to demonstrate here."

"St. George exists?" Asked Alex.

"What a stupid question, my boy! Ask St. George for forgiveness right away! Yes, Saint George is real and always conquering evil in my life!"

George crosses himself like the orthodox: "Spasi, Gospodi Pomilui!" ("Lord, save us and have mercy on us")

In whatever sense he had in this place, George felt that Alex was squeezing his hand tighter.

"But I didn't believe in any of the saints! Or God! Or Jesus! Or the Universe, or Buddha, anything like that! Does that mean I'm going to hell!?"

George, despite everything, still felt himself smile. "My boy, if you are indeed going to hell, they will have to drag your grandfather there alongside you. But I still do not feel as if we are quite dead yet. I do feel that this is a temporary place of existence. A place for us to see what needs to be seen before returning to our world. I guess it's not my time yet to meet St. Peter at the Pearly Heavenly Gates."

"Why?" Alex asked. "What do we need to see here? We were

in the car, and we were driving and talking. You were showing me the medal; it was snowy and icy out, and there was another car and – oh no!" Alex shouted. "Watch out! We crashed! We must have crashed into the other vehicle! We're dead! We are..."

"Hush!" George said gently but with authority. Something that came across the scene had arrested his vision and attention. "Look there, that young boy coming towards us!"

The boy appeared to be around Alex's age, perhaps even younger, with the demeanor of a mature adult. Despite his youth, he walked with solemnity and poise beyond his years, his shoulders held high as if bearing the world's weight. He was dressed in an oversized, worn brown coat that appeared several sizes too big for him, adorned with patches of holes and crude attempts at repairs. His black boots seemed to be on the brink of falling apart. He wore a thick, furry cap adorned with the badge of the double-headed eagle, though it appeared to have seen better days perched atop his head.

"Grandfather's hat," George whispered to himself in wonderment.

"Who is that?" Alex asked. If George was sure he had a mouth, he knew it would have hung open just then in amazement.

"If I didn't know any better," he began. He wanted to choose his words carefully. "I would say that's me." "You?" Alex asked.

As George observed the young man walking through the snowy streets of Sofia before them, he couldn't help but notice the recognition dawning in his grandson's voice. The resemblance between the two was uncanny. The young man had sharp, bony cheeks, albeit thinner and weathered by hunger and deprivation, yet still unmistakably reminiscent of Alex's. His dark blue eyes mirrored Alex's, as did his brown hair, with stray strands peeking out from beneath his cap in a familiar manner. He even walked with a determined stride, much like Alex would when not slouching in a typical teenage manner.

"If that's you," Alex said. "Then, where are we? When are we?" George considered this. "Well, if the "me" we're seeing right now is your age, this year would be – 1948, maybe? As I said, this would be Sofia, in Bulgaria, where I lived back then." George felt Alex squeeze his hand, and George imagined his grandson's eyes scanning this strange past image in front of them with stoic wonder.

In George's mind, waves of deep, crashing memories began to wash over him with an unsettling familiarity. Despite the passage of time, longer than most lifetimes, he recognized the cityscape unfolding before him—the square, the streets of old Sofia—as if he had never left.

In the city's center, George noticed that the century-old synagogue had been revitalized, pulled from the clutches of disrepair through the generous donations of Jewish foundations in Israel.

The largest Sephardic synagogue in the Balkans and Europe stood splendid yet empty. Its grandeur was overshadowed by its lack of visibility and financial prosperity, rendering its members indistinguishable from their average struggling countrymen.

Indeed, Bulgarians had numerous concerns to contend with. They had barely recovered from the aftermath of World War I, during which they suffered significant losses, with nearly two hundred thousand lives sacrificed. Additionally, they grappled with communist terrorists and endured the oppressive tactics of the tsarist government's police force. Bulgaria was psychologically burdened, with its people preoccupied with existing challenges, leaving no room for further turmoil.

Amidst this backdrop, as the rest of Europe was deporting its Jewish populations, Hitler exerted pressure on Tsar Boris III's government to follow suit. City-dwelling Jews were displaced to rural areas and subjected to forced labor, compelled to wear the Star of David while toiling on roads and railways.

When the trains and boats were ready for deportation, ordinary Bulgarian people rose against injustice. However, due to a peculiar combination of ignorance, self-deprecation, and Semitic apathy, Bulgarians often fail to acknowledge or celebrate the fact that all 50,000 Jews in the country were saved, thanks to the courageous actions of the Bulgarian people.

Despite this lack of recognition, few are aware of the profound connection and friendship between the patriarch of the Bulgarian Orthodox Church, Archimandrite Stefan, and Chief Rabbi Daniel Zion. These two men were the actual driving forces behind the rescue operation. Chief Rabbi Daniel Zion implored the Bulgarian Jews to fast and pray, and he exerted pressure on the patriarch and the king before confronting Hitler himself. In a desperate plea, he asked Hitler to send the Bulgarian Jews to Auschwitz, but instead of granting his request, Hitler had him killed.

There are, of course, many Bulgarians like Dimitar Peshev who confront the pro-Nazi government in Sofia, Metropolitan Stefan, and Metropolitan Kiril, who are honored by Yad Vashem as Righteous Among the Nations for their personal acts of humanity and bravery.

He gazed downward and felt a sense of joy, albeit not surprising, as he beheld the snowy, sooty streets materializing beneath where his feet would be. However, he and Alex floated above it all, almost like ghosts. Ahead of them, a young George wrapped his too-large and ragged coat tightly around himself as the biting winter wind began to gust. He was walking toward a long queue of people in front of a nondescript gray concrete building in the corner of the city square. Despite standing still at the back of the line, the younger version of him drew nearer.

George realized he and Alex were drifting toward him, carried by an unseen, ethereal wind beyond their comprehension.

"I don't understand," Alex said. "Why are we seeing this?"

"Well," George began. "You are the one who is seeing this. For me, this is a memory."

"Okay." Alex managed. "Then why am I seeing this?"

"I don't know," George said. "But if old St. George wants you to see my youth played out before us, he and God must certainly have a reason for it." George squeezed whatever served as Alex's hand in this strange state of existence. "But don't worry, son. I can be your guide." Alex was silent for a moment as they drifted toward young George.

"Why is he—why are you in line?" Alex finally asked. George drew his memory back decades.

"It's a bread line," he said. "Bread line?"

"Many foods are challenging to find here. Since the communists came into power, the citizens and workers witnessed many tragic food supply crises. But nobody reads the front pages of Rabotnichesko Delo.

"Worker's Deed," the only Bulgarian daily "Worker's Newspaper" painting the "Bright Future" of the socialist paradise of the Workers' Party."

"The Last Fifty Years of Bulgarian Communism!"

George could tell that he needed to elaborate further.

"According to the coupon category, the quantities and sometimes the qualities differed. The sick also received other coupons for white bread against sick citizens. In contrast, the rest of us at home got coupons for black bread, which was not only a hideous earthy color but turned into a ball of muddy clay if you squeezed it in your hand. Stale bread!"

"Too many deny the true evils of Communism today! Stupid, dirty communists!" Alex responded, shocked.

It's what the West will never understand about the empire of true evil! What are they even teaching today's youth in their history classes? George thought but kept to himself.

"Yes," he said instead. "Before 1944, Bulgaria was a kingdom – or rather Tsardom. It was aligned with the Axis powers during the Second World War. However, in 1944, the People's communist party staged a coup to overthrow a monarchy and establish a communist government. They called it the People's Republic of Bulgaria. But things weren't much better under the communists, as you can see. As a young man, I often spent hours waiting in these bread lines to ensure my family had enough to eat. Or, as close to 'enough' as the government would allow us."

In a moment fraught with tension, Grandpa couldn't resist injecting humor upon seeing Alex's terrified expression. It was his attempt to provide comfort amidst the cultural shock they were experiencing.

In America, we tell people to say "cheese" to help them smile when their picture is taken. Is there something like this in your communist country?" Alexander asked.

"When people on the street hear 'cheese!' they form a breadline. After a long day waiting while resisting depression and hunger, we did tell jokes as medicine for the heart."

"Jokes and anecdotes always save us. Humor in the time of the old regime? Political jokes under Communism can even put you in jail!" George responded.

As the two drifted closer to young George in their spiritual form, George noticed something new—a voice beginning to emerge and rise within their private communication channel. Although it wasn't heard in the traditional sense, George sensed it as their thoughts echoed back and forth toward each other. It was a young man's voice, reminiscent of Alex's but with a raspier, more profound quality, as if weathered by colder air and harsher climates.

Though he didn't see, George could tell that Alex heard it, too.

"Who is that?" Alex asked, but George was listening too intently to respond. The voice was speaking Russian, George knew at once.

"I can tell you what he's saying," he said. "I...I understand what he's saying," Alex said.

Russian voices from the streets broke it, "Da zdravstvuet proletarskii prazdnik 1-ia Mai" (Long live May Day!) "Da zdravstvuet Balgaro–Savetskaia Druzhba" (Long live Bulgarian-Soviet Friendship) "Long Uraaa, Uraaa! Hooray!" Pioneers held the Soviet poster and chanted in exclamations, "Long Uraaa! Uraaa! Hooray!"

Slogans from the Russian Language High School in Sofia marched and chanted May Day Slogans in Russian.

The two ignored the voices for as long as they could, "You do?" George was amazed. "You speak Russian?"

"I mean a little," Alex began, "Mama Margarita would teach me at home..." Alex paused for a minute, "I mean, I didn't think so. But I can understand what he's saying. It's like...I can't explain it."

"I hated to study mandatory Russian Language in school, but it came in handy – it was beneficial when I was looking for a job in Russian Brighton," said George. The two paused for a second.

"It's okay," George said. "I don't think it needs much explaining."

"It's you, isn't it?" Alex asked. "We're hearing your thoughts."

"Yes," George said. The two had drifted so close to the young George that they were almost at the head. "I don't know why, but

I think we're meant to see my story play out here. Or, at least, you are meant to see it." Alex said nothing but took in the wonder of it all. George felt satisfied enough with that, and the two relaxed into the role of mere spectators as the scene played out in front of them as if it were a movie and as if his younger self were some excellent Hollywood star on the screen. And as their voices hushed away, young George's internal thoughts grew louder, so clear that he seemed to be next to them. His thoughts came through so clearly, playing in trilingual: Bulgarian, Russian, English, and seemingly every language and no language but the language of perfect comprehension.

George gave his grandson's hand one last squeeze. He already knew what his young self was about to say. "That's it," Young George thought to himself, though his voice carried across the entire world of the two of his invisible spectators. "I'm leaving."

"I had enough. Let this government be damned! I am going to America!

His grandpa had his favorite Bulgarian saying: "Da be mirno sedialo, da ne bi chudo vidialo," meaning: If it had stayed still, it wouldn't have seen hell" or "If you hadn't gotten involved, you wouldn't have suffered the consequences."

But "If only his youth knew so with his age, he could! But it was too late."

His mind was already in America.

A brief pause as the bread line moved forward half a foot, then stopped again. Young George looked down at the snowy ground and clenched his fists. "I'm going to move to America."

Suddenly, after leaving the capital city of Sofia, George and Alex found themselves in a quaint border village. They were surrounded by the beauty of blossoming fruit trees and the fragrant scent of linden trees. Lying on the grass in a small park, they heard the resonant echo of heavy bells emanating from the village's Orthodox church. It became evident they were in George's hometown, Ljubimetz, on the Greek and Turkish frontier.

It was Easter Sunday of 1948, known as Velik Den, the day of Christ's Resurrection. Villagers flooded the church, busily preparing eggs and Easter bread for blessings.

Seventy-two years had passed since that Easter Sunday, and sixteen-year-old George felt overwhelming joy at seeing his family, friends, brothers, and Svetlana, his girlfriend. However, he realized with sadness that they could not see him despite his longing to reconnect with them after all these years.

In this realm of the spirit, where everything was possible, George and Alex remained invisible to most people. Still, they became visible to some from the other side.

From that day forward, George's life would change irrevocably. Despite the apparent joy surrounding him, he couldn't ignore the fear etched on the faces of his twenty friends. They knew that in just six short hours, they would attempt to escape the border, but tragically, all eighteen of them would be killed.

George alone would survive and escape to tell the harrowing tale of Communist oppression. Yet, he would carry the weight of survivor's guilt for the rest of his life, haunted by the memories of those who didn't make it.

As he lay in the churchyard, surrounded by the blossoming cherry, plum, and apple trees, George was startled by the sudden presence of a goat. Initially frightened by the creature's imposing horns, he was taken aback when the goat burped in his ear and attempted to affectionately kiss him on the cheek with its long pink tongue.

"Baaa! Naaa! Baaa!"

The black goat bleats, burps, and bleaches his face. Goodness, Gracious!

At this time, goats and animals would make good pets, and some kid seemed to have lost his pets!

Suddenly, a group of roughly sixteen to eighteen-year-old children passed by the Orthodox church. George didn't recognize them and approached them, inquiring about where his grandfather Captain Georgiy's old house was in the center of town next to Tzar Liberator Street.

One of the children responded somberly, informing George

that the house was long gone. As he glanced around at the surroundings, George was struck by the beauty of the place, reminiscent of his lost childhood.

The scene also brought to mind the park in South Brooklyn near Brighton Beach, where his son Nicky had grown up—a nostalgic reminder of the passage of time and the fleeting nature of memories.

Under the same cherry blossom tree, George found himself reminiscing about the garden state of New Jersey and the beautiful Cherry Blossom Festival in Washington, DC. The familiar sound of St. George Orthodox Church's bells proclaimed the significance of the day—Easter, the most incredible celebration of Christ's Resurrection, known as Velik Den in Ljubimetz.

As George and Alex stood amidst the villagers, they couldn't help but notice the curious gazes directed their way. To the villagers, they appeared as strangers from different times and centuries. The village boys, dressed in torn, old, dirty shorts and shirts, looked on with fascination and awe at these mysterious visitors. Their sun-bleached clothes bore traces of dirt and blood from their outdoor adventures. Yet, their eyes remained wide open, surprised at the sight of these strangers—aliens, it seemed, in their town for Easter.

The Sofiantzi, residents of Sofia city, regarded George and Alex with fear and apprehension as if they were space travelers or strange creatures from another planet, hesitant to make eye contact with these enigmatic beings.

"Saint George, please protect us from these aliens!" The village boys were praying and making the sign of the holy cross.

Suddenly, George remembered that today was Easter in 1948 when George figured out that he and the group were planning the escape in front of his eyes. They thought nobody would notice their absence when everyone was in the church that Easter Sunday night, and then they would escape the border.

That night, they would already be in Greece. If only George could turn the time back and tell them they have only 3 hours to live. I want them to change their plans for one more day and celebrate with their family that night. Their lives never gonna be the same again!" Oh God, be merciful to their souls!

If only he could tell them not to escape tonight.

Nobody suspected someone in the group would be a traitor – "Judas Iscariot: Who betrayed Jesus with a kiss."

Unfortunately, the son of a secret agent had been following them from the start, and an informant had been planted among them.

# Chapter 3:

# Escape From Home

The colors swirled around the spectators. Before their eyes, the gentle glow of the spring sun in the distant homeland melted into profound darkness, a transition as seamless as the changing of seasons. Walls formed around the spectators first. Second came the feeling of human presence surrounding them. It was then, amidst this ethereal spectacle, that the spectators had a startling revelation – they were peering into the world through the innocent gaze of young George.

"Ah," George stated and pensively.

"What? Where are we?" Alex didn't like the setting. It was an old wooden building. The moonlight filtered through the windows, casting a kaleidoscope of colors across the room. Each beam of light, fragmented by the intricate patterns of stained glass, painted the surroundings with a vibrant tapestry of hues.

"We're in a church," Alex finally figured out. "Why are we in a church in the middle of the night?"

"It's the meeting spot," George said, "We're leaving. What do you mean? Why are you meeting here? Why can't you meet at the border?" Alex's confusion was clear.

The rendezvous point was Kakhovskiat Bunar, his

grandfather's well, nestled just a kilometer away from the border with Greece/Turkey. Within an hour, twenty innocent high school students boldly decided to venture across the border, embarking on a journey without a guarantee of return.

"Sh-sh-sh, don't talk! Here, even the walls have ears! Did you read the origins of 'thought police' in George Orwell's dystopian novel, 1984?"

"Well," George started, "It must be a secret. We're not supposed to leave this place, and if we get caught trying," George seemed to have scared himself with what he was saying. These moments represented some of the most terrifying life-or-death situations they had ever encountered.

Alex stood transfixed, his body locked in place by a surge of realization. He had absorbed enough stories about the difficult journey of emigrants from Mexico to America to grasp the gravity of the situation unfolding before him. He remembered a book he had to read in the sixth grade, "La Linea," about a pair of siblings running over the border to America.

He remembers "The many refugees with no names," the drowned migrants buried in the "Unknown Pauper's graves," killed by cross-border shoutout at the River Maritza. After 1944, many Bulgarians, dissatisfied with the new oppressive Communist regime, massively fled across the border of Turkey and Greece. The small border town, Lyubimetz, has over a hundred people who already escaped. Still, many were killed by soldiers in border shootings.

Alex remembered a classmate with his shortest route from Cuba to the US it was ninety miles. His story is of a Cuban refugee who gets nervous about escaping from Havana to Miami on a self-made boat, far away from the Casto regime.

The scene continued. Young George didn't talk to anyone in the group. He knew what was happening. George and Alex also knew the plan from sharing young George's thoughts.

"Run" was the keyword that young George was thinking of. There were other obstacles, like the light and the fence, but "run" seemed to trump everything.

It seemed like the only thing that mattered. Then, of course, George, when the chips fell, performed with superhuman strength and unstoppable determination, unlike any man I had ever met. Had it not been for him, this book of memoirs would never have been written.

Dead men don't write books.

The night was long. The answers were few and vague. After the first shot of vodka, Franko spoke. "We better make a final decision tonight," he said, turning to George and me. Franko's father was a township judge in the Communist Party system that Franko referred to as a "farce" of Communism. On the contrary,

Franko had access to many legal documents due to his father's position, including the stringent laws and severe penalties associated with the very act they were on the verge of committing. Here, at the border, soldiers were known to enforce these laws ruthlessly, often resorting to lethal force against violators without a moment's hesitation.

It was time to make up his mind. George kissed his necklace—a crucifix—crossed himself, and drank multiple fast shots of vodka to boost his confidence. He believed in vodka courage!

George again told the story:

"Traditionally, that night, my grandfather and his brothers went through the days of Holy Week in the temple of God in Ljubimetz at the main street "Tzar Osvoboditel," which led all the worshipers to the Orthodox Church. 1948, he remembered the Great Saturday: "With the painted Easter eggs in our pockets, we crossed the crowd at the churchyard. Instead of listening to the worship liturgies, together with my friends, we climbed the winding stairs to the bell tower of the smaller of the two dwells, expecting our priest, Father Dimitar, to announce Christ's resurrection for the nine-hundred-and-forty-eighth time. But what unfolded next caught me entirely off guard: around 10 pm, the night erupted into chaos with the unmistakable sound of gunfire echoing from the village's southern edge. Automatic rounds pierced the air, accompanied by jarring explosions that sent shockwaves through the night. In response to the turmoil, my friends and I hastily gathered at the front windows of the church bell tower, straining to peer towards the source of the commotion. Amidst the cacophony of gunfire, firework-like rockets were illuminating the sky in the direction of the turmoil to the South.

Somebody had said a battle had begun between the Bulgarian and Greek military units at the border. At that time, many battles took place on the Greek border between the Royal Army of Britain, who wanted to stop the expansion of Soviet Communism to the Aegean Sea at all costs. Groups of Greek guerrilla partisans often retreated to the Bulgarian territory to prepare for new attacks. Their agents also participated in the actions of the Bulgarian Socialist Government. The atmosphere created by the propaganda – Soviet and Western – was such that no one can predict the beginning of one new Balkan war." The people left the church. Young George was in the middle of the pack, but the spectators could tell he felt alone. We're getting close. Young George thought to himself. A fence came just barely into sight. There was a tower about 700 meters to the left and a spotlight shining over and scanning along the wall coming from that tower. The group closed in on the fence. It was close enough to be seen clearly now. It was a classic chain-link fence. It looked strong, and there was barbed wire on the top.

At this point, everyone was crouched. Two men of fine stature had a rolled-up carpet shared atop their right shoulders.

The spotlight passed before the group approached the high-voltage barbed wire fence. As they approached the fences, the group was near the next obstacle.

"Run" was the parole among them.

Unfortunately, the informant was planted in the group, and the secret agents followed them.

The parole was "run."

The whole group knew in an instant that it was their chance. They dashed to close the distance between them and the fence. The carpet men were in front. With incredible coordination, they threw the carpet to unroll over the barbed wire so it wouldn't cut. Little George waited his turn to jump the fence. The spectators could feel the cold sweat on his palms when it came. George ran up the wall like he had done it a million times. He felt a crunch in his knee as he landed on the ground. He didn't know what it was, but young George knew he had done something to it. He tried to walk it off by taking a few steps forward, but it hurt. He heard it while thinking about what to do for the rest of this trip. The alarm sounded from the distant tower. The trumpets sounded. The kingdom was coming down.

"Run."

The young George thought, forget the knee. Run. The spectators felt the fear young George felt. It was a true "life or death" situation!

On the border zone, the soldiers were shooting without warning. The most important thing was not to panic.

The emergency squad of border soldiers with ferocious dogs was already investigating some other refugees, so he had time to escape by swimming across the river Maritza, "The River of the Dead."

At the age of 16, George was in the best physical shape in his life to run and swim. That's why he was that year's best high school champion in the Haskovo district.

Alex had heard the phrase a million times and now understood it. The "life or death" situation.

He could sense his young grandfather's agony, the connective tissues and joints rattling with each desperate stride as the young man relentlessly battled for just one more step before succumbing to exhaustion. Alex couldn't bear the pain and rush of adrenaline in his body. In his thoughts, he begged for mercy from Saint George. Eventually, it did come; the world's colors around young George blurred and faded.

It was hard to tell whether it was from the pain or the scenes shifting. Still, soon enough, the scene shifted, and young George was limping over to a train station where faceless Greek villagers stood.

They talked, but the speech was gibberish; young George was almost delusional from exhaustion.

He walked into a boxcar at the train's rear, sitting at the station, and lay down. He used the small bag that he had brought with him and passed out.

Thank God there were no soldiers at the Greek border.

George managed to stagger a short distance to the nearest village house. Weakly, he rapped on the door, hoping for salvation, but the silence was deafening. Summoning the last vestiges of his strength, he made one final effort before collapsing unconscious in the shelter of a nearby barn surrounded by the comforting presence of animals.

He was in severe pain.

George doesn't remember anything.

The fear in the morning overwhelmed George, and he got him up by remembering what had happened last night. He was at the point of exhaustion. George took the small army bundle his grandpa gave him and unpacked a compass, half of a loaf of bread (two days' food), and a plastic water bottle.

The compass showed him South!

Keep only South; take the road to Alexanderopolis. George heard the voice of his Greek grandmother, Anastasia, encouraging him.

"Where is Alexanderopolis?" Alex asked. Young George was still repeating: "Keep only South to Alexanderopolis!"

Alex's vivid imagination struggled to comprehend the distressing reality unfolding before him. His grandfather, embodying the resilience of a true stoic soldier, refused to surrender. George pressed on, undeterred by the daunting odds stacked against him. Little did he know, the tragic fate awaited his companions - everyone except the leader met a grim end. In contrast, the leader was apprehended and sentenced to a lengthy imprisonment.

George had no luxury except sleeping during the day and walking at night. Only Alexanderopolis was on his mind.

George knew that at the Greek port of Alexandroupolis — the city of Alexander — where his grandmother, Anastasia, lived, he could take a ship and travel to Italy. "Don't be afraid. Keep only the direction of the South. When you start something, go to the very end. Never give up; you can do it!"

He was used to not eating and working all day in the fields with his grandpa. Often, George would swim in the river all day. Little did he know that the swimming and manual labor made him strong for this moment.

George was the district champion in athletics and swimming.

George didn't know the area.

He was avoiding the villages and following the directions to the South towards Alexanderopolis, the Greek port on the Aegean Sea. He was sleeping during the day and running by night, often hearing his grandpa's voice:

Don't be afraid. Keep only the direction of the South. When you start something, go to the very end. Never give up; you can do it!

That morning, George woke later than usual, his stomach gnawing with hunger pangs. In his slumber, he had been transported to a dreamland filled with the tantalizing aroma of Easter feasts from home, a stark reminder of the comforts he yearned for. Drained of all energy, he lay there, devoid of strength and resolve.

A dark creature from hell approached him during the night with horns pointing toward his face.

It was a wandering goat that woke him up. It stared at him. Suddenly, a voice inside said: "Jump and drink."

George took the goats and started to drink like a baby goat underneath it.

Where are the goats and ships? Can he find food and water?

Transformed into a creature of the wilderness, George seamlessly blended into his surroundings, adapting to the environment like a natural inhabitant. Casting furtive glances around him, he moved with the cautiousness of a startled rabbit, his senses alert to the slightest movement. Amidst the rugged landscape, George caught sight of a group of shepherds, their figures silhouetted against the backdrop of dawn as they unfurled the flag to herald the new day. At that moment, a deep connection to his grandfather's memories coursed through him, grounding him in a sense of belonging. Choosing to take respite from his arduous journey, George spent the day in the company of the shepherds, finding solace in their quiet companionship as they traversed the rugged terrain together.

He was able to steal their food and continue living!

God, knowing everything, will forgive him for his deeds.

"Come on! Come on! Let's go! Stay away from the village."

"Stay away from people," he heard his grandfather directing him.

The connection between his head and legs was long lost. He was mostly on autopilot, but he was out of gas and strength after a long run.

George slept for hours.

George and Alex were speechless.

Alex had no questions. He understood what had happened so far; he just needed to think. Alex had heard all these stories about emigrants, their poverty, and their struggles. Still, he had never really applied these things to his grandfather. He had also never witnessed it firsthand.

Finally, Alex had a question: "Where are we going?"

"To the West! America," George answered. He knew it was a bad answer, but the truth was that he didn't fully understand.

They were moving according to the plan. First, they passed the border with Bulgaria and Greece and crossed the River Maritza – actually, the bloody event happened on this Eastern Orthodox Easter on April 30th, 1948.

What saved me from the midnight shootout? George remembers an old lucky pocket version of the Bible – a gift from his grandfather, which he kept in the left pocket of his jacket with a Bullet stopped exactly on Psalm 91:7 on the sentence: "A thousand may fall at your side, ten thousand at your right hand, but it will not come near you."

Our festive excitement and conversations suddenly froze and stopped when we saw behind our backs the angry faces of my father, Alexander, and their godfather, Pop Stoyan. He came home to look for me after the news of what happened to some of my friends. Without much explanation, my father commands my brothers to go home. He remembered George's middle brother, Dimitar, when he was fourteen. "We left, unfortunately, the exciting sight of colorful fireworks and the approaching midnight of the resurrection of the Lord when we expected everyone to greet each other: "Christ has Risen!" And you were answered with: "Indeed! He is Risen!" or "Christos Voskrese!" and reply with "Voistina Voskrese!" It was midnight.

In the afternoon of the next day, rumors of murder broke out in the village. Some of our citizens had made an attempt to escape across the Greek border, and they were killed as traitors.

The border of Communist Bulgaria was guarded by Granicni Voiski, or Border Army, a specially trained military force.

The border soldier barked out a chilling command, condemning the 18 innocent children to a senseless death. Among them, George's grandfather, George himself, stood as the sole survivor of the harrowing ordeal that claimed the lives of all but two. Ognian, the courageous leader of the group, was apprehended and sentenced to decades behind bars.

In the aftermath of the tragedy, George found himself navigating a world of displacement and uncertainty. He encountered a group of refugees who had embarked on a perilous journey, fleeing through the tumultuous landscapes of Yugoslavia, later passing through Bosnia and Croatia before finally finding sanctuary in France. Along the way, George forged connections with individuals from diverse corners of the globe, their shared experiences of loss and resilience binding them together in solidarity amidst the chaos of displacement.

"Where did I depart on a ship?" George worked his hardest to remember the route.

"Wow. That's a long way." Alex observed.

"Haha, maybe! I slept it off, though." George said with a little bit of cheer. It shook Alex that his grandfather could be the least facetious about such a situation. The colors swirled again, and the boxcar faded away.

As the new scene was compiled, the scent of the sea drifted to our spectators as the image of young George looking out to the sea became clear.

"Where are we?" Alex asked. The scene resembled nothing of the "old country" that was previously described.

"Trieste," George said. He wanted the story to tell itself. He knew that his grandson would appreciate it.

As the young man walked around, he carried a small bag and rubbed the money in his pocket between his thumb and pointer finger. It was clear he was terrified of losing it. Young George continued pacing around the area in front of his boxcar for about fifteen minutes before a woman's face appeared before his.

He was scared – no ID, no official documents, no Bulgarian international passport – if the foreign police caught him, they would return him to the Bulgarian authorities, where he would face a harsh labor camp or even death!

The woman stood tall, her physique betraying an underlying strength forged in the crucible of adversity. Despite her slender frame, it was evident that in the famine-stricken landscape of her homeland - Bulgaria, cultivating a larger physique was a daunting task. Locking eyes with George, she exuded an unwavering intensity that conveyed a silent challenge, a silent assertion of her steadfast resolve. In the quiet exchange of gazes, it became apparent that she would be the one to emerge victorious, prompting George to avert his gaze first. A subtle flicker of satisfaction danced across her features, a testament to her triumph in this unspoken duel of wills.

"Mia," she introduced herself, extending her hand in a gesture of camaraderie.

"George, from Georgiy," the young man said. He shook his hand. "Where are we?" The young George asked.

"Trieste," Mia answered as simply as the old George had. "Where?" Young George was not well-versed in European geography.

"It's a city on the Eastern edge of Italy. We've rounded the Adriatic; most of the trip is over, but we must figure out our own ways."

The feeling of confusion and loss from young George spread to his spectators. How the hell am I going to get to America from here? I don't even know where "here" is!

"Travel with me," Mia said this almost as a command. Young George was immediately aware he was wearing a look of consternation on his face, which triggered Mia's demand.

"Okay." Young George felt overpowered, "Where do we go next?"

"I have no clue," Mia said in her simple manner. "We'll ask."

George felt relaxed for the first time in what felt like days. He felt comradery; he spoke Bulgarian to someone for the first time after his escape, and for a second, George thought he was at home.

The newfound duo strolled through the bustling yard, tracing the faint imprints left by countless travelers before them until they reached the station. With her limited grasp of Italian, Mia and George, attempting to communicate in halting Russian, engaged with passersby in a flurry of nervous exchanges. Despite communication challenges, they persevered through the evening, piecing together a route through the labyrinthine train system that would carry them from Trieste, Italy, to their destination in Brest, France.

The duo boarded the train from there.

Once aboard, Mia and George sat together and talked away the time. They bonded over the old country and their experiences together. It seemed George had forgotten what they had talked about, as the words that came from their mouths were pure feelings. The feeling was a comfort; the two emigrants communicated pure familiarity and comfort to one another in such an unfamiliar place.

As the train came to a halt, George and Mia disembarked, ready to embark on the next leg of their journey. Boarding another train, they settled into their seats, conversing to pass the time and share their stories. With the rhythmic motion of the train lulling them into a sense of tranquility, they eventually succumbed to the gentle embrace of sleep, finding solace in each other's company amidst the uncertainty of their travels.

The two seemed to sleep in sync with one another. Mia would use the young George's shoulder while he laid his head atop hers. The feeling of comfort that came from young George was growing constantly. Mia seemed to represent George's home; her accent, complexion, and even Mia's mannerisms came straight from Sofia.

The last train arrived at the station. The two Bulgarians left together and looked around their new city. They smelled the sea air for the first time since they had left Trieste, but it was different. The air was less humid, and the scent was stronger and almost darker – if "darker" could even be a scent. It was the scent of the Atlantic.

The smell seemed to validate Mia and George's fear of what was to come.

The two repeated their broken communication process to find the right ship to New York City, as many immigrants had in the past.

After obtaining his asylum visa in 1952, George finally arrived in the USA through Newark Liberty Airport. The journey this time was particularly arduous, compounded by the frustration of navigating through a city where neither he nor his companion spoke proper French. To add to their woes, they encountered a less-than-welcoming reception from the locals, who seemed indifferent or rude.

When Mia would ask one of the citizens something or give a "Pardonne Moi!" to get someone's attention, they would walk straight by her like she didn't even exist, no "Oh none, pardon," nothing. Frenchmen hated immigrants and had no desire for them in their country.

Eventually, another emigrant found the two and guided them to the right ship. He was an East German emigrant named Jacob (East German from before Germany reunited). The duo formed a trio as they boarded the boat.

On the boat, the three passengers talked. "So, Russians!" Jacob started.

"Oh no..." Mia and George said in unison. Mia finished the sentence: "Bulgarians. We are escaping what the Soviets have done!"

"Ah... fleeing Communism!" The east Berliner, Jacob, proclaimed. He had a strong but pleasing speaking style characterized by many East Germans.

Jacob went on to tell his story, but the speech was blurred. Clearly, Jacob's story was forgotten by George as he aged. George felt guilty, as he truly cared about Jacob and missed him dearly. The story had something to do with the East German economy, he couldn't remember.

The journey became a catalyst for forging deep connections within the newfound group. Throughout their arduous trek, they shared stories, fears, and hopes, gradually building a sense of camaraderie that transcended language barriers and cultural differences.

From George's recollection, the odyssey spanned nearly three years spent in the Trieste Camp for Refugees before they finally set foot on American soil. Upon their arrival at Liberty Airport Newark, they embarked on the final leg of their journey, boarding a bus bound for the bustling metropolis of New York City.

The three musketeers shared one room to save money and rarely ventured outside that room. Despite the language barrier between the Bulgarians and Germans, they all enjoyed one another's company. George and Mia were obviously closer than either was to Jacob, but he didn't seem to mind.

The scenes of the ship seemed to flow together for our spectators.

"Wow," Alex said, "Is that grandma?"

"No," George laughed,"

It's Mia! Not M-ar-ia!"

George laughed in response to Alex's surprise.

The scene's blurriness stopped. A new one compiled itself; Jacob was out. The spectators didn't know where he had left, but they could tell it would be a while before he could return. The spectators observed the two figures within the room, their presence filling the space with an aura of warmth and joy. Amidst the unassuming setting, the scene appeared to lack a specific focal point, with attention drawn solely to the room's ambiance. Within this intimate setting, Mia and the young George shared a moment of pure, unbridled laughter, their voices harmonizing in a symphony of mirth that echoed throughout the room.

George stopped first. Mia chuckled a little longer before she noticed George looking at her. The two made eye contact for about three seconds. It felt much longer; they seemed to study one another's faces. After a second, the two broke the stare by closing their eyes, leaning into one another, and kissing. The spectators could feel young George's emotions. It seemed like everything had become intensely real. It was like there was a new level of awareness for the spectators.

The ship reached its port soon enough, and the immigrants left for the intake offices at the port.

At this point, the immigrants had to separate, as Mia had to go to the office for women, and Jacob had his own business to attend to.

However, before even embarking on their trip to America, George and Mia had to wait at the camp for displaced refugees in Trieste, Italy, for over a year before the journey could even continue, as they had to be given special legal permission through political asylum to be able to continue in their immigration. Mia left the group and decided to live with extended family in Bulgarian Chicago, IL. George settled in New York City, where he had an uncle who could help him initially.

# Chapter 4

# The First Days in the New World

Around them, the scene began to blur and haze once more into a strange tableau of dancing and bleeding lights and colors.

George was aware of the strange and distant feeling of movement. It was not so much physical movement but rather an internal sensation that his very psyche was being tipped on its balance and led along somewhere by an invisible, cosmic force.

"What's happening?" Alex said. "Where are we going?" George, though, was still holding onto the image of the bridge that was beginning to form in his grandson's mind. The bridge between the past, present, and future – or whatever served in place of either in this strange, timeless existence that they had found themselves in – the demarcation line at the border between his past and his present. At that point, George knew that Alex's bridge was nowhere near complete. At that point, it was nothing more than a vague foundation and a few support beams sticking up in a row out of a steady but relentless current.

But it was a start.

I think St. George still has more to show us," George said.

"Where is this St. George Anyway?" Alex asked. "Who the hell does this guy think he is if he's doing all this to us? Alex screamed as a typical millennial teenager with no respect for the church and traditions of long-dead Saints.

George, in his mental picture of himself, bit his lip in weary anticipation against Alex's perceived blasphemy. But, if the Saint registered it, it had no effect on the scene playing itself out before them.

"Repent right away, my boy, and ask Sveti Georgiy (Saint George) for forgiveness!"

"One should not speak ill of the saints," George said gently. He tried to reach a compassionate tone that was often lost when his elders and church patriarchs spoke on such matters when he was a youth. "The saints do not just watch over us. They are our guide. What they want us to see is what we need to see."

"But why do we need to see this?" Alex shouted. George had a sudden, terrible image of the bridge in Alex's mind, beginning to shake and falter on its newborn foundations.

"Why do you need to see this more likely," George thought to himself. But he steeled his tone and instead said: "The saints have great wisdom beyond ours. They can see much farther than we can. As you travel along a journey, you may not be able to see the road in its entirety. But you follow it under the faith that it will soon carry you to where you want to go."

"But I don't want to go anywhere!" Alex said. The bridge

in his mind continued to shake and buckle under an invisible force that threatened it. "Only back to the car, back to my tennis match! Back to Earth! Back to Montreal!"

George thought things over in his mind. "What you want now is not what you will need in the future. You must trust that the saints know this better than you—"

"But..." Alex began in protest.

But George shushed him. "Wait," George said. "Look!"

Around them, the twirling and multicolored lights were beginning to consolidate once more into a concrete image. George could again make out a soft, gray sky – a winter's sky – and against it was what appeared to be a vast column of buildings, rising to challenge that sky and its sovereignty.

"It's a city," Alex said.

"Yes," George said. He tried to train his eyes – or whatever he was looking at within this state – on the images that were forming in front of him.

"Is this still what the city is called in Bulgaria?" Alex asked.

"Sofia," George said. "But no, this isn't Bulgaria."

"How can you tell?" Alex asked. "I can barely make anything out."

"Well, for one," George said. "There are no such buildings in Bulgaria."

Indeed, the skyline that was forming in front of them shot up to an incredible degree. Coming from the low city line of old-world Bulgaria, these buildings seemed almost impossibly tall. Even the shorter of the buildings so densely clustered together here were significantly taller than the highest golden dome of Sofia's great Alexander Nevsky Cathedral.

"What is this?" Alex asked.

"I believe, if I am not mistaken, that this is New York City!"

Indeed, as the image grew clearer in front of them, the familiar sights of midtown Manhattan soon came into view. In front of them, standing as the centerpiece of the impressive skyline, was the mighty Empire State Building, dwarfing the buildings around it that themselves would dwarf most others. Nearby was the smaller but far more beautiful Chrysler Building, whose elegant silver art deco stylings forged its own magnificent place in the city's skyline, even though it could not compete with its taller and grander rival in terms of sheer height. Across their vision were endless stretches of brownstone buildings, rooftop water tanks, spires and antennae, and windows that glistened despite the overcast day.

"Bozhe Moi – Oh My God!" A young man's voice called from somewhere around them. "How can buildings even get so tall?" "Wait," Alex said. "Who was that? Was that..." "Me?" George said. Indeed, the scene playing out in front of them had the same limited perspective as their previous view of the back of the man's head in the bread line in old Bulgaria.

It was as if they were watching Manhattan emerge from the haze and fog through another person's eyes.

"Are we in your head again?" Alex asked. "I mean, the old you? Or, I guess, the young you, or – gah! This doesn't make any sense!"

"Well," George said. "I'm afraid I can't help you make much sense out of all of this as a whole. But, to answer your first question, yes, I do believe this is once again the view as I saw it all those years ago. When I first arrived in America."

"Wait," Alex said. "If this is New York, where's the World Trade Center?"

George chuckled to himself. "I'm afraid it wasn't built yet when I arrived."

"But I meant the old World Trade Centers," Alex said. "The ones that got destroyed in that terrorist attack."

If he had eyelids in that state (and he wasn't certain that he didn't, though he couldn't feel them), George felt that he may have blinked several times.

"I am talking about the original World Trade Center," George said. "The Twin Towers."

Alex gasped in astonishment. "You mean you came here before them?" He said.

George laughed. "Son, those were built in the '70s. The 1970s." Just how old do you think your grandfather is? He thought. Though, once more, he said nothing.

From the space around them, young George's internal voice once more echoed off of their shared psychic space.

"How do they even stay up?" He thought with a measure of astonishment that matched his young grandson, decades still unborn in the time he lived through just then. "How do they even build them that high?"

"First time I came to America in 'Nu Yawk.' In the 1950's, that's how I said it when I first came here: "Nu Yawk," like a true Bulgarian immigrant. I was in the stomach of a giant metal bird with a tiny window revealing the view of the skyline of the huge emblematic metropolis.

As soon as George stepped onto American soil at the Newark Airport, he began a new day. The sun, though only peeking through the clouds, shone gold onto the boy who had to shield his eyes from the divine spotlight.

For the first time in NEW YORK CITY, understanding the city is like holding sand in your hands: it just can't be perceived as graspable on your first try. It's full of mysteries and secrets that it seemed every average Joe on the street was aware of – just not you.

Believe it or not, besides Mecca, Jerusalem, or maybe Sofia, New York City is the most religious city in the World! You can't enter the place without thinking of the city itself all the time!

George is now still reminded of the whirlpools at the base of Niagara Falls whenever he steps into the city. Full of energy of total acceptance or rejection. Still, with a whirlpool, everything is being swept together – Bulgarians, Europeans, Chinese, Russians, Hispanics – they're all New Yorkers once they step into the city!

New York might be the most densely populated and expensive space on the face of the earth. For 300 years, it's been a port for a small island that took in immigrants through whom the greatest memoirs of success were written. It's a true monument of capitalism – any time of the day, there are streams of people running to do or patronize businesses. Because of such an intense metropolis, many people are made or broken by New York City. "If you can make it here, you can make it anywhere!" Frank Sinatra once sang.

If you have a dream and are going to fight out your heart for it, New York's the place for you.

As God said to Abraham, "Go away from your country, your people, and your father's household to the land I will show you."

"By faith, he made his home in the promised land like a stranger in a foreign country."

This quote, to a New Yorker, is simply confusing. With the unbelievable fusion of cultures, each neighborhood feels like a different country and people – in many ways, it is! This was the best place, George believed, for his new beginning – the cultural, financial, and media capital of the world – New York City.

"Where are you now?" Alex asked. "I mean, the young you? When even was this?"

"A little while after the scene we just saw," George said. "This is when I first arrived in New York."

"That's crazy!" Alex said next to him. "Did, did you get to, like, rebuild your life or something like that?"

"Well, of course," George said. "Otherwise, you wouldn't be here! But it certainly wasn't easy at first. If I recall correctly, when I first came to America, I had exactly $95 in my pocket!"

"$95!" Alex said with amazement. "That's it?"

"Yes," George said. "Mind you, back then, $95 carried a bit more weight than it did in your day, what with inflation and all that. But, still, for someone trying to rebuild his life in a completely new country on the other side of the World from where he was from, it wasn't much at all."

As if to drive this point home, the young George, whose eyes they watched the city through, briefly sent his gaze down to his pockets. There, he pulled a few crumpled dollar bills into his one hand, turning them over with his thumb as if this would enact some alchemy that would grow greater riches from his mere seeds.

"I wish I could have managed to secure a bit more," Young George's inner thoughts said. "But I guess this will have to do." He turned his eyes back to the city, continuing to remark in amazement at the sheer height of the skyscrapers that marked the upper limits of Manhattan. The cloud cover that day had yet to break, and some of the lower edges of the clouds wrapped themselves around the upper heights of the tallest buildings, blurring their highest lights in a dim fog and blending the line between ground and sky.

"I've never seen anything man-made touch the sky from the ground like that," Young George thought. "Only the Balkan Mountains. How have the Americans managed to match what only nature could do?"

"Welcome to Ellis Island!"

"Welcome to the Statue of Liberty"!

The park arranges voice in the cross grade for everybody

on the boat. Alex finally had the day off to visit lower Manhattan after two years of life in New York. He had never visited this iconic place and symbol of US emigration.

He needed to save money in the city, which is very expensive. Still, this Passover, the Jewish part of Brooklyn was closed, so he decided to visit the Ellis Island Museum. George was visiting the Bulgarian Orthodox Church for Easter in Manhattan. After the service, he decided to go to Battery Park to take the cruise boat to Ellis Island and the Statue of Liberty.

This Saturday, George woke up so excited last night. He turned the magic key of nostalgia about his family. Spring and Easter are coming here. He remembers the bloody Easter of 1948, the Great Resurrection Day when he escaped the border four years ago. This morning, something really exciting is supposed to happen today. He thanks God that he is alive and well.

He felt anticipation that morning. It was as though Saint George wanted to surprise him by going to the Ellis Island Museum. He got a free tour and looked at the large pictures of the different ports and ships. The faces from different countries who arrive seeking asylum and refuge. This is the point that he got the idea of searching for his Bulgarian roots.

He was excited for the dream to come true because, for years, he never came to visit this historical place for immigrants.

*Ellis Island. The Island of Hope and Tears.*

To their right, the lights of an amusement park suddenly appeared and flashed on and off in the late morning cloudy light. A roller coaster was rising up slowly on its tracks, preparing for a death-defying descent down to the ground below. "What's that?" Alex asked.

Before Universal Studios in Orlando, it was 'Luna Park' in Coney Island.

"Coney Island," George said. "In Brooklyn. Immigrants coming to New York Harbor by boat would actually see this before the famous Statue of Liberty and Ellis Island. I still remember my first day in Manhattan.

After the Newark Liberty Airport, I took the city bus around to the World Trade Center. I saw the Empire State Building and was able to see the beautiful Times Square bustling!

On either side surrounding them, young George thought: Koi sa tezi hora amerikantzite? (Who are these people, the Americans?) putting a fun park first on the sights for their new children to see! What a country this is already!

"Coney Island is home to Brighton Beach," George told Alex in their spiritual dimension. "That's where most of the Russian and Eastern European immigrants lived after the War. That's where I lived for a time. Even today, you still see signs in

Russian and hear Russian spoken in the shops and on the street corners."

"I've never been there," Alex said sadly.

"Well, I think you're in luck then!" George told him. "I believe we're about to go there just now!" In the viewpoint in front of them, as seen through young George's eyes, the scene changed to a crowded but grimy dock with the omnipresent skyscrapers of Manhattan cast into the background.

A man in a dull uniform appeared in front of them. He held a clipboard and glared at young George (and, by default, old George and Alex watching through young George's eyes). He said something with a crude, official look on his face. But the words that came out sounded like nonsense, a strange jumble of garbled sounds that made little to no sense. Only a few recognizable words appeared in the mesh of fast-paced sounds. George thought he could make out "go," "supposed to," "ship, " and "city," but not much else. Blah blah blah, mumbo-jumbo!

If this damned man would talk just a bit slower! Young George thought.

"Wait, what's he saying?" Alex said. "I can't understand anything coming out of that guy's mouth."

In his own mind, George felt the waves of memory once more carry him. He remembers exactly that interaction, the fast-talking customs official, the slur of incoherent words. The fear and shame that George felt as being just another "dumb" immigrant.

"I didn't speak much English in those days," George told Alex. "I couldn't make much sense of anything these people said at first." George was always craving his father's approval and his manly embrace. His mother, Emma, was gentle and loving but suffering from deep clinical depression at moments due to her childhood trauma. George was alone – no family, no friends – just surviving alone in this jungle called NEW YORK CITY.

George was always in need of proper words while he was trying to find the right phrases in his conversation that butchered the English language. It was stressful to be around him.

George was trying to avoid embarrassing mistakes in English-like sounds that make the difference between words like shit and sheet, bitch and beach, and piss and piece. Especially explaining his address on Brighton Beach. There are some words in English that are very similar to swear words. When he went through what was said, he realized why the native English speakers were in stitches (this means 'cracking up' or laughing a lot)!

"But I speak English!" Alex said. "And I can't understand anything he's saying! It's weird – like, it sounds like English, or at least like English should sound like. But it doesn't make any sense!" "I believe," George began, "that we're hearing things through the ears of my younger self, just as we're seeing through his eyes. We get as much sense as he – as I – could make of it." In front of them, the customs official continued glaring at young George. From the scene in front of them, they heard his mouth open with some hesitation, and a soft, breathy voice appeared, heavily accented, and broke through the incoherent haze around them. "...I..." it began nervously, "...I...do…not... speak...English." No...Angliiski!

George had enormous difficulty "dzeefeecoo tsee," pronouncing certain phrases in his "Georgian" pronunciations. His Bulgarian was fluent, but his English was terribly sounding with his thick Slavic accent.

"Je parle un petit peu français," which it means in English: "I speak a little bit of French." No translator here? He was stammering and stuttering.

"Please Speak English – Only! That is the rule here. You are in America. Can you read the sign? No foreign language here!"

Young George spoke slowly and deliberately, though his accent was so thick that even such a simple sentence was almost incoherent. George's Bulgarian was music in his ears, but his English was simply tortured! It was like Vladimir Nabokov's Pnin and his Pain of the Past in emigration.

"I remember practicing that sentence over and over again on the boat," George told Alex. "Not that it did much good, as you'll see."

The customs officer scowled and pushed a piece of paper in front of young George. He began to speak again, only louder this time, as if the initial problem were only one of volume.

Eventually, after several moments of angry gestures and confused back-and-forths, George managed to get his signature on a few different documents that he couldn't read. George was writing and spelling like an American first grader. G-e-o-r-g-i......K-K-K-a-kh-o-v-s-k-i-y

"I had practiced signing my name in the Latin alphabet instead of Cyrillic," George said. "That looked good enough for these purposes, at least."

The officer asked him a simple question.

George shook his head for "yes" and then nodded for "no." The officer was confused by the two different body gestures, and then he shouted: "Yes or no?!"

Showing his agreement, George says 'yes' in Bulgaria, shaking his head from side to side, a gesture that in many countries means no!

George replies: yes, yes, yes, confirming "yes" with body language and gesticulating like an American: "Yes, yes, sir!"

Young George moved through the lines. Around him, hundreds of people were grouped together in a tightly packed corridor.

Men and women and children, many crying and wailing, many looking around silently with wide, frightened eyes. George suddenly felt in his own heart a well of fear beginning to build. "Wait, what's that?"

Alex said. "Why do I feel frightened right now?"

"I believe that we are feeling the fear of my younger self. I remember how terrifying this all was."

When you immigrate to NEW YORK CITY, you will always remember your first day in your new country – no matter if it was fifty days or fifty years ago.

Like the Bulgarian writer Nikolay Haytov once said: "Edno e da iskadh, drugo e da go mojesh, treto i chetverto da go napravish!"

In English, that means: "It's one thing to want, another to have, and a third to do it."

Imagining your life in a new World is one thing. Sitting on a boat across the Atlantic for a month is something. But actually, being here, in a strange land, whose language you didn't speak, surrounded by people who thought of you as an enemy – as an invader – someone that wants to steal their jobs – that was something else entirely."

The tourists would come and go constantly, but they were different – they had return tickets – they were going home soon.

George was at home – his new one, anyway.

George was a mama's boy who always was fed and taken care of.

Now he was alone! No family, no country! Nothing! Sometimes, in memories and moments of desperation, George felt like: "I have lived my life until now as a passenger on the train line from Sofia to Svilengrad. Like a wholly stopped train at that empty village train station when thoughts were sneaking into my soul while waiting. From long-lost memories, I heard my grandmother, Anastasia's, voice that said: 'My child, the World is big and endless. There is a lot of space for living, but remember, there's only one mother country. Four walls and two suitcases can't make a home. What are we without our Motherland? Invisible! Unappreciated! Unloved! A foreigner! Outlander! Stranger! Alien! Fresh from the boat! Nothing!'"

Grandpa George used to say, with a short temper, "When you walk, there's only one way: forward."

Never look back!

Then, another voice came through the ether. Young George's internal voice, speaking in his native tongue, but fully comprehensible to old George and Alex just the same.

"You scared, pathetic fool!"

He thought to himself. "Have you forgotten your

grandfather?! The Captain? The courage he bore when facing down the Turks at Shipka pass in the Balkans, all those years ago! What would he think, seeing his own grandson as such a sniveling coward that he fears being a stranger himself? You would sicken him!" Though neither of them could see his face, George knew that his younger self had forced his face into a stoic, emotionless façade as he emerged from the customs line into the sights and sounds (and smells) of New York City.

George was a pessimistic person. He always created a negative reality. Coming back from Bulgaria, deep down he felt unworthy of the American happy life.

"What is your narrative, please?" asked his psychoanalyst/psychologist Dr . Jacob.

"I am a negative person by birth."

"But this can be refrained," Doc said. "Here, you can take a new approach to your new life in America."

This psychoanalysis, akin to Freud, assists him in understanding himself better.

George proclaimed: "I still remember my first day in Manhattan, NEW YORK CITY: after Newark Liberty Airport, we visited Times Square, we were all full of exclamations: The group of refugees started to cry: Long live America! Long live our new American life! Uraa! Long live American Freedom and

Independence! Uraaa Uraaa!"

George was so happy to find his new, adoptive country. It was a place where, eventually, his family would be happy, too! We are on the threshold of another exciting world! We are not going back! We are even more scared now than happy! But there is no turning back! This will be a book about our exile without returning. We left our homes, our family, our culture, and so much more.

"Let me tell you, we are trusting here like a little child going into this majestic city, and we believe that the city will treat us nicely and friendly! On the first day!"

For George, it was a memory as well, but he got the sense that Alex could sense it, too. In front of them, George continued to walk, carrying his head high to signify to the surrounding Americans that he bore no fear and to keep from falling into vertigo at the impossibly tall buildings that lay just across the horizon.

"Where did you go from here?" Alex asked.

"Rather than my telling you," George said. "Why don't we just wait and see?"

Next to him, George once more senses the bridge beginning to form in his grandson's mind, the bridge that connects the past, present, and future.

He saw the columns sticking up from out of the water. The

steel support beams lay horizontally across the foundation. And, to his relief, he saw it, stabilized against the heavy wind that battered it, standing tall and strong and awaiting further completion.

# Chapter 5:

# A New Home

Brooklyn, the borough of New York City on the tip of Long Island (which is connected to Manhattan with bridges), is where a lot of the immigrants arriving from Ellis Island would first settle throughout the turn of the 20th century. George and Alex continued spectating the new American as he made his way into the New World.

Brighton Beach: A snapshot of the ex-Soviet diaspora Brighton Beach didn't become a Little Odessa until the 1970s.

The streets of Brighton Beach were lined with empty storefronts and dilapidated buildings, but with the lasting Jewish legacy of Jimmy Carter, during the Cold War US President who brought human rights into foreign policy, and with the relaxation of the Soviet Union's immigration policies, thousands of Soviet Jews from the USSR, especially from Ukraine, settled into the area.

Curious George wandered first into a bakery. "Where is he going?" Asked our indefinitely questioning Alex. "Well, though $95 might have been a lot, for the time being, I'd starve quickly without a job."

"So, you're just going to get one? You're just walking in?

No resume or reference?" Alex questioned in surprise. He had yet to get himself a job in his 18 years, and even the idea of sitting down in an interview terrified the boy. "What else would I do?" George found Alex's questions to be unsatisfiable. It was clear that this was all George could do.

He had no US diploma. He never graduated from Bulgaria. He wasn't even a real adult. But even after 18, George could sit for the GED testing and earn an American high school diploma. George could only be a general laborer who cleaned and mopped floors and washed dishes. Only for food. Not well-paid jobs. The kind of worker that had no path: all they wanted was to afford their needs. But George had an eligible "political asylum status." He just didn't know how it worked and would never ask for help. George was entitled to receive many benefits from the U.S. government.

George felt like a complete stranger in a very strange country.

As this dialogue unfolded, young George faced his first rejection at the hand of the baker. The messy unintelligibility that came out of the baker's mouth made just barely enough sense to allow our three subjects to understand that our young George would have a longer search than anticipated. Though George knew how the story would end, he still hoped deep down that the ending would change, and because of that, it still hurt when he had to hear his first rejection in the New World.

George just felt like he didn't belong there anymore.

The feeling of shame overwhelmed the spectators as well as young George. Though they were only present in spirit, Alex and George could feel the eyes of the baker on their backs just as though they were young George leaving the building. He felt like a laughingstock. Our young George was the fool. However, George later realizes he has an uncle in America all along!

On the phone, his uncle sounded like he wanted to help, but rejection after rejection, it was clear that even his close relatives had to leave George on his own! Rejection from his only relative in NEW YORK CITY.

"You cannot trust anyone." George Kept pondering. "Even St. George left me here."

The world around Alex and George shifted into another hazy tableau of colors as it changed. Only this time, the colors were darker and cooler than ever before. Alex felt the chill of a New York Winter. If he could shiver, he would. The feeling of one's will being broken overcame Alex, crumpling his spirit into a fetal position. George seemed to stand strong (as much as one could while in the ether).

His resolve was unbroken; the grinding down of one's will is the foundation of this man's life and character.

The world's colors were collected again in one scene:

Young George shivering on the side of the early New York streets. He would sleep there. Sometimes, the local bakery would throw spoilt or stale bread out, and George would take his chance at it. The boy was freezing and hungry.

While they watched this scene, Alex broke the silence, "Why did they say no?"

"They didn't like me," responded the grandfather. "Why?"

"The baker, for one, was Italian," George stated in an almost supercilious voice.

"What does that matter? You were friends with an Italian on the ship back in Italy!"

"Most Italians came here about sixty years ago with the old Russians, as well. They were an earlier wave, so they see themselves as truer Americans than me. The Italians and the Russians had an enormous community, so they helped, of course, their own newcomers."

"Who were the old Russians?"

"The old Russians were part of the White Guard Russians and Slavs that immigrated into America in the 1890s – 1920s when political disputes began to grow due to the poor conditions of the motherland. Many of the older waves of European immigrants saw us as invaders of their economy, so they wouldn't like to give me a job. Of course, at the time, I didn't know this. I just figured the man was a bastard. But, as the day went on and I got rejected more and more, I figured it out."

On this day, George visited more bakeries on Brighton Beach Avenue.

One bakery was called "Lord's" Bakery. They both spoke Yiddish and Polish. Ladies were buying the last loaf of traditional fluffy Hallah bread for Shabbat; George never understood why the Jewish Saturday day begins at sunset on Friday.

George loves their babkas (sweet, braided bread that originated in the Jewish communities of Ukraine, Russia, Bulgaria, and Poland). People buy them for Passover and Easter. George came here first to look for a job, but nobody was paying attention since Shabbat was approaching.

Later, he entered the Italian bakery, "Columbus," across the street. He just couldn't find a job.

"Huh," Alex said. Alex grew up in moderate wealth and couldn't even think of a comment to make. Money was never an issue for him. The idea of freezing on the street because someone didn't like that you had come to a place slightly sooner than them was just not something Alex could grasp. He needed time. After another prolonged silence spent watching the cold and youthful form of his grandfather trying to find comfort, Alex couldn't bear it any longer and asked, "Isn't there anywhere you could've gone?

A cheap hotel, hostel, or a homeless shelter?"

"Sure," George responded, slightly perturbed. "But it would've cost me."

"Cost you what?" Alex asked, not quite getting it. "Money, of course," George responded. "About six dollars."

"Why didn't you spend it?" Alex was amazed and grappling with his millennial mindset. "You could've afforded that easily!"

"Well, if I had spent $6 that night, I would have used about eight meals' worth of my money, and I had no clue as to when I would get more. I knew, even then, that if I couldn't eat, then I would've been much worse off." George explained this with a soft and paternal voice. He figured Alex didn't really get it. He was right. Alex had never spent a day in his life where he had no clue where his next meal would come from and couldn't fathom making the choices George had to make. Then, a fact gained power over Alex: they were the same age. While Alex's biggest concern in his life was whether he would do well at a tennis tournament, at around the same time in his life, his grandfather was freezing on the streets of a new country full of people he didn't understand.

The fact that the young George could've gotten warmth and a nice meal at the time but restricted himself for the future shocked Alex even more. He didn't even have to think about it;

Alex knew for a fact that he couldn't resist. The ten minutes that Alex spent in a state even slightly resembling his young grandfather was enough to cripple him emotionally. After that, he would've needed to see a psychologist for a very long time. A night like that would be hell. Alex would rather die. His young mind couldn't process what was going on. Alex couldn't imagine himself in the street with no friends, no family, no food, or home!

*Ohh, my love. Svetla – Svetlana*, young George thought, I miss *Svetlana*. George let out a little chuckle.

The intensity of the situation disturbed Alex. He couldn't understand how George could laugh at his young self in such a situation.

"Who's Svetlana?" He asked.

"Ohh. Back in Bulgaria, she was my first love." George seemed to be remembering the old country admirably now.

"I remember missing her so much. To me, she meant warmth. Ah... Svetlana. Yeah... Svetla. Her name means, well, the root (svet) means a brightness or a shine. She was my "light" when I was lost."

"What about Mia?" Alex felt almost jealous. He had liked Mia and felt she wasn't being valued.

"Well," George began. He felt he was being accused. "I knew Svetlana for quite a while, and to me, Svetlana represented the comfort of home. Mia, I think, represented a comfort being found away from home, and at this point, I don't think I wanted comfort while I was away; I wanted comfort at home. I wanted to go home. To hell with my American dream! But the price was too high, and I couldn't go back."

The consequences of George's exile were clear: he had become disassociated from his past and felt like a "robot" without a soul.

Alex now understood the feeling of being forcibly removed from his natural roots and deposited in a jungle among wild animals here in the Brooklyn Zoo.

The first four years of George's exile were a blur. George's memories of the old words began to break down. George had figured that he was in a state of amnesia. His native language was dissolving on his tongue. George thinks that when he came to the US, something was damaged when it came to his emotional responses to life. He believes that it was because of his loss of everything that he had known before – he believed a contributing factor was also "homesickness," which really just described the hole in his heart that Bulgaria had held for so long. His *chuvsta* (feelings) and the deep emotions of his soul were damaged. At these times, nostalgia cannot evolve, particularly in forced exile. In this case, George entered a depressed state accompanied by feelings of self-pity, resentment, envy, and guilt. To deal with such painful experiences, George would resort to linking things that help him continue having contact with his past while adjusting to his new environment. This "Emigrant's syndrome" is not recognized well by doctors. After many years, though, the effects are clear: You become frozen like a robot; you're separated and dissociated from yourself – good as dead.

Suddenly, the colors around Alex and George shifted to something darker and more incredible as winter in New York City set in. "It's the most wonderful time of the year to visit the Southern Brooklyn, Brighton Beach. To see the bright sights of New York's winter wonderland, hear thrilling Christmas stories on your way to see Saint Nicky, to tell Ded Moroz and Santa Clause your deepest wishes, and get a special good luck sleigh bell – all for a holiday experience you'll cherish forever."

George was alone and sad since he missed all his family, siblings, relatives, and neighbors who celebrated the Eastern Orthodox Christmas (Koleda) traditions back in Bulgaria.

Alex was overcome with despair while George refused to give in, his determination proving to be a cornerstone of his character.

It all merged in one scene: young George shivering on the side of a New York Street, ready to sleep there for the night.

Sometimes, George would take his chance at the stale or

spoilt bread thrown out by the local bakery. He was both cold and hungry.

But he fed his friend first, Buck.

Buck relished kindness, attention, and companionship.

Buck was the homeless dog on the street that George named, just like Buck from Jack London's books, *The White Fang* and *Call of the Wild.* How people are different from the animals. But this was a moment of survival for George on the streets of Brooklyn.

For his grandson Alex, the emigration was from his books and school field trip when they first came to Ellis Island. Alex never understood the immigrants' difficulties and their tears.

Getting this feeling from his young grandfather, Alex now understood what it was like to be uprooted from where you'd grown up and transplanted into foreign soil with blind and unknowing hope that you'll grow.

One day, far before he found a job in the auto shop repair, George went to an antique music store and bought an old used record player to listen to his albums from his friend's brother from Bulgaria.

To George, this music across the Ocean was so normal! So warm! So alive! So beautiful!

Though George knew he could be biased, he couldn't help

but believe that it was wholly superior.

He hated aggressive American music. He hated Woodstock's cultural parties in upstate New York and the idea of "sex, drugs, and rock n' roll."

You might think I'm exaggerating, but I assure you, I'm not.

George lived in a small apartment and began sharing with two orphans from Yugoslavia in a dump, with no possessions in his dwelling, only some Bulgarian food in the refrigerator and dirty clothes around, and his stolen childhood with pictures and newspaper clippings taped to the wall along with the two US presidents: Truman and Eisenhower: When the man who loved roads met the man who changed America taped to the wall to remind him that he is now free and never to look back.

The chilly night air swirled around George and Alex, turning the World into a blur once more. At first, the air felt as though it would tear through Alex's skin and kill him. But slowly, the air warmed to a light chill, and the next scene came about. The scene was peaceful. Despite the air being 50 degrees (F) at the warmest, there was warmth and comfort around the viewers and young George. Our young immigrant was looking out at the water of a beach. He had the same clothes as the night before. They were even dirtier than before, but the boy looked clean. He looked renewed. "What's happening?" Alex asked. He was relieved the previous experience had ended, and the feeling that he was taking away from young George's perspective bordered on euphoria.

He had to know what had brought it about.

"I remember this moment," George said.

"I'll never forget it; this memory will always be clear as day." George enjoyed the scene for a minute as though he hadn't begun a thought, then he broke,

"This...This is the moment where I realized I was going to be okay."

"Why did you think that?" "I got a job."

What does it mean to have a job in America?

George fondly recalls the melodic strains of "If I Were A Rich Man" from the beloved musical "Fiddler on the Roof" during his youthful days as a nineteenth-year-old immigrant. He deeply resonated with Tevye's plight in Anatevka, finding parallels to his own journey in Tzarist Russia. Originating from a Yiddish monologue by Sholem Aleichem titled "If I Were A Rothschildld," the song held profound significance for him. Reflecting on its message, George acknowledges the dignity in poverty, yet candidly admits the struggles it entails. As he navigated life in America, he couldn't help but ponder the allure of wealth. Slowly, George found himself drawn to the notion that perhaps prosperity held its own merits in this land of opportunity.

"How do you survive in the shadows in the booming

economy?" asked George.

I've already survived the Bulgarian communist system, learning from his father how to bribe and go around the black markets in Sofia. He adapts faster to Brighton Beach in Brooklyn. George was big and strong. He could find a quick job with the Italians and later the Russian mafia. But he prefers to work with his hands.

In the 1970s, Soviet Union Russians delivered to America not only the Russian Jews but a lot of criminals undercover KBG sleeper agents who, with fake IDs, adapted to the community. Cheaper rent, next to the beach, get free money for education, and move to quiet suburbs of New Jersey, Long Island, or Upstate New York, far away from the City.

"C'mon, baby, it's capitalism," said George's Russian buddy.

If you make it to NEW YORK CITY, you can make it anywhere. Brighton Beach became the Wild West. Instead of being a gangster involved in requiring activity, he chooses to do business on how to fix cars.

He didn't join the crime family and groups. In the 1990s, waves were highly educated with technical skills trained in communist bureaucracy. For the USSR, it was Brain Drain, but for the USA, it was Brain Gain!

The USA is one big candy store. Big orchids with fruits open to eat the goods; Soviet Russian emigrants just didn't care. They are not afraid of what will be punished. They survived the Soviet system already trained and quickly learned how to work around the American system, too. But George preferred to work an honest job with his hands.

No mafia jobs for him.

Alex understood the comfort. It wasn't a feeling of warmth or a specific pleasure; it was the feeling of absence. It was the feeling of the cold night being over. From this, Alex learned something.

Alex learned just a little bit about what it was like to struggle. "Where do you work? Where are we now?" Alex continued his questioning after some introspection while looking at a storefront sign that had its name in both the English and the Cyrillic alphabet.

"We're looking out over Brighton Beach, Coney Island. This is where many Russian immigrants, new and old, came in search of economic success and stability." "Wow. It's nice." Alex observed. The chilly wind blew softly and carried a salty aroma and taste to the young George's mouth. The wind pushed young George just enough that he had to lean forward against it; this gave him the feeling of facing something down, of overcoming opposition. It was a physical representation of our young immigrant's determination. A little introspection on Alex's part followed, and it left silence between the spectators' line of communication. Once, the silence had its fill, and it felt like St. Georgiy's will had been carried out. Alex spoke: "What's your job?"

"Same it's always been," George responded simply. "Fixing cars. Among other things." "Really?" Said Alex in slight disbelief. "You've been doing that since you got here?"

"Of course, what else would I have been doing? I didn't apply for government benefits; I felt it was necessary to *contribute* to society. I would say that it was a good job to start off with, too. I started fixing cars for anyone on the street – just minor things like flat tires or changing brakes and lights. At the most, it was an oil change. Eventually, word of mouth worked, and I got lucky." The word "lucky" shook Alex. He was lucky. This "luck" his grandfather spoke of wasn't luck; no true fortune had fallen on him. This "luck" was the absence of doom. This broke another epiphany for Alex; living (in a human condition, at least) was lucky. It was a stroke of luck for his grandfather to be able to eat and not freeze on the street. This was the fight of an immigrant. Alex, at that point, remembered how his grandfather George had been trying to teach him how to fix his old car in the backyard. " Why does it seem like fewer guys in the US know how to work with their hands- like carpentry, car repairs, or just fixing things?

Back in Bulgaria, every man head of the household must be like a certified mechanic, plumber, or electrician."

One day, George met a group of young people from "Jews for Jesus" in a fiery argument with the Lubavitcher Rabbi's "Jews for Judaism" on the boardwalk in Brighton Beach.

The argument was: "Who is the Real Messiah?"

It was a Saturday/Shabbat, and the rabbi thought that George was a Soviet Jew and started to convert him to Judaism, but with his "Georgian" English, he started to explain that he was "Orthodox" but Christian.

The black-hatted Hasidic said a prayer, thinking George's parents were that religion before Lenin's Revolution. The rabbi thought that he was coming from an Orthodox Jewish family from some forgotten shtetl in Eastern Europe to bring the captive free from the lost tribes of Israel.

The whirlwind returned. St. Georgiy had more plans. The scene turned from its idyllic image to a mess of colors into the black that represented such a lack of light that it could barely even be given the title of black. The black remained. From the darkness was the garage where young George was working. It was night, and the feeling of exhaustion overcame the two spectators' spirits. The image assembled more, and a clear scene was eventually set. It was of young George, alone in the shop.

"I remember this." George introduced the scene, "This was at the end of my first week."

"Why is it important?" Alex was confused as to why this day was a stop in the review of his grandfather's life.

"It was when I knew what was in the future. Maybe for the first time in my life."

"I'm tired. I want to quit; why am I here?" Young George's thoughts broke right as George finished "speaking."

"It sounds uncertain." Alex contributed.

"No," George said flatly, leading into his next thought. "I thought it was terrible, but you'll see how this ends. I might've thought anything, but I know how I felt." The scene continued. Young George finished up work. He left the garage and visited an office in the front where it could be assumed his boss was working.

The change in the scenes between rooms was like flipping through surveillance cameras; at one point, the two spectators could see everything unfold in one room, and then, in a second, everything was happening in the next. It was like the beginning of a scene in a movie where the protagonist enters the room. The "cameras" switched from watching young George while he left the room into the manager's office.

"It is time for you to go?" The manager said to young George as he stepped into the office. He handed him his paycheck in an envelope. He was a large man. He was portly, but it was clear he had a strong build that gave him a decent bit of structure. You don't fit here.

"So, they just shoot me. Ex…squeeze me. I mean, excuse me. I can't believe it. They fired me… "

"The owner's son, the shop's Manager, Igor, didn't like me, some clients complained. That's all! Not the father, but the son hated me. This guy treated me like complete shit? Fuhgeddaboudit!"

"Wow. His English is really clear. I mean, there are some confusing words sometimes, but wow! Have you learned it by now?" Alex was relieved that he could understand the man's dialogue.

"No," George said. "He's speaking Russian. That's Dimitri; he's an old Russian. He's the one that opened the auto shop and hired me."

"Oh. I thought the old immigrants didn't like new waves?" "They don't, but we Slavs liked one another. Russian-speaking Soviet Russian and Ukrainian Jews, Kazakhs, Kyrgyz, Tajiks, Uzbeks, Armenians, Georgians, Uzbeks, and Eastern Europeans have joined them. Because of a common Russian World in Brighton, we helped each other out." "That sounds kinda racist..." Alex didn't quite understand the bond that their culture initiated.

He didn't have much of culture himself besides the wisps of American culture displayed in his upbringing.

It was a little pay, but I learned a lot." Said George flatly. "And I thought it was kind of silly at the time, but a shop runs easier when you all speak the same language accents and understand how you all think a little better."

"It was a little." Said George flatly. "And I thought it was kind of silly at the time, but a shop runs easier when you all speak the same language and understand how you all think a little better."

"I guess." Alex felt a little defeated.

While their conversation went on, they watched young George leave the shop and bike home. The shop was about three miles from young George's residence. As he biked home, our viewers could feel the cold air in young George's lungs, and they could feel the soreness rising in his legs as exhaustion slowly overcame him. After about three minutes of biking, images began flashing. They were the images of the cars young George had worked on earlier that day. Alex and George understood that much, at least. There were no thoughts in our young George's head, just the images and the feelings they gave off.

There were really two feelings in the images: excitement and anxiety. It was clear that the excitement wasn't only present in anticipation of fixing the cars but also in overcoming the anxiety.

As young George was biking home, he was lost in his mind – in the images of the cars he had fixed. "Who was that client who made a complaint against him? He did such a good job that day!"

Once young George focused back on the road, it was too late. He was already half a second away from crashing into an older woman. Old lady Babushka was screaming in Russian, "What do you think you're doing, durak?!" The angry babushka, dressed in a headscarf, angrily shook her fist at George, who dared to cross her path with his bike.

The woman was displeased and armed with her cane. Witnesses saw the young man being smacked over the head with the old woman's stick. Clearly, he would not be fighting back!

Alex and George were speechless as they heard young George be assaulted by a tirade of English-not-quite-English words. The only words that seemed to make sense were basic pronouns and profanities he had learned through nasty addresses from pedestrians while he was a "street urchin." George and Alex could feel the fear young George felt. If they had eyes, they would've cried. The warmth and familiarity of the shop had fully left the spectators. This was a strange place that didn't speak their language, and there was no leaving. This place, no matter how much work is done, is not home. Young George ran away, and with the blurring of the surroundings from the speed of his bike came the blurs from another change in scenes.

The new scene was of a door. It was a small house with green paint and white awnings. As the scene continued, young George approached the front door and opened it. Alex remembered this. This was his grandfather's house. The whites of the accents were sharper and cleaner, and the green paint was lacking dirt, but this was his grandfather's house; he knew it.

"This is your first house." Alex chipped in.

"Yep," George said simply and with pride. "This is the first time I saw the inside after buying it." Alex was amazed. This was not the first time he had seen the inside. He had been given a myriad of opportunities to appreciate the beauty of the house, which George bought as is and saved money by fixing up. But only then did it seem so beautiful. Maybe it was because he saw the house as young George did, maybe it was because it was the first time that he had seen the house when it looked so new, or maybe it was because he finally understood the struggle his young grandfather overcame to get there.

The scene continued without young George in it. The spectator continued to watch the room as different people appeared in it. "Who are these people?" Alex asked.

"Your family," George said in his usual paternally simple tone. "From the old country. You just don't remember them; most passed before you were born, or at least before you were old enough to remember them."

Alex felt sad. Not only because he never got to meet the people that young George felt so strongly about but also because of the warmth he felt from these relatives of his. This was home, home sweet home. Young George hadn't gone home. Home had come to him.

"How'd they get here?" Alex asked while still in awe of the people and the comfort they brought.

"I brought them here. In my dream, I sent them letter after letter with any money I could spare in hopes they would use it for food or save it to come. Apparently, they did the latter."

"Wow." Alex was in awe of his grandfather's tenacity once again.

"It was risky too..." George continued, but he seemed to have gotten lost in thought.

"Why's that?" Alex asked, bringing him back to his train of thought. He saw his grandpa storing his cash. Ben Franklin bills in stacks under his mattress. Why do you stash your money there; why not in the bank? Grandpa, you are sleeping on it – literally.

"US Dollars were illegal in Communist Bulgaria. It was seen illegally in the new system. It was "counter-revolutionary" to have a lot of money." Especially American hard currency.

"What would've happened if they were caught?"

"I don't know," George told his grandson pensively.

"However, I can tell you that the secret police controlled all aspects of life and that if you were caught, you could get sent to a prison camp. Have you heard of the book 1984? Well, I lived all that back in 1948..."

"Oh," Alex said, "I didn't know." He was uncomfortable. The situation that his grandfather overcame him more and more every time he heard about it, time and time again!

It was crushing him. This emigrant's survival was foreign to him. Alex was part of the Millennials – the *me, me, me* generation.

# Chapter 6:

# Success

Two years since George came to Brooklyn, he remembered one particular Saturday. These were his "orphan years" in America.

"I felt the nature, the breeze, the freedom of the seagulls in New York Harbor walking on the boardwalk of Brighton Beach," George would think in recollection. He felt trapped in the country while walking. It was like he was under heavy anesthesia during a long and transforming surgery. "I cannot live in this depressing state anymore. I am stuck in prison at this low-level life. I should not live only to survive. My life should not be a list of things I must get done in order to keep living it!"

Have you ever wondered how to live a simple life and be happy even under stress? Life in America would be full of extreme hardship.

Many of the emigrants had to endure many things: low wages, poor working conditions, and overcrowded living situations. Yes, it was better than their place of origin. Yet, if life was too hard, many immigrants went back home. George had clinical depression, and he had it regarding longing for his lost country and how to make peace in loneliness.

"I cry for no reason in my life of suffering. It brings me to the darkness of Dostoevsky's *Underground Man*. I think I have internalized the vigor of Dostoevsky's character a little bit too literally."

When I was reading Tolstoy and Dostoevsky finally understood myself entirely. From the very start each and every description in the books I have the same feelings. I always thought that they were talking about me.

In New York City, on the pedestal of the "Freedom Monument," the Statue of Liberty, George remembered its last engraved verse from the Jewish-American writer Emma Lazarus' "The New Colossus": "Give me your weary people, all eager to sigh freely, thrown into need. Poor and orphans, Expelled from distant shores! Send them, homeless and humiliated, to me! I raise my torch in front of the Golden Gate!"

The scene ended. Everything was fast-forwarded and blurred.

George's speech with his uncle went from a clear business conversation to blurred nonsense to Blah Blah talk.

Though the scene and its visual aspects changed, the gibberish continued. It was about his uncle's advice and guarantee in the bank.

Everything came together visually until the scene was

clear.

They were at the "Emigrant" Bank. It was clear where the gibberish was coming from; it was the customers and tellers at the bank. The gibberish seemed to make more sense to young George, but the mundanity of the speech kept Alex from even trying to listen in.

The scene followed young George while he spoke to a secretary and was asked to take a seat. Due to the fast talk, all George understood was: "Seat... suppose... Soon."

Alex was confused by what the woman said, but he figured it to mean, "Please take a seat; I suppose they'll see you soon."

"Why are you at a bank?" Alex asked.

"I need a business loan," George said flatly. He seemed a little perturbed.

"Why?" Alex pushed.

"I needed it???

To open the Auto shop."

George clearly didn't want to say much more, so Alex figured he would just watch. A bell rang, and the secretary raised her head, "John Balkins... See you... in # 104." Young George understood this fine. He got up and took his briefcase (it was cheap, clearly), which he held with a sense of uncertainty. He entered the office and greeted its occupant before taking a seat.

"So... A loan? For an Auto shop?" said the fat man. He was a portly man, but not like Dimitri; he was softer than him. It was clear this man had not fought like George or Dimitri.

"Yes." young George said. The ethereal spectators could feel the shame young George got from saying that.

Not just because he didn't like asking for money but because he was trying to hide his accent.

This was a difficult task, though young George was about twenty-five at the time and had been in the country for eight to nine years. His English was far from perfect, and he had trouble speaking it fluently, let alone as though he were a native. Young George also knew that if it was clear that he immigrated as recently as he had, the loan would be refused quicker than he could understand what had happened.

The loan advisor was quicker with the questions than young George had expected, "What profits?" Was all that young George could understand from the man's quick speech in the first question. Though he didn't fully understand the question, young George knew what to do. He clicked open the cheap case and pulled out a piece of paper with a set of numbers from Dimitri's shop: "These are the profits from a shop in a similar area." Young George had practiced that line for hours the night before with his relatives at home. There was just a slight accent. Most of the previous night's practice was covering it up. He knew the numbers were promising enough to justify a loan, and the loaner's change in expression justified that fact. "Where are you from?" The loaner asked directly. George was plenty familiar with that question.

The American policy at this period was to attract more emigrants from Western and Northern Europe but not from Eastern and South Europe. Slavs or Italians were not favorable. They had difficulty adapting to the Anglo-Saxon language and culture. Americans were afraid that instead of English, Brighton would become more Russian speaking.

"He can't ask that!" Alex shot out. "That discriminatory. I learned this in school; I remember that much."

George chuckled. "Oh boy. This is long before those laws came into place."

"Oh." Alex felt defeated once more, not just because he understood the fact but also because he was feeling young George's emotions at the moment.

"What country were you born in?"

"Bulgaria." Young George answered bravely.

"What did you say: Slovenia?"

"No! Bulgaria!" What? Bolivia?

As a college-educated person who failed to identify one of the Balkan countries in Europe, there's no hope they'll know where or what Bulgaria is. Most Americans associate Bulgaria with the Black Sea or with the Greek Island in the south.

Never heard about it. But you're an American citizen now.

"Good, son. People love you, Rusky bastards running their shops."

The fat man responded with a light chuckle. "I think we have an offer for you." Today is your lucky day!

The spectators could feel young George's rage.

"25% down."

Young George stood up and shook the man's hand. It's a deal! "What happened?" Alex asked.

"We got a loan," George said with a hint of pride.

"From him?! Why would you take a loan from him? There were plenty of banks, right? Get it from somewhere else!" Young George's rage had clearly rubbed off on Alex.

"We can't. This is the sixteenth try." George said flatly. He knew Alex didn't know any better, but the idea that he could've chosen not to take such a debasement against his home country perturbed him.

George had made appointments with twenty different

banks. Refusal after refusal. George understood what "no" meant, but he wasn't taking it! Eventually, he got his dream loan! George was a stubborn young man.

He couldn't be beaten!

"Oh." Alex was once again in a defeated mood.

The scene followed young George getting into his car and driving home. He didn't seem happy, but an exciting mood overcame the two viewers. The car ride seemed long (and it was), but the mood peaked when young George pulled into the driveway. He walked up the wooden steps to the door, opened it, and found his family and friends waiting. So, George had actually shown a document to prove his uncle as a guarantor and showed his bank's savings in another document. Thanks to this, he was able to get the loan. That was his lucky day. He felt like he was swimming with the bank's sharks, and he got it!

At this moment, he wanted to share his joy with his parents back in Bulgaria since he didn't know they were in prison because of his defective son.

"I got the loan." Young George announced in a slightly raised voice. All his friends and guests erupted. They cheered and congratulated him. The men shook his hand as firmly as a man could, and the women pounced on young George to hug and congratulate him. George felt pride. Dinner had been prepared in anticipation of the event. A whole baby lamb had been roasted. It smelled so good that Alex began to wish he had a stomach so that he could enjoy it.

It was May 6th, Georgiovden (St George Day)— his name day celebration. The Saint from the wall's hand-painted icon in his house as if winking at him as a sign of his intervention on this day.Glory to God! Thank you, Sveti Georgiy, the Victorious.

The bright lights and faces of the house shifted into a blur.

The new scene composed itself into a garage. Young George carried himself differently here. It was as if he owned the place – mainly because he did. Young George was proud of himself. He was a young man with great success in the Bulgarian community.

He would like his parents and grandparents to see him now. To celebrate his achievements.

"Wow," Alex said. "This is your business? You built this?!"

"Yes, showing the sign of the repair shop. It was Nicky's auto-body repairs on Coney Island Avenue, and this was his happiest day in America!"

George said with pride, "Well, it was mostly built when I got the place, but it's mine, nonetheless. And this isn't even the best part of this memory!"

"What's the best part?"

"You'll see," George said confidently.

Soon after the older young George finished talking to a repairman, a woman approached him. "Hello, my Chevy's broken down, and I need a man." The woman was clearly also an immigrant but elegant. She had a thick Italian accent, and it was clear that her English was imperfect. The final attribute, she was beautiful. Maybe it was just how young George saw her, but the woman was a glowing aphroditic image.

"Is that... grandma?" Alex asked. He was stunned.

He hadn't seen a photo of his grandmother when she was young that wasn't incredibly grainy and monochrome. He had never even thought that his grandmother could look like a young woman. "Yep," George answered with pride.

"That's her." At this moment, George remembered Maria, who was sitting in the hospital room, holding his hand at his death bed as she prayed for his (quick) recovery." She was a devoted catholic, praying – "Hail Mary, full of grace, the Lord is with thee; spiritual mother to those in need, I fervently request your heavenly intercession for George and Alex, who are ill and seek God's miraculous assistance. You truly care for the sick and offer them your compassionate support in powerful acts of healing!"

The scene skipped a bit to our young George inspecting the

woman's car. As the owner of the shop, this was not commonplace, but he decided he would make an exception. "Da." "Yes, Ma'am!" the young man said, "The radiator is cracked; you didn't cool her."

"What does that mean?" the woman asked.

"Three days and about $200," George said flatly.

"You can do it in one day for $170." The woman responded with a hint of aggression due to the extreme summer heat. "Come on. Don't bullshit me." The young lady's attitude grabbed hold of George's attention and interest instantly.

"Ooh," Alex commented. George chuckled. He was clearly entertained by the vivacious personality of his young wife.

When a woman first meets a man, she is, in a sense, "scanning" a man – to gauge her instant attraction to him and whether she wants to see him again...

Something like love at first sight.

"Oh. Maria was always such a strong businesswoman with intuition. She could buy the Mona Lisa for a dime if they gave her the time!"

The scenes skipped again. It was two days later. Maria was back for her car, a Chevy Bel Air, and George was talking to her in front of the car. The spectators felt uncomfortable and nervous, just as the young George did, but it was clear he was trying to seem cool while leaning on the hood of the car. Maria had paid for the repairs inside, so all that was left for her to do was drive away. George did a free tune-up, too.

The conversation blurred until young George said, "Call you sometimes?" Maria handed him a slip of paper, tapped his knee, and walked to the driver's door of the car.

George was happy to see Maria in her stylish red car fixed with an exclusive smile, expressing great satisfaction. The first time George saw her, he was impressed, and he silently followed her for a while until she got her car keys back. She walked so graciously – her long, beautifully shaped hips. Her red skirt swung from side to side, barely covering her long legs. The heels made her legs look even longer and firmer, and her breasts were the perfect size. She was stunning, even without makeup!

George followed her like he was in a dream. She was simply out of his league. She looked like Sophia Loren. The stunning Italian icon!

"La bella figura." is about possessing dignity, warmth, kindness, and politeness.

"Amore Mio: Maria, my love," George thought – but such a visceral statement would get a reaction from anyone.

What about this Italian kissing? What a difference between the pious Bulgarian man and the exciting Italian woman.

"Ciao," she said before she drove off. The spectators felt

pride. George in his younger self's ability to attract such a woman, and Alex from the pride his young grandfather was feeling. The scene sped up again. Now, it was going over the romantic scenes of the couple. George worshiped Maria.

Even going to the grocery store, Maria looked stunning and was the envy of all the men who passed the couple by. To many locals, she was even known as "Maria Karenina" around Brighton Beach. It showed the two of them on their first date. The conversations they had weren't clear, and neither spectator could make out the words being spoken, but the feeling of comfort and affection was obvious from the start. After the first date, a montage ensued. The affectionate moments that created the foundation of the love in the two immigrants' relationship are shown to both the spectators. George almost became jealous of Maria's family while they did their pleasant face-kiss greetings. Sometimes, the jealousy peaked, and he would lash out or drink.

Even at the worst, though, the morning routine of George waking up early to make his love breakfast in bed and going out late to buy her a new set of flowers and chocolates. George and Alex were mesmerized. George was overcome emotionally.

Remember the wonders of his youth and how he loved spending it with his wife would've made him cry if he could. He felt like he was in love again. He missed her immensely and wished he could be with her.

He hoped that St. George would allow them to see one another once more. He began praying for it in his head. He still didn't know whether or not his grandson could hear him, but he didn't quite care. Alex was having trouble processing. He had never seen his grandparents young, and their passive elderly love was far less intense than the love they showed early in their relationship. He wished he could see his grandma again so that he could feel as though he understood her in a new way. Sadly, that was a possibility that had passed him by, as she had passed a few years prior to this story. The montage continued until a feeling of tension was created in a new scene.

Maria was gone, and George was sitting alone. He was looking down in a chair, and across a large leather-bound desk from him was a big Italian man. He had black hair that was slicked back with hair grease or some other product – George never quite knew.

The man's face wore an expression of stern consternation with a mustache planted in the middle. He was thin but well-built. It was clear he grew up with physical labor before his present situation.

"So." The man's voice broke the silence of the room and scared everyone but himself. "You want to marry my daughter." Young George looked the man straight in the eyes and repressed his nerves as much as he could.

"Yes. I love her."

George laughed aloud, "Ohhh." He laughed again. "Oh. I can't believe I didn't lose my mind! Hahaha. I left my home to make something out of nothing, and I swear this still might just have been the scariest experience of my life."

Maria's father sat there. He stared at the boy just long enough to make him wonder if he would die that day until he burst into laughter. He laughed a bold and proud laugh like Saint Nicholas.

"Mi piaci. I like you. You have my blessing." Young George shot up.

"Oh, thank you. I promise you will have pride in this decision." He leaned over quickly to shake the Father's hand. He was ecstatic.

"If you hurt her," the father began.

"I won't." Young George interrupted.

"If you hurt her, I'll shoot you in the mouth." Young George froze for just a second. He had no intentions of ever bringing harm to Maria, his love, but such a visceral statement would beget a reaction from anyone.

"You must worry not about that. I love her." Young George. After his initial reaction, he didn't worry so much about the consequence of hurting his love. His reason for repeating this promise was a concern of another sort. It was a concern that anyone would think that he would bring harm to his love, and our spectators knew that.

Maria's father nodded. The nod acted as an apology to young George. It was an apology for asserting that the young man would hurt his love. He said, "You may be my son-in-law.

I look forward to it."

The scene blurred. St. George's will tore away that version of George and the father of his love and set up a new George with a new situation to manage his way through. Before the scene was even set, a feeling of joy and comfort overcame the spectators.

Compared to previous feelings of comfort in George and Alex's adventure, this one was tenfold any other moment. After a couple of seconds, the scene was set, and it was beautiful.

The scene was that of a wedding. Specifically, the one to establish the eternal union between George and Maria, his love. Their Roman Catholic wedding wasn't just one of the biggest commitments that two people had made in their lives; it is also considered to be one of the most important aspects of their religious family life.

George and Alex were silent while watching the bride walk the aisle to the groom. The tradition of the Roman Catholic Church is one in which a married couple commits themselves to each other "till death do [they] part." The wedding is known as the sacrament of matrimony, which Catholics believe to be a "channel of God's grace." They said their vows and kissed. The feeling of that moment could only be described as magical. George wore a handsome brown suit. It was all that he could afford at the time. Maria's father had paid for most of the wedding. The bride and groom stood together and took a photo, which, decades later, still sits on the right side of George's desk. He loved that photo. He loved that day. And George felt his prayer had been answered by being given the gift of reliving this day.

As the wedding died down, the scene started shifting. George was sad to have to leave but content with what he had been given. George was thinking for himself at that age.

Life in exile is not that romantic at all. As a matter of fact, it isn't easy, *especially for Maria. She had to take care of all the housework – cooking, cleaning, and taking care of the newborn baby.* Maria was in constant pain. Physical and emotional.

For three years, the two lost emigrant souls, George and Maria, found themselves raising their infant – Nicky, the firstborn. George was working all day, managing his auto shop. He was a student at the "University of Diversity."

This was my moment in life. Nobody taught me, but this auto shop experience started my success, and the skills I developed helped me build my American Dream. Maria was so stressed as a first-time mother. She understood that she was sacrificing them to open opportunities for her baby boy and their future kids.

"This is America, Maria," George would start some evenings, "Buckle up, young lady, there's no time to waste! It's a luxury we cannot afford! Work, Work, and only Work to achieve our dreams! Only Hard work! There is nothing like Julius Caesar saying, *'I came, I saw, I conquered.'* Nothing like that!"

George, as an alpha male immigrant, was pretty aggressive in conversation in the family, but Maria didn't buy that. He will be the boss only in his business, but not in her house.

George was attracted to Maria as an independent woman, but he got angry when he learned that independent women do not submit that easily. Maria didn't allow the old country respect and submissiveness in her house.

"Wow," Alex said. He felt that, through this experience, he understood his grandfather now. Alex had always loved his grandfather, but his old-world accent and mannerisms had always made him terribly unrelatable, extremely weird, strange – even alien!

Alex just didn't get his grandfather.

But now, after seeing his grandfather grow up, fight struggles that Alex couldn't even imagine beforehand, and fall in love, he felt as though this experience had made Grandpa George a part of him.

The scene finished shifting. The next scene didn't move. It was a still image. The image was of a pregnant Maria standing in the kitchen of their house. It was the morning, and the light from the recently risen sun shone in behind her to give her a glow that was deifying, to say the least. Next to the Bulgarian wooden carving icon "The Virgin Holy Mother of God."

"Ah." George started. "I remember this moment. I don't think I'll ever forget it."

George stopped and thought for a second. "This was when I realized that I was going to be a father for the first time. And – that it was going to be alright because I was married to a beautiful, amazing woman."

George sounded like he was crying. If it was possible, he would be.

Alex couldn't imagine his grandfather crying, even after all of this. He had always been such a stern, disciplined man.

The colors of the scene slipped away. In its depth, George could hear the lyrics of the song, "If I can make it there, I'll make it anywhere. It's up to you. New York, New York," a famous song that George believed to embody the feeling of the city.

Let's make a toast: 'I did it my way,' America's anthem of George's self-determination.

"How I made it in America, my way." The words from the famous song, *"My Way!"* sang out.

A new ensemble of colors assembled themselves. They aligned to form a beautiful image of a happy baby boy in the hands of young George. "Nikolaschka," or Kolyia, Nikolas - namesake for Maria's late father. Or Nicky, the diminutive for Nikolay.

"That's," Alex began. George finished his sentence, "Your father."

# Chapter 7:

# The Blessed Child

Alex and George gazed at the cherub's first seconds of life.

At Coney Island Hospital on Ocean (so-called "Russian") Parkway, baby Nikolay was born just before Christmas.

Like baby Jesus– he was a gift to the World. Everyone here celebrates Hebrew Hanukkah, also known as the Festival of Lights, in the Jewish part of Brighton.

"So that's my dad," Alex said, breaking the admirative silence.

"Yeah," George responded. It was barely a word, barely English, but it meant everything.

That one word said everything it needed to about how George felt. It said, "That's my boy. My beautiful, beautiful baby boy Kolychka." George had relived this moment in his head a million times. He had thought through every second of it as he acted out his fatherhood, but seeing it was just different. George thanked God in his head. He wished he could thank Him more.

George wished he had the time to say a million prayers in thanks for the gift of truly reliving this moment. Such a beautiful moment made George feel the car wreck was almost worth it!

Almost. At this moment, George remembered this situation.

The Brighton Bulgarian community took a large chunk of George's neighborhood, and as a result, they celebrated Bulgarian Koledari and New Year with the Russian Ded Moroz in English - Santa Claus or Grandpa Frost.

They always gave gifts to their children on the atheist New Year instead of Christmas in Bulgarian – Koleda. They all would write wishes for each other on small pieces of paper called kasmeti for the traditional 'Banitsa,' which was a traditional feta cheese pie.

Back in the communist time that George lived through, they always gave gifts to their children before New Year's Eve around 9pm and watched the New Year Special program on the Bulgarian channel – BG TV – Novogodishna programa.

At 12:58 PM, they drink sovetskoe shampanskoe champagne from the USSR on the 1st of January. After midnight, they eat banitsa, for which grandma wrote happy wishes and hid them in tin foil that was put into the feta pie. Each wish would include something like happiness, health, traveling, or success over the next year.

George was lost in the trap of his memories.

The moment had changed: Am I alive? George thought. At this moment, the scene of the hospital and George's newborn son faded just enough for him to see past it into another location.

The scene was still in a hospital, but it was a completely different place. The feeling of the room was different, too. Instead of George's relief and pure joy in the delivery room, this one had an unbelievable tension. It was the tension that made George scared even to think – let alone say something.

As the scene cleared up, George could see himself clearly enough. He was lying there unconscious in a bed with medical personnel surrounding him.

George's body was hooked up to a heart monitor that was beeping steadily. It didn't take him long to figure out what was going on – I'm in a coma, George thought as he began to panic. As George panicked, everything around him blurred just a little; it was the universe falling apart around him. As the blurring ended and the universe around him came back into focus, George could see his heart monitor and that it was flatlining. Am I going to die?! George's panic took over once again. The people in the room, George's son, daughter-in-law, and friends, looked even more panicked than George himself.

They flew around him, and the tension in the room tripled; everyone could feel their worst fears coming to life. George began to hyperventilate, and just as he did, the monitor started beeping again. At first, the monitor resembled an alarmingly quick pulse, but soon enough, the rate slowed and steadied.

At first, the monitors resembled an alarmingly quick pulse.

Then someone was shoving a mask on George's face to force him to breathe...

Someone put some medicine into his IV...

George knew how to fight for his life but understood the need to relax and finish his spiritual tours with Alexander that were guided by his grandpa, the captain. It was such a roller-coaster.

At this point, George knew what was going on- he was fighting for his life. This realization marked the beginning of George's third wave of panic. He watched the heart monitor accelerate. With the increase in speed, it seemed the monitor was growing in noise as well. George looked for anything that could calm him down and only realized that he was completely alone. Alex was gone. The only thing left to accompany George in his panic was the black-not-quite-black ether that surrounded him in the middle of a tunnel, completely dark – like someone turned off the lights. Another door opened at another time across the Atlantic Ocean.

George was born premature – so tiny that his mother, Emma, was holding him with fear. His father, the general town physician, Dr. Alexander, came into the birthing house to assist with the delivery because he appeared unexpectedly before his time. It was a problematic situation. "Georgiy – Goshko – my boy! He will live, or he will die!" It's up to him! And God's Will for his life! From the beginning, George was a fighter and survivor! He knew how to fight! From Sofia to New York for the second wave of his uncertainty back and forth.

His son Nicky was born in Coney Island Hospital. Big boy, almost a 9-pounder. That December, it was freezing, so he decided to procrastinate his birth due to freezing temperatures and snow on December 18th 1961.

His nursery room was painted blue over the crib, and dozens of adorable blue onesies were perfectly folded in a dresser drawer. So, where's the baby? Don't sweat an overdue baby. He came just before Christmas as a gift from God into this international, dysfunctional emigrant family.

Many times, both parents had problems over how to raise their precious only child. It was the battlefield between the Eastern and Western Roman Empires.

It was the Clash of the Empires. From his mother's side, Nikolas was loved, and Maria represented the grace, big-heartedness, and gentleness in his life.

On his paternal side, George came from a long background – a line of Orthodox church priests, officers, soldiers, and disciplinarians, which meant that the "laws and rules" in his family were Gospel. If your disciplinarian father tells you to take the trash out, you're probably quick to follow their instructions. Parents should not be fighting in front of their children. They need to sort themselves out and respect others inside the house. Strongly suggest that they stop arguing or take their anger somewhere else as it's your home, too. Who would want to listen to this for ages?! You could step in and tell them to be quiet and stop the noise! How can you last through all this screaming in both foreign languages?!

Heated arguments every night, like

"What is wrong with you, Georgio, all the time?

Eh Basta Georgio - Stop it!

Enough Silenzio - Shut Fuck up!

Nicky is in his room!

Oh, mamma Mia - OMG, Oh, Goodness gracious

I Provide for you, but you never respect me as the man of the house!

What a stubborn man! Ma che fai - What are you doing?

Ah, Idiota - Oh, Idiot! Stop, Stop!

Va'a farti fottere - "Go screw yourself."

Eventually, every argument finished with unresolved issues or would be finished with the alarming word:

"Divorzio," "Razvod (in Bulgarian) — divorce!" which traumatized the little boy.

George tries to explain his joke, stuttering: "I just! I just!"

Maria replied: "He thinks he is so just, perfect like Jesus! Always right! Almost Saint! St. Georgio! The holy man of God!"

She said that with bitter sarcasm and satire.

George responded: "Maria! Listen. You are always picking his side. Why Maria? Why always protect him from whom? From me? His father? You are my wife. We need to stand together – to make decisions together!"

Many times, Nikky craved his father's approval and the embrace of a man. Maria is gentle and loving but sometimes suffers from deep depression due to her alcoholic Italian father's abuse. She hated this type of macho man like her Italian papa.

Nicky, as a student in Abraham Lincoln Hight School, was always in need of proper words, trying to find the right phrases in his conversation. It was stressful to be around him.

He was suffering from low self-esteem.

Maria often repeated the Balkan saying: "The man may be the head of the household. But the woman is the neck, and she can turn the head whichever way she pleases. Heheh!" She was laughing.

*Love and Hate* was an emigrant Kakhovskiy family tale.

The divorce rate in America today is more than fifty percent. I don't understand why Leo Tolstoy is making a big deal about Anna Karenina's divorce.

This was during a different epoch compared to today. For America, divorce is something normal and tough. Nicky, after listening to the following heated arguments of his parents who were arguing because of him, didn't understand the complicated life and difficulty of coming and settling in America with George's humble beginning. For him, family was his most precious possession as an emigrant. For him, it wasn't easy to settle anywhere. George's family was above his business.

George was always angry, and at the end of the week, it's not easy to balance the sheets and payroll of all your employees while making sure your family is okay, too. Sometimes, Maria just couldn't control George's demons, which would leave him slamming the door and screaming. Fuhgeddaboudit!

His "emergency exit" was drinking at his friend's bar. The alcohol would relax him and his body. He needed to relax. He needed to play more with his kid. George had contracted a fear and anxiety around the word "tomorrow." "What will happen tomorrow?" George was worried about what could happen to his family or business. Every night that he lost his temper, he would put a band-aid on the wound and would cover his shame with lavish gifts, flowers and chocolate, and restaurant reservations on the next day. Sometimes, it was simply paying attention to Maria with kind, loving words.

It was difficult for his ego to say, "I'm sorry, I was wrong last night! Please forgive me, Maria!"

The next day, after all this, George was asking Koliychka (little Nicky) in his joke's manners: "Who do you love more, Kolya (diminutive of Nikolay), your mom or your dad? Why? Why?"

"Who do you love more, Mom or Dad?"

Nicky: "Both. It's not fair! I don't know. I'm confused. I don't know who loves me most. I love you equally!"

"Mahahha!" It was his constant stupid joke.

George remembers his parents: "My father, hands down, was always busy in the hospital. My mother is very dear to me; don't get me wrong, but she was abusive. Half the time she beat me, I didn't understand why – I probably deserved it. She was a teacher.

When proper parenting is abandoned, their children suffer, like today's kids. Children do not need buddies or pals or friends – they need parents. Lax parents, of course, produce woke kids. Look at the emigrants who had the right methods to raise kids in America.

My father was just the opposite. He was always slow and thoughtful, at least to me. He explained things. If he thought you didn't understand, there would be a quiz. There was never a punishment without first there being an understanding of the problem in all its facets. The only time he even raised his voice was for safety issues. If he yelled, "Stop! Freeze!" everyone, my mother included, turned to stone. He was always in control. In his hospital and his family."

"Alex!" George shouted hopelessly into the ether. In this

story, George's voice had never been as shaky or uncertain as this moment. He sounded like a fourteen-year-old boy.

"Alex?!" George shouted again. This time, George's voice was more solid, but it had gained a level of certainty that served to say, "Was the boy even really here, to begin with?"

"Alex!"

This time, George's voice was breaking again, but not in a fourteen-year-old way as before. This time, George was breaking down into tears. He was alone. There's no one left to accompany me in my fight for my life. George thought as he began to forfeit into the ether. George simply sat there for a few minutes to focus on the confusion: "Am I in a coma? I'm fighting for my life. I'm alone. Sveti Georgiy, please save me!"

Suddenly, George met the angry face of Vasiliy, the Red Demon, in the darkness. George could see his red, evil, burning eyes. Like another Red Socialist Soviet Revolution, his gang of devils called George to follow Vasiliy's lead. They promised to bring him to his grandpa, Captain Georgiy. They were moving into the ever-increasing darkness. The strange group of demons started to scream and abuse George, shouting evil words, kicking and beating him, pulling him around, and subduing him – unable to move as he seeped into a deep depression. *I... even lost...Alex.*

Welcome to my kingdom of darkness! Finally, you're in

my hand! Your grandson Alex, too. Both of you will be here, dead forever! I have been plotting this for years and years!

George was fighting to overcome Vasiliy's fear and challenge. He fervently prayed: "St. George! Please help me. Please save us!"

The demon's face turned red with rage. "There is no saint or god here! Your god is dead! He is not alive; you belong to me, in hell forever! You will pay for everything that your grand grandfather and my brother Georgiy stole from me!"

George murmured repeatedly, "Even if I shall walk in the valleys of the shadows of death, I will not be afraid of evil because you are with me; your rod and your staff, they comfort me!"

"If even I pass at the gates of hell, I will call upon the name of the Lord, and He Will save me from hell."

Eventually, both hospital scenes faded away, and all was dark. From the darkness, a voice-cracked shout emerged.

"Hello?!" It was Alex, "Hello! Hello! Somebody! Please! Help!" The fear of losing his grandpa overtook him.

The two joined one another again.

"I think I was watching myself...I think you and I are still in a coma!" Alex was clearly showing his anxiety much more than his grandfather.

After this life-threatening spiritual fight, George focused on his lifeless body in the hospital. He was still viewing himself in the wrong place.

In what world am I? George asked about the level of anatomy, brain oxygen deprivation, hypoxia, coma, or seizures…

"We are moving to brain death. Wake up, Albert Einstein! Don't stock in death. Move up to higher dimensions! Don't give up, my boy!"

*"Move up! Go higher! There is "life" beyond the veil."*
Alex thought.

"Yes. I think we are." George was calm now (or at least trying to make it seem like he was) and was speaking in a reflective tone. "What are we going to do?" Alex was panicked, and George knew there was nothing he could do. Look up!

"Wait. See what St. George has for us."

George figured that being direct would be the best option in this situation. George and Alex were so focused on one another that they didn't even realize that the scene had changed around them.

The scene of newborn Nicky faded away, and a new one composed itself.

The new scene was set in the living room of George's house, but the furniture was off. The couch was shifted about four feet from the TV more than what it usually was, and the armchair that usually sat perpendicular to the TV was also scooted back a little bit – one side was pushed back more than the other so that the chair was facing slightly away from the television. All of these adjustments were made for one thing – the crib.

Christmas is the celebration of God's passionate pursuit of humankind. God is breaking into the brokenness of this world with His love and power. The birth of Jesus in Bethlehem's manger reveals how God works to bring about His purposes in the World. He was the real reason for the season. Baby Nicky was the Christmas Gift from god to these young parents.

A crib or cradle is a bed for a baby. A manger is a stone feeding trough for animals but is featured in the nativity scene as a bed for baby Jesus.

In the crib was a happy and beautiful baby boy. While Alex and George watched the room, young George walked into the room and loomed over the crib. The perspective of the scene snapped so that our spectators were watching through the eyes of the newly paternal George. Through George's eyes, baby Nicky came into view. He was stunning. The young George watched the new boy giggle and explore the new World with his eyes before locking them onto his father.

The little boy giggled a little bit before pushing out a phrase, "Dadaaa! Tati! ta ta tata." In Bulgarian, "Tati" means daddy, a diminutive for father.

Pride washed over the new father. He couldn't believe it. That was his son's first word; *he* was his son's first word!

This moment once again made George almost feel as though his whole predicament was worth it. George still feels frequent pride for this moment more than 30 years later.

Our spectators watched with astonishment while baby Nicky gazed back at them with that silly, not-a-worry-in-the-world smile that babies often give.

"That's a person," George thought. The concept was clear, but Nicky's words gave that idea a new meaning. I'm really creating a person. I'm giving them ideas and knowledge of great things, like right and wrong! A feeling of fear struck young George as he knew that it might be too easy to mess it up. What if it learns the wrong things from me? God knows I make mistakes; what if he takes the wrong things away from them?! After the brief panic, George's confidence returned because he was so excited to teach this human everything he could about the world.

Young and old George watched alongside Alex with pride as the baby existed simply. They couldn't take their eyes off baby Nicky. Eventually, the image shifted back to a third-person view of the living room, and the crib faded away. After that, the furniture was realigned, and the living room looked as it always had. After a moment of looking at a still room, a little boy ran into view. At this point, George recalled Nicky's favorite book in the third grade. Time Machine by H.G. Wells. The novella from 1895 was known for popularizing the concept of traveling through time.

It was funny because George realized that, more or less, he and his grandson were traveling through time as well! In the basement of their house, Nicky had this self-created imaginary laboratory where he did his experiments to discover his time machine and to find a new like in the other Universe. He wanted to become "the scientist" who started to build his time machine while learning from the science fiction magazine by Isaac Asimov.

Asimov was a Russian-born American writer and professor of biochemistry at Boston University. During his lifetime, Asimov was considered one of the "Big Three" science fiction writers in the USA. Nicky was inspired by the work of John Vincent Atanasoff, one of the great Americans (with Bulgarian roots). He was known as the father of the modern computer.

The kids in the classroom stopped laughing so much at his funny Slavic accents because they saw a future science fiction writer in him. Slowly, his accent faded away and was replaced by strong English! Ultimately, Nicky gained fame through his science teacher.

George fears that, later in life, the Americans will never accept Nicky into their inner circles.

There was a gap between us and them.

George could almost see the look of fear and disapproval whenever he would try to talk about his son's little time-traveling adventures in front of his friends. Nicky's massive bag used to be engorged with different books and diagrams for his next sci-fi adventure! Nicky would imagine that his busy parents were on different planets while they were away at work and that they were on a spaceship back every day before they two arrived for dinner. As he grew older, going to Lincoln High School, he could hear the aircrafts taking off from JFK Airport. Nicky imagined that his bus would turn into a plane and take him to Bulgaria (a magical place – according to his father) instead of school, which he despised, but we'll get to that in due time.

The boy had a massive backpack for his body, which came from George and Maria's one-size-fits-all mentality.

Both of the parents grew up poor, and the idea of purchasing an expensive bag just to buy another one the next year when the boy grew out of it was ridiculous. Aside from the backpack, the boy was wearing khaki shorts and a blue polo shirt. Maria thought this look made the boy seem very polite. Along with his clothes, little Nicky was carrying two blue velcro shoes. Nicky had blonde hair and blue eyes. He was a husky boy, but most of the chub was offset by his height, which was decently tall for a 5-year-old. The boy's cheekbones were strong despite the softness his complexion had gained from his build.

Young Nicky swung the backpack off his left shoulder into his right arm and plopped down onto the soft blue couch before setting his bag on the floor. Once seated, Nicky began strapping the velcro shoes onto his feet. Upon finishing up the right and second shoe, a thirty-something-year-old George walked into the room. "Kolya, you are ready?" the young father asked.

"Ah! I remember this image – Nicky's first day at school!" The much older George chipped in. Nicky enthusiastically nodded his head, got up from the couch, and ran outside of the field of our spectators' view. George followed with a casual gait, and the scene faded slowly into darkness.

A new scene slowly composed itself. The scene consisted of young Nicky hugging his father in a small and colorful classroom. Eventually, the father released his son, wished him well, and told the boy to behave. Young George walked to the entrance of the classroom and waved goodbye to his son before disappearing.

Once his father left, Nicky ran around and attempted to socialize, as little kids do. Nicky went first to a much thinner and slightly shorter brown-haired boy. Nicky approached the boy and said, "Hey! I'm Nicky! Can I be your friend?"

The boy looked uncomfortable and ran away, as our

socially inept children do when they don't quite know how to handle a situation.

George and Alex were enraged. They didn't know how to handle such rudeness and isolation. The two could feel the embarrassment and reasonless shame the young boy felt.

"What was that?" Alex couldn't understand why Nicky was just ignored like that.

"I don't know..." George was angrier than he had been in a long time. He wanted to discipline the little bastard who had just treated his son so terribly.

The scene reset to Nicky approaching the boy again. But this time, our spectators were watching the situation unfold through the eyes of the brown-haired boy. George and Alex watched the husky little blonde boy approach them.

Nicky spoke again, "Ey, As Sam Nik!" "Hey, I'm Nicky!" In English). Discomfort overcame the two viewers. It must have been coming from the boy through whose eyes they were watching. They realized that Nicky's fluent introduction was just an illusion – It was what Nicky thought that he was saying.

"What was that?" Alex was shocked, "was that English?" he continued. When Nicky spoke to others in his class, it sounded like Pnin's wild and funny broken English from the well-known book *Pnin* by Vladimir Nabokov.

"I guess Nicky picked up on my Bulgarian..." George said with shame. He had no idea that raising his bilingual American son with a Bulgarian influence would have that effect in school.

The scene continued, and the two spirits were forced to watch our ugly-duckling waddle about socially in pathetic attempts to make friends. By about ten minutes after the first attempt with the brown-haired boy, Nicky was a nervous wreck.

Nicky feels comfortable at home, where someone like his mama loves him. He always feels small, insignificant, not essential! In his eyes, his father – George, was significant; the powerful, strong Nicky didn't have good self-esteem.

Nonna is the Italian word for grandmother. Nonna is a term of endearment, meaning "little grandmother."

Occasionally, nonna will be shortened to "Nonni," but "Nonni" is also the word for grandparents in the plural.

But Niko loved to be spoiled by his plump little Italian grandma, Nonna, in "Little Italy," Manhattan, when every time he visited on the weekend, he gained a few pounds right away, which made his mama Maria mad about how grandma showed him with true love by gorging her grandson on her little food stamps program money.

Mamma Mia would always say, "Mather! Please stop overfeeding Nicky every time!" It made Maria very mad to see how grandma showed her love by gorging her grandson, cooking all sorts of Italian dishes for him on her little EBT program money.

Nicky was tall and big (chubby) in school. At first contact, he intimidated his classmates, but in his heart, he was a gentle giant: a big Teddy Bear – which disarmed many of their feelings of intimidation but only showed weakness to the others.

They called him names: "Mad Bulgarian scientist" or stinky Russian bear. So many times, he explained that he is not Russian, his parents are not communists, didn't come from the Soviet Union, the Empire of Evil, but they still labeled him as commie – short for damn communist.

George was watching Fox News religiously and supporting the upcoming candidate for Elections for the American president, a famous star of many cowboy movies in Hollywood, against the "Mighty Peanut" from Georgia.

George believes that Ronald Reagan will "tear down" the Berlin Wall so he can go back home.

On the other hand, Maria was watching CNN's liberal news network, like most Italians in Brooklyn, and arguing about who would be the new American president from John Kennedy's democrats.

# Chapter 8:

# Growing Pains

The spectators were forced to focus on Nicky's face. Everything around it disappeared. The boy's face slowly shifted. His jaw dropped, and he grew into his cheekbones; Nicky's hair darkened, and his eyes seemed smaller as their sockets grew and widened. Nicky's backpack was the same as before, but after the years we watched Nicky grow, the bag sat much more confidently on his shoulders despite the heft added by the dense books Nicky had decided to pack.

Once Nicky finished growing, the newest scene put itself together. The scene was of Nicky and his father walking to school.

Nicky was big and tall – one head above all his classmates, still chubby and clumsy, and George wanted to sign him up for sports. Of course, the Bulgarian popular sport of wrestling, or American football – even basketball!

George was busy in the auto shop but decided to take Nicky to private lessons at the Brighton Beach Tennis Center. The Russian tennis coach was a client of George's. He knew that the Russian was a tough coach, so he decided to check him out. Individual sports demand that you are responsible for surviving on the court by yourself – Nicky liked that fact.

"Oh my my! Bozhe moi! Time flies by so fast! This is Nicky's first day of middle school!" George was happy to recognize the memory. The previous scene had made George insecure that there was more of a disconnect between him and his young son than he realized. "I insisted on walking the boy to school that day! Oh, how I embarrassed the boy! Hahaha!" George was more than pleased to relive this memory. The boy and his father walked to the big metal doors that served as the gate to Nicky's inferno.

Upon Nicky and his father's arrival, Nicky turned to our young George, "Okay, Dad, you walked me in. I'll do fine from here!"

George remembered that any perturbation from Nicky's new-world freshness was washed out by the pride he felt for his little boy that day.

"Okay, okay, fine," George said to his son, giving him a grand hug for a goodbye while Nicky's peers and fellow students walked by.

Emigrant parents don't give up easily. Interestingly enough, Maria found the neighbors – a friend of her friend, a Russian grandma/babushka, to pair their children in a small group to protect each other from the American classroom bully since they were terrible.

Once again, George waved goodbye and disappeared. It was clear at this point that the scenes that George and Nicky were seeing had gone beyond just the struggles of a young George. The scene continued with Nicky looking at his student schedule and finding his first class. Nicky's first class was science. When he arrived, there were few seats left for him; he picked the one in the middle. The class had a few minutes until it started, so Nicky decided he would try to make some friends. George and Alex watched through Nicky's eyes as he sought out a potential friend but saw intimidating glares anywhere he looked. It was clear to our spectators that Nicky felt he did not belong. After a few intimidating instances of eye contact, Nicky gave up on socializing and decided to wait for the late bell.

Eventually, the bell rang, and the teacher, Mrs. Cooper, walked in and started talking. Even when everyone was focused on the teacher and her syllabus, Nicky felt uncomfortable and out of place. After a minute of basking in the feeling of discomfort, George and Alex were allowed to move on to the next scene.

The following scene was set in the cafeteria. First, the image of sixth-grade Nicky carrying a Styrofoam tray while walking was established, but soon after that, his surroundings became more solid. After having the scene set, our spectators began viewing everything through Nicky's eyes.

Through Nicky's eyes, our spectators walked down the

aisles formed by the space in between the long and crowded lunch tables. They could feel Nicky's discomfort; for most of the scene, Nicky was gazing at the ground, but every few steps Nicky took, he would glance up and try to make initiating eye contact, but every time someone's full face came into view, it would contort into a disgusting scowl that seemed to say, "Don't talk to me, I'll freaking kill you!" This made George and, in turn, Nicky furious. "How dare they treat my boy like that?! These little punks need some discipline!" George thought.

"Why do they seem so pissed?" Alex asked. He didn't think George really knew, but he couldn't figure it out either and was hoping for some perspective.

The two were still (as if they had another choice) and speechless for a moment. After some time, George calmed down a little, though he was still furious, and the scene began to shift. The scene shifted so that the same event was replaying, but this time, the point-of-view was through the eyes of one of the glaring peers. George and Alex were then watching their boy, Nicky, walk down the aisle, and the scene was a very different situation than they thought. Americans frame George and Nicky in categories that identify them "in the group of *others*," the outsiderness of the outsiders – the strangers, the aliens, the foreigners.

George's real emigrant experience as a writer allows him to be hurt and traumatized deeply enough to become an author one day.

With nobody to help you in life, you simply need to go through the system to become a real American in this "nowhere land" called the United Nations (UN of Brooklyn).

George and Maria had a very intense family dynamic, so Nicky became a rare "product" of international multicultural patents. The process of alienation and assimilation into the new American culture.

With the desire to belong to something greater than itself, Nicky was thinking: "I am half Italian and half Bulgarian, or American? But my father George always reminds me, 'You must be proud that you are Bulgarian!'"

"These Italians are not really white people." George made a mistake.

"Is this your stupid joke again? You gotta be kidding me!"

"Why do some cultures frown on smiling? Look at all George's Bulgarian photos. They were stone-faced." You can hear Maria's pitched voice.

George playfully replied, "Oh no, no, sorry! Just kidding! But the Italians have great food! For them, 'La Famiglia e Tutto' means Family is Everything."

"Bulgarians are the scariest white people I ever meet in Brooklyn," Maria would say.

You can hear Maria's voice from the kitchen.

A long time ago, George learned how to be a gentleman. He was big on funny people and light on funny jokes. George made a mistake, and he is regretting it. Brooklyn is full of Italians, but it is a miracle to find only one Bulgarian whom their entire family celebrated.

But Brighton Beach was a little bit of Russia in our backyard.

For one, Nicky was walking weirdly; he was obviously very conscious of how he looked while he was walking because the way he was moving his legs gave the boy a weird gait that changed every five or so steps. Nicky was also clearly rather sweaty; his forehead gave a glint from its perspiration, and a darker tone of his blue shirt's color was visible around Nicky's armpits. It's obvious to anyone observing that Nicky simply wasn't socially functional. Among other things, Nicky was also doing something with his eyes. Frequently, Nicky would glance up and then shoot his eyes back down with a slight blush as though he had just looked up to catch someone in a changing room. Eventually, Nicky reached our spectator. Nicky glanced up to make eye contact with our framing device boy, George, and Alex could feel the boy's mouth curve to make a smile and then watched Nicky's eyes shoot down, and his blush worsened. Alex and George then realized that the children weren't the problem.

Instead of rage, George then felt helplessness overwhelm him. George couldn't help but feel guilty for the situation that his son was in, but he knew he couldn't do anything to fix it, especially since it had passed. The idea that Nicky was happy and married in the future gave George just enough comfort to hold onto and not fall apart.

After Nicky passed the spectators, the perspective of the point-of-view snapped to an overhead third person. From the third person, we could see Nicky walk over to an empty part of the lunch room and eat quietly alone. From the other side of the room, we can see a person stand up with their tray and walk over to Nicky. The boy sat down with confidence and good posture. Immediately as the boy sat down, he made direct eye contact with Nicky, accommodated by a simple-looking smile.

Alex and George had no clues to this, but they could just tell that this was the boy through whose eyes they were just watching Nicky.

After sitting down and making brief eye contact before Nicky glanced down and away, the boy spoke:

"Hey! I'm Eli." The boy had a polite tone to him that conveyed just enough excitement to meet someone new.

"I'm Nicky," he spoke. Though he didn't stutter, Nicky felt he had done something wrong in his introduction; his own voice made him cringe.

"Ah, Eli!" George said as though he were welcoming the boy into his home. "So, this is where he came from!"

"Eli?" Alex asked.

"Oh yes, Eli, Elias. His Russian buddy! Ilya! Of course, I remember Ilyusha." George started like that and answered Alex's question perfectly, "These boys have been best friends since... well, since now, it seems!"

Mamma Maria was working behind the scenes; Eli's mother had instructed him to look for Nicky, the tallest boy, during lunch.

They liked each other for the first time. Both of their mothers allowed them to play after school in the front part of their residence building. They were emigrants' kids and spoke the same language that they knew before still attending class after school— English as a Second Language (ESL), in Brighton Beach Library, South Brooklyn. The boys continued their things through the lunch period—Nicky was sitting uncomfortably and eating his lunch while Eli was trying his best to tear Nicky out of his shell. It was clear by the end of the lunch period that the two had enjoyed the interaction greatly despite the discomfort.

Our spectators breathed easy for a moment after seeing that the scene had a happy ending.

After a second of living in the relief mood that the scene gave off, a new one composed itself. This scene was simply Nicky and Eli talking. The spectators couldn't hear what they were saying, but they could understand the feeling that was growing, the comfort of a friend. From this scene, more continued. These scenes were the same when broken down to their anatomy- Nicky would always sit down with a packed lunch from his frugal parents and look around for a bit, waiting for his friend to show up (though they were friends, Nicky was still easily uncomfortable and he found that eating was an easy way to fill the silence. Nicky also liked the idea of only eating lunch with his friend, not alone), then, once Eli got his lunch, he would appear at the other end of the long table the two sat at. From there, the two would eat and talk for the remainder of the half-hour. After our spectators watched a few of these scenes, a new one abruptly started.

Eli and Nicky were inseparable all over the school, sitting together. In the classroom, at the last table, like Tom and Jerry— the best friend's cartoon. When Nicky was introduced by the teacher, she was pronouncing his first name. The first name was easier. His last name was always difficult to pronounce. The teacher had to excuse herself if she pronounced it incorrectly and ask him to repeat it again and again.

"Your last name, please say your name."

And Nicky started nervously with a stammer:

"Kakh...Kokh Kakhovskiy"

"Mwahh hahah! What he just said: 'cock.;'"

The class bully behind him exclaimed, "Okay, Dickkie!" The whole group in the back laughed at Nicky.

Nicky didn't understand why they were laughing at any time when he said his last name.

The reason you discriminate against foreign accents starts with what they do to your brain. Why do people laugh when someone speaks broken or unclear English? Why do they have to laugh about Nicky's pronunciation of his last name all the time? Nicky took his small pocket dictionary to check and learn what was so funny about the word. It was a new word for him; he had never really heard it before. Eli, who was sitting next to him, turned against the bully: "Idi na huiy! "Go to a dick."

Using his bad Russian in the same context as the English term, "fuck off—" "Blyat, Idi na huiy," said his Russian friend Eli!

"Don't pay attention to these bastards! Don't give a fuck!"

When Nicky found the best Russian boyfriend, a new Russian girl showed up in their classroom in the middle of the school year.

Anna was a Ukrainian girl from Kyiv, USSR. Nicky fell in love at first sight with this modern-day Russian Princess. She was Tolstoy's modern-day Anna Karenina as a new student. He was helping her with English so that she wouldn't have to feel like he did in the beginning.

At a parent/teacher conference, it was discussed how Nicky is improving with English, Science, and History. He even started to read Leo Tolstoy in Bulgarian. George discovered the Russian Classics in Brighton's bookstore. The English teachers were very impressed. Before he knew who William Shakespeare was, he had read Tolstoy, Dostoevsky, Turgenev, and Pushkin in Bulgarian.

He remembered his first scientific project adventure in a small scratch book novella about traveling to new planets.

His new science teacher was Ms. Lubavitch, an Orthodox Jewish woman.

Ms. Lubavitch loved him from the moment of his school presentation in class. He was accepted, not as a fat Bulgarian boy, not as a child of emigrants, but as Nicky—Geek and Nerd—the scientist.

This scene started, as usual. Nicky sat down and placed his blue plastic lunch box before him on the table and then waited for his friend. Eventually, Eli appeared down the aisle, but this time, two other boys were with him. Eli reached the table and sat down, "Hey Nicky, these are my friends, Marcos and Noe!" The three boys looked at each other. Nicky panicked. He had just gotten comfortable with one person! How could he handle two more on top of that?! Noe and Marcos seemed calm. The three of them exchanged apathetic "Heys" and didn't speak much after that. At least, the three of them didn't speak; Eli, Marcos, and Noe continued talking without speaking much to Nicky at all. Of course, speaking of Nicky was a different story entirely. At the point that the boys were speaking of Nicky instead of to him, Eli had excluded himself from the conversation. There were two main topics of conversation regarding Nicky. First was the sweat. Nicky was a nervous person, and nervous people sweat. When two unfamiliar people came by, Nicky's nervous sweat kicked in and left two semi-ovals below his arms.

Usually, Nicky would cover up any stains, sweat or otherwise, with a sweatshirt or hoodie that he kept in his locker. Sadly, Nicky couldn't just walk out of lunch, so he had to bear down until the next period. The second was Nicky's lunch. Unlike most kids, Nicky brought his lunch. This was for two main reasons.

George and Maria were a couple consisting of an immigrant and the child of an immigrant. Even with financial comfort, wasting money was a non-option. "Lunch costs $2 a day. That's more than $40 a month! Why would we pay that when you could eat my home-cooked food for free instead?" Maria would lament whenever Nicky tried to convince her to give him lunch money. You're an Italian, for God's sake! There couldn't possibly be a reason to want some plastic instead of this food." George would chip in, both as an argument and as a passive reminder to Nicky that his mother would be inconsolable if it seemed he didn't like her food. To waste is a sin! Think about all the people who couldn't even afford enough food for them to waste!

These reasons were given whenever Nicky tried to appeal for lunch money, so there he was, eating leftover Fettuccine Alfredo with homemade garlic bread. This was Nicky's favorite dinner, but a day old and chilled, the dish peaked at home. Still enjoyable. Even though the pasta was more than familiar to many of Nicky's peers, it was still seen as weird while trying to get the smell of garlic off his breather, which brings us back to a far too obvious point and giggle given by Marcos (or Noe—Nicky didn't quite remember who was who) to Noe. Our spectators were forced to watch this embarrassing interaction for the remaining half hour before St. Georgiy finally allowed the two to move on from the secondhand embarrassment and anger that they were feeling.

The new scene wasn't much of a change from the previous few. It started with Nicky, a little more anxiously, eating his lunch. As Nicky was eating lunch instead of waiting for his "friend," Eli appeared down the aisle, walked over, and sat down.

"Where are your friends?" Nicky couldn't help but ask after a couple of quiet minutes.

"Oh, those guys suck. Not my friends." Eli didn't make eye contact while he was saying this. He never said it, but it was clear he felt terrible for the previous day.

Our spectators could feel Nicky's mood; it was euphoric. Someone outside of his family not only cared about him but cared for him enough to give up his friends for Nicky! This might have been Nicky's first bout of social confidence in a long time.

Alex and George watched the boy have an amazing lunch with his friend; it was the best conversation they had seen. Once lunch ended, Nicky and Eli walked together down the hall.

Eventually, they went different ways, and a moment later, Nicky reached his locker and began taking his books out for his next class, Math. While Nicky was doing this, a tall brown-haired boy with a solid jaw loomed over him. The boy ripped the book out of Nicky's hands and threw it at the wall at the other end of the hallway. It took about two seconds for Nicky to register exactly what had just happened. The boy with his varsity wrestling jacket kicked Nicky's right side so that he was pushed into the wall of lockers; Nicky hit his head against the metal, and one of the hinges cut Nicky's arm right below the end of the sleeve of his t-shirt.

The boy laughed, muttered, "Fucking Commie," and walked off looking pleased.

Like Mama Maria always said, ignore the bad boys, and be polite (we are Europeans – very cultured people. Do not pay attention to these savages and hooligans)

On the contrary, George prefers to teach him a lesson on

how to protect himself and hit without anybody noticing these bully bastards.

Nicky didn't say anything. He was clearly displeased, but just as clearly, this was commonplace, and Nicky had given up on any dramatics.

While Alex and George watched Nicky recollect himself, they felt a new feeling from Nicky. It was hatred. Nicky felt hatred toward his "homeland." He hated every one of his father's values. It wasn't home to him; it wasn't something he understood how to love. Nicky's homeland only brought him consequences, and he hated it for that (Like he had a choice of where to be born).

Why is Nicky always so different? For one day only, he wanted to be "normal" like anybody else. To be accepted, to be appreciated, to be loved. At least George was trying to integrate into American culture in his family.

His Bulgarian neighbor often screamed from the kitchen to his son. *Ivane. Do not speak English here!* In our house, we speak only Bulgarian. We are not stupid Americans. People who work in the Bulgarian community listen to the same music, eat the same Bulgarian food, and hate the country with its door open wide for them. We all came to their country silly, not the opposite.

Americans are more generous than Europeans – by a large margin! America the generous: the U.S. leads the globe in giving. Americans are the most generous people in the World, a study says...

George concludes, "We will never mix with these stupid Americans. What melting pot do they love to speak about? It's impossible! There is an old Bulgarian saying: 'Each toad to know its bog.' 'Every cobbler must stick to his last.' 'Every frog to know its pond.' We can't mix with them. It's a different pond. Our blood is thick – we are oil, Americans are water. Why don't oil and water mix?! That's all! We are here, and they are there – at a safe distance – far, far away."

# Chapter 9:

# Turmoil and New Hope

George felt guilty once again. He didn't understand the effect that insisting his culture upon his son would have on the boy. George came from a long military family background, army rules, commands, and perseverance, and ancestors of fighters and protectors. George often said, "My father beat me because he loved me, and that's why I became a real man."

George was trying to teach his son Nicky to be tough to survive in the New York "Jungle" lifestyle. Far too many have never known any discipline, have never had any clearly defined boundaries set before them, and have never heard the word "No." And in far too many homes, far too many kids are being raised without a father, which makes all this even more difficult.

Nicky does not need buddies or friends–he needs parents. Yes, parents can be friendly and someone kids like to hang around with, but they also need to act like parents. And that means doing parental things, including setting boundaries, providing discipline when needed, and steering a child in the way he should go.

George and Maria had a very harsh family dynamic, so Nicky became a rare product of an international relationship. Nicky was a victim of alienation and exclusion due to his forced integration into both his parents' cultures.

Sometimes, George didn't know how to express himself as an Introvert. He often struggles to put his thoughts into words. As a child, he would stammer in school. Whenever he tried as a little kid, he would freeze, unable to express himself properly. Usually, this is from his family upbringing. He developed "compleksi" complexes.

As a teenager, George always compared himself to others and felt that he didn't measure up. He developed an inferiority complex.

Children who grow up surrounded by strong adults, especially those who tend to care for them, may grow up feeling weak and incapable of caring for themselves without parental assistance. This can be made worse in situations where children are deliberately made to feel small and helpless. They are unable to "carry their cross."

George's life in America was extreme. There was a lot of stress, a lot of eagerness, confusion, anxiety, and hopefulness to become an adult overnight. George was always stressed out to the max.

I don't know; maybe Nicky inherited this condition from me, but Nicky doesn't stammer or stutter at all. Maria, however, was as loving, gentle, and protective as an Italian mamma can be. For Nikolay's Birthday, George bought him a large stuffed toy Lion and laid it next to him on his bed to remind him about the

Bulgarian symbol of bravery. The feeling of hate and disowning his culture gave George a flashback. He remembered how they fought.

"What are you thinking about, Grandpa?" Alex offered the question mainly for an "I'm here for you" sentiment, but George answered after a moment of thinking.

"When Nicky was older, late into his High School, we fought–A lot." As George spoke, an image of his younger self and Nicky arguing composed around them. The two were in the living room, circling each other while exchanging verbal blows. Both were angry, but it was clear they simply figured that the other just didn't get what they were saying.

Often, Nicky wanted to talk back to his father, "Please don't dump your Bulgarian culture and tradition on me! Making me feel guilty that I don't date a stupid Bulgarian girl so I can create a Bulgarian family and produce a Bulgarian baby! I am an American, Dad. I am more interested in American girls. I am in a position to take the best of both Worlds...Don't push me to hate everything Bulgarian and Russian."

All my father's friends were Bulgarians or Russians. We, as a family, live in a close Bulgarian emigrant community in the heart of Russian Brighton. As a student, Nicky never left this inner circle. Soon, he must break out and experience the American culture outside of foreign Brooklyn.

Nicky's best "Brighton Beach" memory about his father's parenting was the shadow of Slavic accents, which were mostly Eastern European. More specifically, he had a stupid Bulgarian accent, which he hated! Best parenting with "accent" between two worlds, George tried to keep his Bulgarian identity for himself and, on the other hand, slowly assimilate with the new culture.

Nicky always thought of his dad as an outsider, a foreigner with the shadow of a Slavic accent. Even when they go to the Yankee Stadium, Nicky would get up and sing the National Anthem at the Yankees game. He put his hand on the heart proudly.

George was always keeping his old "culture," emphatic, with his accent on certain words like "kultura."

Then Nicky looked at him:

"Pap, Paap, Paapa...! You know better than that," but George refused to get up. This day was the famous final between the New York Yankees team and the New York Mets based in Flushing, Queens when the Mets won two World Series.

Yes, he repeated the word "kultura" (culture) that anyone could understand, like the people sitting next to him, American Italian, Mexican, Brazilian, Bulgarian, or Colombian.

Kultura is a word borrowed from the Latin *cultūra* from *cultus*. Sometimes, George would reference "Evropeiska kultura, or "European-based Culture." There's an old saying: "Americans live to work; Europeans work to live." America is a land of immigrants who come from a rich heritage of European culture.

The man next to George and Nicky asked the boy, "What is your nationality, son?"

Nicky would get up and proudly announce, "I am an American." "You mean American with Bulgarian Roots?"

"No. I am an American!" and Nicky proudly put his right hand next to the heart. Nicky hated his last name. He preferred Mickey Mantle, who was the best New York Yankees player of the 1960s.

As this scene was composed, George realized that he had some control.

So, he made a point of refining his mental image and telling the story as clearly as he could.

George continued, "One day, we just fought too much." The fight scene continued. Neither spectator could hear what the father and son were yelling about; they just watched the mannerisms exchanged between George and Nicky. At this point, Nicky stood at a tall 6'2", and his build was dense enough to give the impression of a well-established young man. Because of this, the fight wasn't between a man and a boy; it was between two adults (especially since this was a couple of months past Nicky's 18th birthday). The two men stopped pacing around the living room. One went into a bedroom while the other continued shouting in its direction. A few minutes later, the young man came out of the bedroom with a large gym bag over his shoulder. The father's shouting grew louder while they made their way to the door. The boy walked out the door, looked at the man, and said something calmly. The old man closed the door while the boy turned and walked away.

At first, the young George walked back into the living room with a peeved "so there!" expression, but after a couple of minutes, his expression broke, and he was sad. My son is gone, he thought. I've driven my own son away! I'm horrible. George felt pathetic, both in the past and present.

Maria said, "Don't put him down; he isn't a child anymore. He is a smart boy; what do you want from him?"

I can't tell you how crazy Mama Maria feels when the children have to leave the nest. The safe place they had known at this point for so many years.

Maria was overprotective of Nicky. Every time George tried to discipline him, she always defended him. No matter what, she only said that "Only Stupid "Scorpio" can say or do this!

Eh, Idiota (Italian) - Oh, idiot! Why does everyone hate scorpios?

George was a Scorpio, the worst of all signs. He didn't believe in this zodiac; this was all Maria's New Age nonsense, occultism!

She was a Cancer and would say that George is "broody, irrationally secretive, and...Scorpio told me we are too guarded and expect other people to read our minds. Scorps are self-centered, judgmental."

When Maria read everyone's Astro Charts and consulted with her girlfriends who read her palm and Tarot cards, she was deeply taken into the idea of witchcraft as a method of navigating her relationships.

They remember their neighbors couldn't kick their children out of the apartment for more than 30 years. What good is it? At least Nicky is a very responsible young man! You need to trust more that he is a capable young man to make it in life. Everyone has their American Dream. Maria's favorite proverb says: "If you give a man a fish, you feed him for a day. If you teach a man to fish, you feed him for a lifetime." Teach your son skills & you will not regret it.

The scene went dark, and so did our spectators' surroundings. Alex was furious. He couldn't believe what his grandfather had done. After watching Nicky being destroyed socially, what Alex had just seen hurt even worse. "This boy has a lot of "Chutzpah," George's Jewish neighbor said once.

George always said with pride: "Teach your son to have Courage, Faith, Chutzpah, and Humility—and the world will be His!"

"But be gentle with love and wisdom," Maria would add with pride!

"Why did he leave?" Alex felt a little broken from watching his father be forced out like that.

"Well," George started sheepishly, "I told him that if he was going to live in my house, he was going to do things my way. I guess he didn't want to do things my way... "

"It's not all rainbows when your parents treat you terribly and blame you for their unhappiness. Thirty years later, they become loving grandparents, but the damage is already done," said Nicky.

Alex asks why grandparents are nicer to their grandkids than their kids.

"My perfect agape–love didn't come till you really appeared as my first grandson!"

Later, Nicky had a sister, but George loved the girl differently–George protected her. As a strong alpha male emigrant, business owner, and strong father, he pushed his son away when Nicky stopped talking to him and left the house.

Nicky and his sister Emily's live were in Brooklyn. They were about the protection of their mother. Growing up, they both saw the world from the inside of their own immigrant heads and cultures. George would tell Maria that it was to protect Emily, who would go on to write a book about *Another Brooklyn*—one of immigrants and the experience with her brother in the 60s, a time of sex, drugs, and rock and roll.

"So you kicked him out?" Alex couldn't believe what he was hearing.

"I guess. He said he was leaving when I told him 'my house, my rules,' but it was clear that it was my fault. I didn't understand how unique my immigrant beliefs were. He was an American, and I needed to understand that Bulgaria was far, far away."

The two watched young George sit sadly for what felt like forever. St. George allowed the two to feel his young George's emotions as he had before. It was worse than Alex could've imagined and even more terrible than George remembered.

Eventually, the scene faded away, and everything was darker- than-dark again.

After an even longer pensive moment, Alex spoke up, "What was Nicky like in high school? I feel like we've skipped that part..." As Nicky said this, the scene recomposed to show a young Nicky. The young man was clearly a freshman or in a similar age range. In this image, Nicky had grown a bit. He looked even less husky than before, and his jaw had become stronger. Besides that, the boy looked tired. Nicky had the same backpack as before. But this time, it was especially bulky because he had packed it well with books- both for school (he had chosen almost exclusively advanced subjects) and pleasure (Nicky had become an avid sci-fi fan ever since discovering the "Dune" books). The boy felt terrible- Alex and George could feel it. The boy was walking from school and had just gotten into his father's car. As they rode home, Nicky looked over at George and felt a connection to his father, but it was lacking. Nicky and George didn't talk on the way home.

George didn't know how to express his love for his son. He thought that true love comes from the heart, not from the mouth and lips.

The boy needs to be trained to become a man. "Coming from a communist regime, you have to fight, you have to assimilate, you have to overcome, and you have to survive and thrive to achieve the American dream," George would say. He wanted his son to struggle to survive.

When the two arrived home, they got out of the car and went into the house. George opened the door and entered first, with Nicky trailing behind. As they entered the house, the two greeted their family. On the couch facing the TV was uncle Andrey looking at Nicky. He was a husky man with balding black hair. At the time, Andrey was sporting a white tank top. On the red chair that usually faced perpendicular to the couch sat Auntie Yordanka. The brother-sister trio of George, Yordie, and Andrey was as dynamic as a trio could get. When Nicky entered the house, Andrey turned from a heated (Bulgarian) conversation to greet little Nicky. The spectators could feel comfort between the man and woman but couldn't help but feel a disconnect. It was clear that Nicky didn't find the Bulgarian aspects of the situation desirable.

As much as the family could emulate a Bulgarian environment, Nicky was an American- Nicky grew up speaking English to his American peers (the good and bad ones); he received an American education and learned to enjoy things the American way. Nicky was an American whose dad was from elsewhere as far as he was concerned. After greeting his aunt and uncle, Nicky continued to the kitchen where his little mother (she had never grown past 5'6", while Nicky was nearing 6' 2") was sweating lightly from the stove.

On the stove was a white cream slowly reducing in a saucepan with water waiting to boil next to it–Nicky's favorite. After giving his mother a hug, Nicky headed to his room until dinner. When Nicky crossed the threshold into his room, the scene fell apart into wisps of images, and our spectators were given a chance to think about what they had seen. Nothing was too out of the ordinary, but the feeling Nicky got when he stepped into the house was something new.

George was the most taken aback by it.

He had no idea that his son didn't feel fully at home all the time. The idea that Nicky would be stretched between American culture and the culture of his homeland was new, and George felt truly guilty about that. Eventually, the two's introspection ended, and the second scene was composed. It was similar to the previous one, but the feeling grew. Nicky still loved his family, but the Bulgarian expressions were even more foreign to him. Alex and George figured out what was happening and prepared to watch the remaining scenes from Nicky's high school development.

And that's what happened. George and Alex watched two more rounds of Nicky gaining a disconnect from his culture. George was devastated while he watched this- George felt as though he was watching one of the last remaining elements of his homeland burn to the ground. Alex, however, wasn't too phased. He knew that his father loved his family, and there wasn't even hate when he felt what his father did–just unfamiliarity. Alex did know that George felt otherwise, so he kept his mouth shut and let George grieve.

Nicky decided to visit his parents on May 6, Georgiovden/St George's Day. George's name day and celebration of Bulgarian Army and Bravery. George had a big party–He knew how to prepare a whole roasted lamb!

"We need to celebrate and be glad, for this, your son was dead and is alive; he was lost and now is found."

George was raised in sports, the same tennis lessons Alex picked up from his father, and he wanted Nicolay at a very early age in school to practice individual sports like tennis to teach him "not to give up easily in real life" "No pain, no gain" is a proverb, used since the 1980s This was George's motto too.

George was a serious man–that's why he was able to open his first business and be successful. Many American parents were easy to their kids, like, "It's OK, don't worry, it doesn't matter, you fail; so what! Take it easy. So, math is not your subject! Do whatever you like!"

Sometimes, George thinks about why American parents are so hesitant to discipline their children. Instead, they coddle and spoil them.

For George, education was very important, combined with the competitive Bulgarian culture of education. All these things were very important to him!

George and Maria cooked Nicky's favorite food.

For years, Nicky never missed a birthday, Christmas, or New Year's celebration to be with his family. He didn't even call. Maria was so worried about what had happened to him. She finally found his phone numbers from friends and called. "We all are worried. Where are you? Come home, take the 'knife from my heart!' If you don't come, I will kill myself; there is no reason to live in this lonely world!"

Nicky became rebellious; he wanted to change his crazy last family name, "Kakhovskiy," to something more

Americanized. *Just imagine this name on my diploma or credit card*, he would think.

Adult children are many times more likely to be estranged from their fathers than their mothers. Nicky didn't have a good relationship with "the old man."

Uncle Andrew shared with Nicky at the table when George went to the store: "Please don't pay attention to George. He is a good man. He loves you out of fear for your good and future. This is the old emigrant mentality–life is a constant struggle! He always needs to find a battle and conquer it!

How many immigrant families want whatever you have? The property, business, family, and education?!

The newly "fresh off the boat" Eastern Europe emigrants live in a ghetto in the public assistance buildings. On government sponsorship, most of them were using the system.

"Your father provides a house for you. Don't be hard on him or yourself!" So finally, after one year's absence, Nicky returned home. Everybody was so happy. George invited all his friends, relatives, and neighbors to a celebration welcome party. This was the happiest moment in his family. Finally, Nicky was home. The table was set up, and everybody was already celebrating his homecoming. The lost son who came home again!

But there is more to the story than meets the eye…much more.

Suddenly, George came from the kitchen, showing everybody the most expensive bottle of Bulgarian wine, "Mavrud," pointing to the bottles and shouting, "Oh-ho-ho, Opah!" (with fun slang) as loudly as he possibly can, pouring and filling all glasses in cheers and blessings for Nicolas returning home.

George had an 'expensive Bulgarian soul.' He didn't care about money or riches; he worried primarily about his family, friendship, camaraderie, and the Bulgarian community. "For health and cheers for his son, Nicky's future."

Raising all cups, they would cheer: "na zdravie!" (let's drink to health!)

"To your health, Zhora Alexandrovich, and for the health of your son, Nicolay! Drink to the bottom! Na zdorovie!" His Russian friends would cry.

"Long live Bulgaria! Na zdrave," the Bulgarians would cheer, Na zdorovie being the Bulgarian cheer for your health.

"God was in control. He was the boss of his destiny and would not let any powers above heaven and below the earth separate him from his beloved son."


All his neighbor's relatives and friends came to celebrate George, his son's homecoming. His Bulgarian hospitality was very well-known among his friends. Maria was so happy to see his son coming too–after three bottles of vodka disappeared. Funny expressions like: "Bulgaria after three glasses of vodka." Ironizing the nationalist slogan "Bulgaria on three Seas" by connecting the patriotic exaltation songs that are often contained in it with the characteristic of some patriots in a state of alcoholic intoxication raving about the distant Bulgarian ancient glorious past.

On this holiday, like St. George's Day, all Bulgarians all over the World raise a toast, which is always done with eyes locked together, saying: "Cheers," "Let's drink to health," or "na zdrave!"

George has asked himself, and has been asked this, a million times in America:

Take a look at George's name–what if it was something more American? Less "foreign." "My name is Georgiy Kakhovskiy, but I inherited my father's name instead of an American 'middle name.'" The patronymic (otchestvo) part of a Russian person's name is derived from the father's first name and usually serves as a middle name for Russians. Patronymics are used in both formal and informal speech.

His workers always address their bass with their first name and patronymic. In Brighton, they'd call me Zhora (Yes, Zhora, the boss–diminutive of George), Aleksandrovitch (son of Alexander), and Kakhovskiy. The last name came from the Kakhovka Village Reservoir (the Kakhovka Dam on the Dnieper River in Ukraine). Kakhovskiy was the namesake of General Count Vasily, with Kakhovskiy being his grandfather. He was also known as the founder of the village of Kakhovka in Ukraine.

In 1787, the Tsarina Catherine the Great personally founded with Prince Potemkin, her Commander-in-Chief of the Imperial Army - Yekaterinoslav, when General Count Vasiliy Kakhovskiy was appointed as governor on the territory of Modern Dnipro in the Russian Empire and governed the city of Yekaterinoslav (the glory of Catherine).

Now try to fill out that paperwork and get someone to pronounce your surname at the Department of Motor Vehicles–the DMV. When George would tell an officer or his newer American friends his full name, they'd stutter.

Every time someone asks him to repeat it again and again. "How many times do I need to spell my name?! It takes five minutes of a tongue twister to be embarrassed and to explain it again and again, my dumb foreign surname. Just forget about it. I've had enough! Goodness gracious. Just call me Mr. K."

"Prosti Amerikanci" "Stupid Americans!"He murmured in his own tongue.

*But I don't want to change my last name. It means the World to me.*

Eventually, he'd just given up.

But as life is in the USA without a social safety net like in Europe, if one problem appears, like an economic recession (like during Jimmy Carter's presidency), it can close your business and throw you out of recovery for many years.

George comes from an oppressive communist regime. His father, Alexander, pushed him in life in this way at a young age. But it's good for you; one day, you will understand that when you become a father, you will probably have the same challenge with your son.

Some kids, like your classmates, had a horrible life. Their father left the family and never came back. This is devastating for some; even the death of your favorite pet can damage you for life. Just when the two thought it was over, a new scene composed itself. This scene went as usual, but George wasn't there, and Nicky was close to two years older than the previous.

This time, when Nicky stepped into the house, he was overwhelmed with the feeling of home. Uncle Andrey and Auntie Yordie were sitting in their usual spots, having their usual heated conversation. But this time, the words felt endearing. Nicky grabbed Andrey's hand and held it for a second while his uncle said something to him.

Nicky chuckled, spoke some Bulgarian that he knew was subpar, and walked over to the other side of the room to give his auntie a hug. After chipping into the conversation a little more, Nicky left for the kitchen to say hello to his mother. When he went in there, the old woman spoke to him with pleasure and softness. It was clear that Nicky was home here. Nicky returned to the living room with Andrey and Yordanka to continue their conversation.

After about ten minutes, George entered the house and greeted his son with a hug. They chatted for a second before setting the table together.

"Ah, I remember this! It was a couple of weeks after Nicky came back. It was the best of times..." George said, reminiscing the times when he had his young son living with him.

"What happened to bring him back?" Alex asked.

George: "I didn't know it was a mandate of American culture that we teach boys to be independent. So, he was supposed to raise Nicky to be a good man, not a 'real' man.

"I understood that he was a man..." George said in a tone of contemplation. As George finished that sentence, a new scene composed itself around him. It was George walking into an apartment building. The man looked tired and obviously wasn't quite there. The descriptor "young George" no longer fits the man. The man got into the elevator and went to the fourth floor. Out of the elevator, George walked down the hallway and took a turn before arriving at the apartment. Our spectators could feel the tension from our subject as he became closer and closer to the door. Eventually, the anxiety peaked when George knocked on the thin, white piece of wood. Eventually (after 12 seconds of eternity), the locks of the door rattled, and it opened to reveal a young man. At this point, Nicky was an adult. He had a firm stature and jaw. He wasn't as husky as he was as a kid, but he was far from thin. Nicky gazed at George with a soft complexion after registering that his father had just appeared.

Nicky left a boy and returned as a grown man. George kept him in prayer during these hardships. Like his grandpa said, "Train up a child in the way he should go, and when he is old, he will not depart from it." "Dad!" Nicky sounded pleased. Nicky hugged his father and said, "Please come in! I just made coffee," before moving to allow his father into his home. George obliged with a look of pleasant surprise. Nikolay led George to a light green couch in the same room as the entrance. Nicky's apartment was far from lavish, but for a young man, it looked fantastic.

"Did you say when you are doing your 'heating party' for your apartment? Why in the summer?

"You mean my apartment warming party that I was talking about?" They both laughed.

George was confused about some words.

George still remembers this Saturday night when Nicky left the house.

That night, his parents were at the edge of razvod/divorce, but after Nicky left the house, they both found themselves sad and alone and guilty, so they came together, as never before, to solve why they had to fight all this time just to gain Nicky's audience and approval for what college to choose after they see him back. They were very happy, saying *Daddy is a very good husband. He's doing everything right; he doesn't drink too much lately, so let's celebrate at Nicky's new apartment*!

The effect of George's discipline on his son was obvious because he always followed the scriptures, "Those who spare the rod of discipline hate their children. Those who love their children care enough to discipline them."

George smelled him from a distance and checked his eyes for marijuana use. As a father, he had to be strong and keep his son in the right direction before Nicky left the house.

When Nicky didn't come back, they worried and worried about their son.

He showed his parents that he was able to support himself both in work and study.

They asked him how he was in school, and he said his 3.6 GPA shows that he has very good (5) and excellent (6) marks, equivalent to an American −A and A+.

For the first time, his father saw him as prosperous and encouraged him to improve his studies.

Nicky is definitely grown up. In his first year at college, his father looked at him as an incapable human being, but later, he changed a lot and was able to keep up his studies well.

Maria asked him what the grades of the other children in college were. "What kind of grades do you have?" She would ask.

Nobody talks about grades here, Mom!  The fact that they don't talk about this in school is totally unacceptable. What kind of education is this?

It was mostly Russians and Eastern Europeans.

"We are so happy that you and your sister Emily are doing very well in school. She was in middle school and a good student. She was always reading books in the library. Her mother was to make sure that she brought her home from school and brought her to the library to do her homework. You have to understand that you are our pride because you're our future–the next generation!

The pride of the immigrant family!"

This is very important for George and Maria.

George was so proud as an immigrant living in Brighton Beach!

At Kingsborough Community College in Manhattan Beach in Brooklyn, New York. They have all the Russian and Chinese ex-communist history professors Ph.D. They have everything they want here and culture from all over the World, but George was saving money and thinking about how to provide for his son so that he could buy him a nice car and house next to his on Brighton so that they will all be together and going to Orthodox church since they were not many Bulgarian communities in this part of South Brooklyn. George didn't want to live in this poor "projects" ghetto–where the new Russian refugee community settled first.

For Nicky, it was important to be part of the American chosen culture in the college, not to stay near the stinky immigrants who were born back in Eastern Europe.

Nicky was interested in the American way to learn business and management. He doesn't pay attention to the political campus on the right or on the left. For him, it was important to know that America was going against the Soviet Union in the Cold War, and finally, a new old president, a cowboy from California, was elected after the good-failing Democrat, Jimmy Carter.

Nicky knew that his father was an immigrant, but he had sympathy with the right and with the conservative values who were afraid of the liberal Democrats and compared them with communists, who had the best propaganda, brainwashing, and branding on their children.

Nicky didn't take his father's American dream to become a medical doctor in honor of his grandfather, Dr. Alexander, or a lawyer after the choice of his mother. Maria wanted him to become a businessman. New Yorkers vote overwhelmingly for Democratic politicians, but immigrants from the former Soviet Bloc are an exception, perhaps because the Russian immigrants to the "borough" of Staten Island were flocking to the Republican Party, saying that the national democrats' "socialistic" policies remind them too much of the top-down oligarchy fled in their native land.

He still keeps his Eastern European heritage while studying

history and languages, but his main call is to go into business. He has a girlfriend–his parents were very happy to meet her, so they invited both of them on May 6 during George Day/ Georgovden to celebrate in honor of his father, George.

Nicky, while thinking, said: "I am a 19-year-old second-generation immigrant. Post-communist, post-dysfunctional family guy. For me, it's very important to pursue the American dream. In my mind, I was materialistic, without any possessions. I would like to know it, to touch it, to feel it, to hold it, and to possess it. My Ambitious education brings me closer to my American dream and far away from emigrant losers who just arrived fresh from the boat. I appreciate everything my parents have done for me, but I don't want to think and be like them at all."

The most important is that I have a girlfriend after my miserable teenage stupid years in Brighton, where everything was Russian.

I am not rushing anywhere. I want to live my life slowly as the excitement of my first American dream sexual "intercourse," and make it more fun and memorable with the girl I love when I lost my virginity.

Every weekend, he traveled to Manhattan. He was meeting and dating beautiful girls. Here in NEW YORK CITY, you don't need to travel abroad. All nationalities and cultures are here under your feet.

Nicky was happy that his family was together again.

Nicky and George in Brighton Beach–the Bulgarian emigrants blended beautifully with the Russian ones.

They always talk loudly. They are not angry; this is the way they talk–always at a high volume, and they look like they are arguing–but this is a normal conversation for them.

Nicky still remembers the first phone, which came with an answering machine as a man of the house. George left the first message:

"Hello, we are not home–I will be back soon, and I will find you."

Exactly like Arnold Schwarzenegger's *The Terminator.*

Nicky said: "Pops, change this message on the machine. All my friends were scared to call back. They thought they got some KBG hotline, and nobody called us back or left a message."

Finally, Nicky changed it when his father was on vacation and put a better message because the people who called them always hung up.

George still remembers his baby Nikolisha's first tooth that he kept in his documents box. George didn't want to spend money on a dentist, so he tied the boy's tooth to the door and slammed it shut.

So easy to see. Nicky was scared and surprised that suddenly he took it out pain-free! His father saved this tooth and showed it to him after they moved to Chicago. George and Maria saved every curl of the first haircuts of the children, keeping every small piece of artifact from their childhood. He was the man of the house and sometimes was strange about the children learning that and understood him completely even without talking. What is next, funny moments?

Nicky made the TV louder.

"I cannot see anything from here!" It was before the remote control.

"I don't understand why I have a head."

"Do you mean you got a headache?" Nicky always finishes his sentence the way George wanted.

Also: "Why am I getting so old? It's a never-ending process. Or my father died the next day." He meant years ago.

"Bring me these carrots for Thanksgiving–something that I like."

"Do you mean this sweet potato?"

"Hahah! They would all laugh at his 'senior moments.'"

George's Bulgarian family in Brighton Beach, Brooklyn, made it so that you had to compete with everybody coming from Eastern European emigrants, especially from the former Soviet Union, particularly in tennis competitions. It's serious. It's not for fun.

When his son grew up, George decided to put Nicky into

private tennis lessons. One of his favorite clients was his coach. He was known as a torturous coach, but all his players reached the state finals. Americans were coming to play only for fun, so their children enjoyed playing tennis so the parents could have time for themselves so they could go shopping at the Kings Plaza Shopping Mall, but playing tennis for Nicky was different: It's not just for a good time/fun. Mostly, you sign up to become a professional tennis player, so whatever he did, his father, Nicky, made sure that Alex was following all age group rankings. Nicky personally picked the most sadistic tennis coach for Alex (called him Gestapo). He was very strict and very un-merciful if you didn't follow his system of training.

The coach was engaging in slight child abuse. Bulgarians and the Russians were always shoulder to shoulder in sports like wrestling and weightlifting, but also in tennis.

"Why do your parents pay if you're showing no improvement?!" he would shout.

Alex hated that he didn't have a normal childhood. From school to college, almost every summer, he was practicing at camps in the Catskill Mountains. There was no time to waste on silly or dangerous things like drugs. Every Saturday and Sunday, Alex had scheduled training and competitions.

This was not for fun at all. He would not be a professional tennis player, but you have to give your best to make sure that you are on top since George was paying good money!

Plus, since Nicky's parents were paying from their pocket for private lessons, in the future, this will help Alex develop a sense of competition. Fighting individually on the court by himself. Nicky got Tennis Scholarships for his College Education! No pain, no gain! This was George's motto!

After he got old, George called the kids and Nicky and Emily on the phone many times: "Where is your mama? Where is she?! It is my lunchtime! She knows that I have to eat lunch now!"

"I don't know that I am in college," said Nicky, "She's probably doing grocery shopping or with the red-haired lady on the fifth floor talking, or with that eastern european roma fortuneteller from Hungary, Maria is studying our horoscopes to know about our future. Don't worry, Pap, she will call you later."

"She knows that it's time for me to eat."

"Please, Pap, open the refrigerator and get something small to eat till she comes home."

George was the man of the house, and Maria was his maidservant housewife. She didn't let me know where she was going. I'm starving, and why she suddenly disappeared from him at the moment he needed her to serve him his favorite Bulgarian food.

For George, this was a ritual–a tradition to sit comfortably.

It has to be served properly and presented in the proper

etiquette. He was the man of the house. He has to say a prayer in the Orthodox Grace manner and cross himself so he can eat normally and enjoy a cup of red wine. Cheers! George was certain that wine helped with his arthritis and cleaned out his arteries. If you see Bulgarians talking louder, this is normal for them. They're not mad. They are not angry. This is the way they talk only in high volume. Similarly, Russians and Germans also have a hard and loud language.

You have to remember Bulgaria is a part of the Balkans. All major wars started in this area.

Remember that the Root of the Balkan troubles is a history of ethnic skirmishes. "If there is ever another war started in Europe, it will come out of some damned silly thing in the Balkans." Never forget the Bosnian 'Sarajevo' and the memories of wars.

This is the way they talk. There's nothing wrong with that. George was the same, screaming out of his lungs, talking with Maria. They loved each other, but they had tough love.

Many Bulgarians had a hard life during communism, so they had to learn to cope.

Maria was born in Little Italy in Manhattan. She was an American, but she loved her Italian culture. She never understood the lonely Slavic soul and the difficulty that they had to endure. Both souls were so different, but they had one American dream for both their kids, and the only thing for the immigrants was their family, so they did everything to keep their families together and take care of their children the way they were taught by their parents back in the old school.

Let's go back to Nicky's homecoming :

George sat alone, looking around for a second before Nicky returned with a mug for his father.

Nicky was grown up. He was humble and happy to see his parents, spend time with his father, watch his favorite Bulgarian show, and help him around the house. Even listening to the same "mantra," the same old story and father's advice repeated a million times.

He understood what George did for him to escape communism so that he could live a better life in America.

After their second or third glass of vodka, their conversations were smooth and pleasant! It was like nothing happened!

"Nicky," George started. He wanted to tell his son that everyone missed him and that he needed to come home, but after seeing his son taking care of himself as he was, George was overwhelmed with one thought, and he needed to say it: "I was wrong. You're a man, and you can clearly take care of yourself!" George said as he gestured around the small apartment. "I came to ask you to come home, but you've changed my mind. You're a man." George couldn't get that thought out of his head, "I've raised a man!"

The idea shocked him before he continued with a deep breath.

"You're my son, and I want to grow old with you around...would you join us for dinner? Surely you miss us too?"

The more George spoke, the more Nicky felt like crying. He had clearly missed his father, along with the rest of his family. Nicky hugged and held his father before saying, "More than anything in the World. I'd love to."

Content. Everyone who watched this scene, present or not, felt strongly content with the World at that moment.

"So," George started again, "How'd you get here?!" The fact that his son could properly provide for himself (in the ways that he was) was still quite surprising to George. From there, the father and son began catching up. Once again, our spectators couldn't understand the words that either person was saying, but they could understand the feeling: mutual respect. This was the feeling that both our spectators could tell was missing from the start, and from it, they knew that all was well.

"Wow." Alex had never felt something like this. The closest he had gotten to it was winning a tennis tournament or some other vein accomplishment, but this feeling was a hundred-fold compared to any of those.

Soon, the two men's talking faded away, and the two spectators thought to themselves for a minute before speaking. From his thoughts, Alex spoke, "So it's a happy ending?"

"Yeah, more or less..." George still felt guilty for a couple of reasons.

First, George realized that he had never truly understood his son's struggle. He had just pushed it off as "New World comfort."

Second, George had still kicked his son out of his house. Throughout George's entire experience as a parent, he had heard about the horrid parents who drove their kids from their homes to fend for themselves. The fact that George was one of these horrid parents of whispers and second-hand stories for even a short time devastated him personally.

Alex understood that, though all was well now, George still felt extremely guilty, and Alex respected that.

"So, what happened after that?" Alex asked.

"Well, he worked for a little bit to take care of himself, but eventually, he went to college and lived a little off of me and your grandmother while working to keep himself out of debt!"

"Wow!" Alex, at this point, completely forgot about college. It seemed insignificant in the scheme of things. "What did he study?" Alex was a little ashamed for knowing so little about his father.

"History- Eastern European History specifically. Kingsborough College (the City University of New York–CUNY), in South Brooklyn."

Alex could feel a grin creeping up on George's face as he said that. When he heard "Eastern European History," Alex quickly had flashbacks to the myriad of fun facts his father had told him about his grandfather and homeland. It was at this point that Alex realized how much George and Nicky's upbringing affected his own.

The ensemble of lights arranged themselves again to show a small dorm room that our spectators could quickly imagine was Nicky's. A thinner blond boy first walked into the room before Nicky went into it. Besides the blond boy, two bags and George accompanied Nicky. One of the bags was a large duffle, and the other was a backpack. It wasn't the same bag as we had seen previously, but it had the same blue and orange color scheme.

Nicky obviously missed his old bag when he was shopping for a new one and just wanted the closest thing to what he had lost. George was properly old- this was the beginning of George's present and final era, and this was right when George was becoming an "old man."

Though he had always been an "old man" in the nobility of spirit, at this point, George's personality was being actualized. Despite George's age, he was carrying a quite heavy cardboard box. Once Nicky and George both set down their luggage, Nicky greeted his new roommate. The boy's name was Sam. He seemed affable, but Nicky resented the boy because he knew he would miss living alone in his apartment. Of course, the fault was really on the university and its residency requirements. Still, Sammy was the physical representation of Nicky's displeasure, and he couldn't help but dislike the boy a little because of that.

Sam was nice, but nothing to write home about. He was a very stereotypical college student. After the scene resolved and George did his usual wave before disappearing, Nicky and Sam got along a little more before playing some video games and becoming clear friends. "Wow," Alex said. This was the first time a scene with that format had ended happily or with any kind of social success.

"Yeah," George started.

"He had really grown since then..." This made both George and Alex unbelievably proud. Alex understood that it was absurd to feel pride for his father becoming a social person (as a matter of fact, when Alex thought back to his father in social situations, Nicky was by far the most fluent and affable person he had ever seen handle any situation), but he felt pride, nonetheless. The scene sped along. With the speed came a few new scenes. First was Nicky's first college party. It was a nice house despite the massive mess. It was clearly a frat house. Nicky started off drinking very little, but as the night progressed, Nicky became drunk for the first time. Nothing bad happened, but the first impression of alcohol was a lasting one. After the scene went black, a new one composed itself.

This scene was one of Nicky's first hangovers. Alex had never been drunk before, so he was not only gifted with his first experience with drunkenness but also its consequences–this time in the form of a vicious hangover headache.

"Ahh," Alex exclaimed to the smallest (unidentifiable) noise in the background. George felt this pain as well, but his grandson's reaction was entertaining enough for him to give off a chuckle.

George was entertained by both his grandson's first reaction to alcohol as well as the vision of Nicky's first time drinking. Though he did envy the college kids, Nicky drank with them for stealing his first drink.

After the party experience, the next vision contained Nicky moving out of his dorm. George remembered that this was because the dorm fees were steep, and an apartment was more convenient for a few reasons beyond just the cost. Sam and Nicky said goodbye to one another; they had known each other for less than a year, but there was a clear feeling of comfort and premature nostalgia that came from the boy when Nicky talked to him. Once they said goodbye, Nicky and Sam went their separate ways. Nicky left for his car, where he had packed his other things and where he had his father sitting in the passenger seat. Nicky drove off about four blocks to the new student housing apartments.

Nicky and George spent the next few hours unpacking and talking about whatever would come to their minds. At this point in the development of their relationship, Nicky and George were both expert conversationalists, but just as well, they were both very comfortable with silence between one another.

Once they were unpacked, George didn't leave. Instead, George waited with his son for about an hour before Maria arrived. Soon after, Maria, Andrey, and Yordie arrived. Maria helped Nicky with preparations for dinner while Andrey and Yordie sat and chatted about whatever they could come up with while sitting on the couch. Once Nicky and Maria finished making dinner (with George spectating and commenting the whole time), everyone sat around the small table and ate. The group had drinks after dinner and chatted even more as a group. Finally, everyone congratulated Nicky on his new apartment and left one by one. Nicky felt a new wave of accomplishment while he was doing some light cleaning in his apartment–it was something our spectators had felt earlier. Nicky felt comfort, not just in having a home where he felt he belonged, but it also came from pride in creating a home in which others felt comfort.

Our spectators recognized this unique feeling and warmth from the earlier scene of young George's first home in America. Eventually, our spectators fully took in the feeling, and the scene faded into black. George was proud of his son. He forgot about that experience until then. When he thought back to it, George remembered getting this feeling secondhand. It was a point of immense pride for his son at that time, and from there, he trusted his son even more.

The scene skipped to the final representation of Nicky's college life: his graduation. Nicky had decided to attend the graduation ceremony (thanks to the pressures of his family) and was sitting in the third row when his name was called. Nicky walked up to the stage, took his diploma, and shook his dean's hand before turning to the crowd and giving a short wave while trying to find his family. Eventually, he found his parents and extended family cheering with the crowd that surrounded them. At this point, Nicky felt yet another bout of unbelievable pride. At this point, even our spectators felt amazed about the world.

After this event, a new one came across. The new scene was more intense. When the scene was composed, it showed George and Nicky sitting together over a drink, but neither was drunk.

There was a feeling of both tension and excitement between the two. George was the first to speak, "So, this is what you want to do in life?" George said. His tone wasn't accusatory or judgmental, just cautious.

"Yes," Nicky started, "I think so." This gave George

immense pride. He stared into his son's eyes with a stern look before saying:

"Let's do business, then!" George stood and shook his son's hand before pulling Nicky into his embrace. George was on the verge of crying.

"What happened?"

Alex was beyond curious.

"Nicky and I decided what he was going to do after college," George began before going into a moment of quiet contemplation. "We decided to open a shop in Chicago. There's a Bulgarian community there that Nicky was interested in becoming connected with" (It was clear at this point that Nicky was beyond comfortable with his culture) "as well as a flourishing Italian community that Maria was more than ecstatic to gain a connection with (she had trouble feeling at home since the passing of her parents)," Nicky remembered the image of the strong Italian man who had become so affable in giving his blessing for George and Maria's marriage. He felt remorse to hear that he had passed (though he knew it was coming, considering Nicky had never met the man). His grandpa Nikolas, Nicky's namesake.

The scene skipped to an image of George and Nicky signing a document together. From there, it showed George, Nicky, and the rest of their family packing up the house Nicky had grown up in and moving the boxes to the truck. Maria was on the brink of tears because of the required process of accepting that her little boy's days of a time machine and spaceship stories were over. He's a man now. Once all the things were packed away with Nicky's stuff, the truck took off with George and the gang trailing behind in a car.

The scene skipped the car ride to Chicago from Brighton Beach and simply composed a scene consisting of the two–George and Nicky. The two were looking at the sunrise down a narrow city street in front of their shop. The two had to wake up early to get to work on the shop- they could only afford a few days without any profit if they wanted the shop to be a success. Our spectators basked in the wonderful feeling of owning and building something. Both George and Nicky had felt this way, but this time was different- it was more intense than any other time.

After the beautiful feeling had sunk in for the spectators, an image of a thriving and functional auto shop in downtown Chicago, above the men working on the cars and the customers they were talking to, read a big red sign, "The Bulgarians" in Italian. After looking into the bustling shop, however, you could see two men, one young and one old, having a strained conversation. It was about money; most understand that people talk a certain way about money, and these two men were talking that way. "We don't have enough!" George said frustratedly.

"We do, and we'll have more after we go through with it! Look at how amazing such a shop can run!" Nicky responded both quickly and with great excitement.

"But it won't be ours!" The passion was clear in George's voice. "What's going on?" Alex asked. He was far too used to that question by now.

Our present-day George sighed, "Nicky wanted to branch out. He saw our success in our first shop and, with it, an opportunity." "Branch out?" Alex asked.

"Yes," George answered shortly before explaining, "He wanted to open shops across the state with our same name. He figured that people would flock to them because they trusted us." Alex realized that this was the true beginning of his father's career. And he knew how this ended- or at least he thought he did.

"So what happened after this?" Alex was ready to hear the story about how George and his father became great businessmen.

"I said no," George said rather firmly. He clearly didn't regret that decision.

"What do you mean, 'no?'" Alex asked.

"I said no. I told your father that if he wanted to open another shop, he could do it, and he could do it with his own money." George had the contrary tone of a politician in a debate.

"I Bvlgari" auto shop started from George's Brighton Beach location:

"Nicky's."

"So he did?" Alex knew the answer at this point.

"Yep," George started, "and soon enough, I was dragged into helping him manage the regions. I'll admit, he was right–those shops were as successful as one could be, but that little shop in Schiller Park and Des Plaines Chicago will always be the real 'I Bvlgari,' no matter what happens–to us or to it!"

George clearly felt passionate about the issue, and Alex could feel that.

Eventually, the argument between the two men ended exactly as George said it would. George said, "If you would like to do it, you may do it! You may absolutely take your share of the profit and waste it away on some knockoff of what we built!" George had obviously downplayed how angry he was when the whole ordeal unfolded. Nicky responded with a simple, "I think I will." He was clearly far too confident in his business model, but he was still quite polite.

There was one final scene in Nicky's saga that St. George condescended to show our viewers: Nicky was walking into one of his shops. Instead of the common mechanic's jeans and t-shirt, Nicky was wearing his suit. It was clear from this attire that Nicky was not at the shop to work. He was there to manage and make sure that everything was running smoothly. As Nicky was talking to the receptionist at the front desk, a woman appeared behind him. She tapped his shoulder, and when he turned around, he saw the most beautiful woman in the world.

"Is that...Mom?" Alex was surprised. He had never heard the full story of how his parents met, just abbreviations of the situation.

"Yep," George said, "That's your mother. Isn't it amazing how both my son and I met the loves of our lives at these shops?!" I swear it's some kind of blessing that allows these things to happen!" The idea of love at first sight wasn't new to either of the subjects (Nicky and Margarita). Since Shakespeare's days, this idea has been around. It was only then that the two understood it.

Alex and George appreciated the moment for a while before Alex spoke up, "So, we know what happens from here; we both lived through it! Where do we go from here?"

"I don't know..." George was concerned. His adventure through his son's life almost made him forget the terrifying scenes that he and his grandson had seen of themselves in the hospital. "I guess the only way to go from here is back or in the future!"

# Chapter 10:

## Captain Georgiy and Nurse Anastasia

George and Alex thought about what would be next to come, and that came exactly. The scene fell apart from the romance, and it composed itself back in Europe, but this place was new… "Where are we?" Alex asked. His grandfather seemed to have been able to answer that question with ease every time he had asked it in the past.

"Not a clue in the World," George responded simply. He knew at this point that what happened in this fictional World wouldn't hurt them and that, so far, it's served as an educator for the both of them, so George had taken on an exciting attitude after seeing the beauty that was his son's life. The background of the new scene lost its blur. At this point, George and Alex could tell they were in an old hospital- a very old hospital. George recognized the hospital as before his time. George figured the hotel must've been from the 1800s to be as old as it seemed. Beyond its antiquity, the main characteristic of the hospital was its general disarray. The hospital not only looked like it had been assembled in a matter of days, but it clearly was taking in more people than it was meant to handle. Nurses were rushing through the corridors with bedpans, and doctors were making the briefest of visits to each of their patients. Eventually, the perspective moved along the corridor into the general ward that held at least 50 men being attended to. All of them had at least one brutal wound and were checked to make sure that none had a contagious disease that could spread to their roommates.

Despite this, many young men were coughing, and some were dead in their beds. Eventually, the smell of the room reached our spectators and made them gag (in spirit, at least).

A teenage boy was carrying a freshly printed newspaper and shouting, "Plovdiv was in Russian hands! Constantinople is next!"

It was January 2, 1978. The Russian forces left the liberated city of Pazardzhik. According to intelligence provided by Bulgarians, Suleyman Pasha's group retreated in two directions: Pazardzhik-Peshtera and Pazardzhik-Plovdiv.

On the night of January 3, the column of Major-General Pavel Shuvalov crossed the Maritsa River through a ford to the village of Airene, and at the same time, the cavalry unit with the commander, Major-General Daniil Krasnov, approached Plovdiv on the left bank of the river. The Ottoman defenses were breached.

On the morning of January 4, 1878, Lieutenant General Yosif Gurko entered the city with his entire staff and announced the liberation of Plovdiv.

A prayer service was held.

The main Russian forces immediately moved to attack the

covering Ottoman forces in the area. Suleiman Pasha's group was diverted from the direction of Plovdiv-Edrin and directed to the Rhodopes, where it disintegrated as an organized military force. Constantinople, the Ottoman capital, will next be in the hands of the Russians. The perspective became more specific until it focused on a man. His hair was black, and on his face was a beard that was as thick as one could get (usually, that would be a good thing, but since the young man had neglected to take care of it, the beard looked ratty and unmanageable). Despite the beard, our boy still looked quite young. The shock of war had just reached him, and it was clear on his face. George recognized the face immediately- it was his Grandfather Georgiy. George could recall the face not because of personal familiarity but because of the photo his father had taken of him while telling him great stories of his grandfather's feats.

While the man was lying there, our spectators could feel the tension in Georgiy's leg. It was clear there was something wrong with it. Our spectators couldn't tell if the tension was mercifully numbed by St. George or if it was the result of what Georgiy was feeling from the anesthetics. Regardless- the tension in George's leg was what had landed him there. As Georgiy lay there, a nurse eventually approached him. The woman's name was Anastasia. She had blond hair and was about 5'8". Lieutenant Georgiy Kakhovskiy–6 '2". At the end of the war, he was promoted to Captain.

Ana was born in Alexandroupolis, Greece (200 km) from the Bulgarian border, the ancestor of grand grandma Anastasia, who served in the Balkan Red Cross as an army nurse. She saved the life of the wounded Russian military correspondent lieutenant.

While the tall and graceful woman was washing over George's leg with a cloth, George looked at her and made eye contact once she glanced up at him. After making eye contact, the nurse quickly glanced back down and blushed with a slight smile.

There was a love-at-first-sight chemistry between the two. "And that," George started matter-of-factly, "was my grandmother, Anastasia."

As though St.George was saying, "Correct," the scene quickly changed to another. The new scene held George and Anastasia cheering in the street. George grabbed his love and kissed her. Our spectators could feel the pure jubilance rushing through the two lovers.

"And this," George said like he was doing well on trivia night, "Must've been the end of the war, in which my grandfather became Captain Georgiy Kakhovskiy!"

"What war was this?" Alex was ready to revisit history with his grandfather once more.

"The Russian-Turkish war. It only lasted about a year, but it greatly changed the geography of Europe! The Russians expanded West and acquired a set of territories in the Balkans.

Those territories included our homeland- Bulgaria! This war might've been the first time our family stepped foot in my homeland!" (Alex wanted to point out the irony that, though George didn't claim Ukraine as his homeland, he seemed excited to deem Bulgaria to be Alex's homeland, considering it was George's birthplace.

"Where'd the war come from?" Alex asked.

"Well..." George was compiling all of his historical knowledge, "In the short of it- the Ottoman Empire refused to forfeit what was asked of them during a peace conference, which upset Russia (the nation to which they were supposed to forfeit things) and started a war. In 1877, a series of Balkan events brought Europe to the brink of a new war. Most countries around these two nations promised not to interrupt because they figured it would be a poor choice for their citizens and economy." George took a breath to figure out what else to say, "The long of it: well, ask your father. He studied the material and was given a degree for it, so he'd probably be able to cover the myriad of nuances better than me!" The obvious subtext of that statement was, "Ask your father if you ever can," but neither spectator pointed that out.

They were both more than aware of the situation and felt it strongly upon hearing that statement.

George regretted saying anything. A War correspondent story of Captain Georgiy: He was first engaged to his sweetheart Natasha. His first fiancé was from a Nobel Aristocratic family. She was killed in 1877 at the beginning of the Russian-Turkish War on the Caucus front. Lieutenant Georgiy was sent to the Bulgarian front. He was wounded and sent to the battlefield hospital near Plovdiv, where he met his soulmate, Anastasia.

God sent an angel of a nurse of Greek origin who became his wife. She was dishonored by her Greek father because she was not engaging according to the traditions in his hometown of Alexandroupolis. She fell in love and married "for love," which was very rare and rebellious for a young woman like her. Her Greek father rejected her, but later, he gave her his blessings in marriage to the Russian hero (he was also an Eastern Orthodox Christian).

Eventually, the scene composed once again of an even more jubilant event: a wedding! At the end of the aisle, Georgiy stood waiting with excitement while his beautiful Ana walked slowly to him. The Orthodox priest gave his speech, the couple gave their vows, and the two kissed once more into matrimony. The spectators were given brief glances at the reception and the couple's retreat to their honeymoon. After our spectators truly appreciated the wedding, two simple images appeared. The first was of a loving group of people adoring a pregnant Anastasia.

The image was clearly a part of the real world, but it looked as though it was from the Renaissance, with the different looks of affection on each person's face that crowded around the woman sitting solidly in the center of the image. The second image was similar, but instead of being set in the couple's house like the previous image, this one was set in another hospital (It seems there are too many hospitals in our spectators' recent lives). But this was a happy hospital scene. It was George's turn to witness his father's first moments. There were no words to describe and thank the Lord for young Alexander's appearance. Alexander was a variant of a Greek word meaning the defender of the people.

# Chapter 11:

# The Story of Dr. Alexander and Emma

The story of George's father is a complicated and dramatic one, much like that of George himself.

To begin it's known that Alexander was born to Captain George. Ambiguously known is that Alexander was born in the city of Ljubimetz, Bulgaria, and spent much of his young life there. Once Alexander began showing signs of a young man, however, he was quickly shipped off to the prestigious Seraphim Military Academy (translated from Russian, of course), where the boy learned to be a proper citizen in the immense power that was pre-revolutionary Russia. Sadly for Alexander, since he was sent to his academy in the mid-1910s, Great Russia was only properly pre-revolutionary for a matter of 11 months after Alexander's arrival before it was overcome by violent and vicious revolutionaries—the Bolsheviks. The revolution was swift, and the revolutionaries targeted grand government institutions such as the very academy that Alexander was attending, especially because it was in the interests of the pre-revolutionary so-called white Guard, or Royal Army.

Alexander knew that because of his situation. He needed to escape the mainland to his family and home.

Now, the story of this heroic man's escape had been told

and retold to his family and descendants. The way the story went, as George swore, he recalled it, included Alexander running and hiding in the forest amidst the harsh winter to a freezing sea.

The occasion, as St. George recalled it to our dear subjects, simply followed Alexander illegally boarding a French ship that was being patrolled after being overtaken by the revolutionaries. Regardless, the odds were narrow for Alexander's safe escape from the nation, just less dramatic.

Lieutenant Alexander was the last officer allowed aboard a crowded French ship. With teary eyes, the boy thought that this might be the last time he saw my lovely Russia! Goodbye! Royal loyalty officer recited in French:

"Quelle Histoire Dans Cette Partie du monde (what a history in this part of the world?)."

"C'est merveilleux et Magnifique (this is wonderful and magnificent!)"

Au revoir la Russie! Goodbye, Russia!

*Quelle histoire dans cetter parite du monde. C'est merveilleux et magnifique!*

Upon his escape, Alexander landed in Sevastopol. From there, a ship sailed the Black Sea to Varna port before finally arriving at his rendezvous with his family in Sofia. From there, Alexander finished his development into manhood before leaving his homeland once more to attend the prestigious Sorbonne

Medical University in Paris, where Alexander departed from his status as a simple man to an educated one. Not long after establishing his career as a surgeon back in his homeland, Alexander and his wife, whom he married immediately upon his return from medical school, had a child. This child was the first of a few, but his significance to this story is great, considering he was Georgiy or George, the namesake of his father and one of our two subjects of this story as a whole. Soon after the birth of our brilliant boy George (the vision of which gave George a brief moment of intense existential consideration), the wave of socialist revolutionaries chased Alexander down in Bulgaria–the "People's Party" had taken over.

The Bolshevik's reign continued as they ravaged much of Europe. Alexander's firstborn, Georgiy, wed long before Vasiliy. Because of this, when his father passes, the man will inherit everything. The laws of the old World promised what was left behind to the married men of a man's descendants almost exclusively and with the highest priority. Allowed by the comfort of his wealth, Georgiy moved to his life. The mad Vasiliy joined underground Marxist groups, where the philosophy of Marx was revealed to him as the true Paradise on Earth for the masses–justice and freedom of expression for all. Later, he joined an underground group of Jewish "intelligentsia," and he was against Leon Trotsky. Finally, he became a loyal red commissar to Stalin. Vasiliy was so mad and angry with his brother (like Jacob and Esau, he believed that the brother stalled his father's birthright and inheritance) with his own hands he killed his mother, Mariya, confiscated all his property and lands and killed his brother who refused to join to the Bolsheviks.

After the Russian Civil War, Vasiliy was looking to kill Alexander Georgiy's son, so he moved later to work as a Soviet Ambassador and attaché in Sofia. For the following years, Alexander and Emma struggled to raise their children under the oppression and starvation that the People's Party and communism brought upon them. Upon his coming of age, Alexander's son, George, decided that he, too, would be leaving the country to become a man. The boy fled and disappeared for months on end. Alexander and his wife assumed their eldest son had been killed at the Greek border, and his body disappeared. As all hope was lost, a man arrived at Alexander's practice. With the man was a package wrapped in manilla-colored paper. With the package was a set of new shoes that George figured his father would find stunning, some American money, along with a note reading, "Hello, father! I have settled in an apartment in the beautiful Brighton Beach in New York. I've sent along means to pay for your tickets and to help with your travels along the body of Europe!"

Alexander was ecstatic. He quickly hid the note and the included bills and put on the shoes after checking to make sure there were no American maker's marks. Alexander left his office early to go home and find Emma to tell her the good news–their son was alive, and they were moving to America. But since George escaped illegally to the Bulgarian-Greek border and committed treason. For his parents to move to America legally was impossible–This was the life of a young people in this oppressive regime, breaking us to submission for forgetting who we are, our individual patriotic past, so that we become a mass of people easy to control. Dr. Alexander had only one choice given by the communists to send his family to Ljubimetz, a deep province where his parents lived, and medical staff, doctors, and teachers were in shortage. Hence, Alexander and Emma moved to live with their elderly parents, Georgiy and Anastasya, when little Georgiy started school. He met his sweetheart, Svetlana. At sixteen years old, he finally escaped Bulgaria.

George's parents were followed by "State security" "Darzhavna sigurnost, an oppressive force that would arrest, imprison, torture, and even execute those who they thought opposed their cause. Under the People's Republic of Bulgaria, their secret service was closely related to the KGB. He was extremely harassed and repressed because of George after he was declared a criminal in his motherland, where he received a sentence to death due to treason. Instead, his parents were aggressively arrested and thrown to prison because of the escape of their son George.

Another memory from Bulgaria:

George and Maria had their firstborn, Nicky, and a younger

daughter, Emily. George was the firstborn and had two brothers, Dimitar and Drago (children of Alexander and Emma). Andrey and Yordanka are children of his uncle Ivan (cousins from his mother's side), whose father came to America before 1944. After the communist regime, he remembers a "Moment when George moved to study in Ljubimetz from Sofia. He was alone in the neighborhood. Nobody wanted to find friends because his father was anti-revolutionary; after 1945, they fired him from Sofia Hospital, he lost his private medical practice, confiscated his big house on Khan Asparuh Street because he graduated Medicine in a Western country like France after his son George escaped the communist put him in jail, beat him to submission broke his spirit till proudly called before "monsieur" became "tovarish–" one of many comrades without individuality only brick of the wall "Another Brick in the Wall" after the famous Pink Floyd's 1970.

George had this dream for the future of new family discoveries as soon as George and Alex were transported to Sofia, Bulgaria, in 2020. But George always prefers to highlight the fact that he had survived because of his mother's warmth, love, and prayers.

George is utterly grateful that he was born in the house of Emma and Alexander. In addition, he was truly thankful for absconding from Bulgaria, as it was a significant circumstance that molded his life. It gave George experiences that money cannot buy.

"I am sure," Alex replied with a smile.

George kept quiet. It had been only some hours, and he could already feel as if I were gathering the missing pieces of his lost Bulgarian rhapsody. Then, all of a sudden, all of his fears had evaporated into thin air. George and Alex were transported into the future when Dimitar (George's middle brother) unexpectedly died during the COVID pandemic in 2020 under strange circumstances. George was under pressure to make a dangerous decision against medical advice to travel to Sofia with Alex in order to say goodbye to his brother at his funeral. Over the short time, he was able to sell the house with Dimitar's sons. It was the only time that they would be able to get a good deal. Later, he visited Ljubimetz at the frontier, where he met his old girlfriend, Svetlana, for the first time since he was sixteen—and fled over the Greek border. When he arrived in Sofia, George was scared to look like a stranger in the city, and he wasn't sure if the locals would accept him and understand his love for his birthplace. George didn't want them to think of him as a greedy son who had returned to cash the fortunes of his ancestor.

There was a memory in the old house when Little Georgie was ten years old. One night, his father was late, and his mother was not home. Georgie was afraid.

When they finally sat down to eat, he took one of his son's hands in his own and very softly intoned, "Almighty God, we give you our sincere thanks. For food in a world where many walked hungry; for faith in a world where many walk in fear; for friends in a world where many walk alone. Amen."

As a religious expression of any kind was forbidden, George naturally felt uneasy during the moments of whispered prayers. George believed that, during communism, walls had ears, and they could hear and report every conversation to state security.

George can still feel the fear he had felt whenever his father prayed before dinner. When the indoctrinated teachers had much more say than his parents, communism was already there. George was obligated to report his parents as a faithful Dimitrovski pioneer in school and what was going on in his family. The notion of social justice at that time was merely written on paper. It reminded George of George Orwell's popular rejoinder, "Everyone is equal, but some are more equal than others."

As George had read George Orwell's 1984 plenty of times. He was certain Big Brother was watching him. So, George paused for a moment and tossed a question at his grandson:

"Is America becoming Orwell's nightmare, Alex?"

"I don't know...but Americans have become numb to a loss of personal privacy on an unparalleled scale," Alexander replied. "We cannot deny that everyone's activities on streets and in public places are routinely captured on tape."

George smiled at him. He was happy that they were on the same page. Many people feel nostalgic for socialism.

They claimed at that time that there were no poor or rich people, as everyone was equal. George begged to differ. According to the facts, in 1980, the BCP (Bulgarian Communist Party) – Nomenklatura–was concentrating incomes comparable to those of the British aristocracy. George told Alexander one of his memories of one night when the red communist guard had shown up at his doorstep. The members of Komsomol had come to arrest George's father as someone had filed a report against him that he was playing Beethoven and Bach, which was a crime in the eyes of the regime. Hence, they took it as their responsibility to punish his family for enlightenment.

George's father was fond of playing the French antique piano that once belonged to his grandfather, who had brought it from Odessa, Ukraine. George's mother would often help him practice his music lessons on it after school. As the security militia had marched into the house, George remembered they were screaming, "You filthy aristocrat bourgeois! Stop polluting the air with your poisoned Western music."

The ten guards had searched the whole house by turning everything upside down. It seemed as if a traitor had lived among us. The guards had searched for anti-revolutionary books and letters. They had thrown them in the courtyard, yelling:

"Long live the Bulgarian Communist Party. Huraayyy! Urrraaa!" George was a young boy at that time. After the guards left, he leaped from my bed and ran to his mother's room. George was terrified by the sight of wisps of smoke curling up in the air from the heaps of half-burned books and music records. With its charred sides and tangles of snapped strings popping up from inside, the piano looked like a wrecked piece of trash. The ashes were falling in the courtyard like snow, covering pieces of clothing and papers that were strewn everywhere. At the front door, there was a carpet of shattered glass that glimmered in the morning light as icy crystals. George was trying to get out when the neighbor grabbed him by his clothes.

"What are you up to now, stupid boy?" she had asked.

"I am going out to salvage some of our belongings," George had replied courageously.

"No way, you can't do that!" she had commanded before pulling him inside.

"But I see our radio," the boy had protested.

On the ground under the willow tree lay their old tube-brand radio 'Orfeus' with its brown plastic cowling seeming to be intact. It was his father's favorite Soviet-era radio with which he liked to illegally listen to Western stations (such as The Voice of America, BBC, and Radio Free Europe). As George stood silently staring at their house in horror, he heard his mother's cry, "George, don't you go out there! It's dangerous! Somebody can report you."

The only thing my family was able to recover was an old leather doctor's bag in my father's room. The bag had my grandfather's hundred-and-forty-two-year-old lost manuscript, which hid his father's medical records and other official papers. Unfortunately, the guards had overlooked it as they were aware that my father worked in a government hospital in the town. Hence, they had left it alone, deeming it to be a dull and dreary thing to set ablaze.

After communism took hold in 1944, the sizable aristocratic house on Khan Asparuh Street in the center of Sofia was considered to be huge for George's family. Hence, the government ordered two more families to live in the house. As lawful owners of the property, George's family was only left with one big room and a shared kitchen. The actions of each family were observed and reported all the time. The government eventually expelled us to the countryside with time because a big boss from Moscow wanted to settle in our house. Along with another family, my family relocated to a small town, 'Ljubimetz,' in the Haskovo Province, southern-central Bulgaria, where my grandparents lived due to a shortage of doctors and teachers.

At that time, George was a ten-year-old boy. His mother used to teach French and classical music; the areas of her interest made the family suspicious and unwanted by the regime. George's father had also graduated as a doctor from the prestigious Sorbonne University in Paris, France. In addition, his father's brother had long immigrated to the United States. All of the facts and circumstances were enough for the government to declare us the spies of the West and the enemies of the state.

One day, the Komsomol members surrounded George in the school courtyard, and they were yelling because they had figured out about his piano lessons. One of them started to beat George in order to turn him into a disabled person. George received many injuries on his left arm. They wanted to break the arm off of his body. Naturally, the first piano that George owned was burned, and the State Conservatory confiscated George's grandfather's classical French piano. The piano was given to a communist mother and her only daughter. Back in those days, all the belongings of the upper class were handed into the hands of the lower class because it was seen as if they legally deserved it. After all, the communists chanted about equality between all the classes. The communists would force the people to chant their slogans and continue to beat them until they submitted and corrected their nonconformist behaviors. Some of the people were also sent to correction facilities, where they had to endure a great deal of mental and physical torture. The reason that George received such brutal treatment was that he was born into a family of traitors and deserters. George's Ukrainian grandfather's surname, Kakhovskiy, was already well known because of his articles and reports against the Royal Russian generals, and the fact that his father had attempted to publish *his* father's manuscripts in 1889 did not sit well with the government.

Hence, George's identity was a hurdle in his path to

acquiring an education. George was almost a black sheep for people around him because of his ancestry. Some of George's ancestors had the red privilege because they were simple peasants and poor workers who had climbed up the corporate ladder under the government of BCP (Bulgarian Communist Party). But George knew that he had a tiny chance of getting a quality education and making a decent livelihood for himself in Bulgaria because of his relations. George's file always had a black spot in the section on hereditary characteristics. Hence, escaping to America in search of a better future became the boy's dream.

"The only other thing I was able to find from the basement that day was my broken toy train, Alex," George said, wiping his tears. "It was my first (French) toy, my oriental train that my father had bought for me. I always played with it when I was in kindergarten." The memory of George's toy train often gets entangled with his memory of staying under the bridge of the Maritza River in the town of Ljubimetz. It was the place from where the Oriental Express passed every day at 6:00pm before crossing the border of Bulgaria and Greece. George used to think while looking at the bridge that one day, he would make use of the bridge to escape from Bulgaria forever. But, all that time, George was unable to understand that he was trying to get away from the oppressive communist regime, not his homeland.

"I am surprised, Grandpa," Alex said. "I am speechless." George smiled at him. He knew it wasn't easy to grasp for his grandson, who had been born and bred in a completely different World.

"Well… that's just the start of my story," George replied.

"Why don't you get some rest now? We have a long day ahead of us?" Alexander said as he stood up.

George nodded. He needed to shut his eyes and lie down. He needed to rest.

At that moment, George understood the way a person perceives their world. In line with our world, there is an entirely unknown reality of the past and future born into our own universe and exists only in our brains. I think it is much more real than the real one. It is full of such unusual, unseen, and non-existent things. I can imagine and see various things through closed eyelids, yet I can only see what comes from our experience. As we break it, we rediscover it, and we continue to carry it within us. I remember when someone presented a painting entitled 'The sun through my closed eyelids' in our Art Club's annual exhibition. The painting merely had a sun, nothing too special, but the picture was red, and it was about happiness and well-being.

As I kept my eyes closed, I found myself dwelling in the past. I had a feeling that I was born on an old passenger train on the Sofia Ljubemetz line. The train had halted at a vacant country station. I could feel thoughts continuing to creep into my soul as I waited alone in the compartment. I sank into my memories. I heard the voice of my grandmother, who would always tell me, "My child, the World is big and endless, with plenty of places to live. But don't ever forget your homeland. The four walls and a suitcase do not make a home."

While my grandfather used to say, "When you go, there is only one direction forward in life. Never look back."

But then, his grandfather learned from his experience, and when a person became confused in his life for a long time and struggled to find an answer to his questions, he had to stop for a while and look for his lost home.

He finally realized the importance of taking time out to sit and think before going forward with his endeavors. It is said that any change of home, city, or country is akin to the loss of a loved one – a deep trauma that subsides over time. But it has a tendency to pop up in the mind like an old, unhealed wound of the soul.

In this sense, emigration had been a real torture for people. Not many people understand that it is a journey that separates people from each other because the World is big, and the journey is endless. However, George was grateful–utterly grateful to God, who protected him from the heavy fires of bullets on the border of Greece on the bloody Orthodox Easter in 1948. So, George will continue the circle of life to tell the story to the next generation. After hours of thinking, another scene of memories opened in front of the two's eyes:

"Now is the best time to sell the house at the market price as the property has reached thrice its value," said the real estate agent.

It was in the future. Alex and George were visiting Sofia, Bulgaria!

Alexander's two nephews and George found a great deal and sold the old house.

After the agent took leave, all of the family members decided to clean the old house room by room. Vasil, George's nephew, urged him to take some rest, but he thought his adrenaline was rushing in his body as George felt energetic to become a part of the cleaning crusade. George didn't tell them, but it was a chance for George to connect with his memories.

Each and every room in the house had a cluster of memories for George, and he was ready to take a dive. After dividing the rooms, George followed Alex down the basement. As they reached the bottom of the creaky stairs, Alex flicked on the switch, turning on the lights. George was shocked by the sight of a mountain of cardboard boxes staring at him.

He found a book about *Dracula* by Bram Stoker, published in 1897. His granduncle's favorite book was there.

George was surprised that the Important boss from Moscow who lived in his father's house was tovarish Vassiliy Kakhovskiy, who confiscated his brother's property. The memory of Vassiliy, the demon looks like his presence is still here.

"Does dracula still exist?" sometimes George thinks about him all the time because upon entering the basement, the appearance of the book about dracula on the old shelf in the home library shows that something is happening in the old haunted house. There was Paranormal activity in a house – strange noises, an apparition sighting –an event or experience that can't be explained by the laws of science.

"If you're-experiencing these scary events, your home may be haunted. However, a good ghost hunter errs on the side of caution. What may feel like classic paranormal activity or signs of a haunted house can often be explained by logic."

Alex downloads an app for ghosts on his phone: "Is the demon of Vassiliy still here?".

After the funeral, leaving St George church Alexander always played jokes on his grandpa. Because after the funeral, it was too heavy for his spiritual atmosphere, like a gray blanket of depression was trying to cover everyone. Alexander tries to cheer up his grandpa, who drifts away often in his memory. In every church, George and Alex would light a candle at the altar and ask the priest for a blessing or put garlic in their pockets, which was an old superstition that would keep the demons away. Surely, he would "knock on wood" to ward off bad luck from something he had just said.

Alexander's mother Rita was so angry with his grandpa for not leaving him alone on his beloved Bulgarian trip during the Covid pandemic.

Alex was born as an American freeman and had nothing to do with his lost childhood in Bulgaria - a third-world Balkan country. "The Stress, anxiety, fear, depression & darkness in Bulgaria are really heavy"!

Was thinking Alexander all the stories he heard here are coming directly from Hell. So far he didn't hear something positive or a story with a happy ending! Since Alexander traveled from America, Germany through Romania & Bulgaria and later to Greece & Turkey; Enthusiasm, happiness & enjoyment slowly disappear and give place to melancholy, confusion, fear, depression & sadness.

A grandpa's relative said to Alex one time: " My funny-talking boy, you think all these life stories are too heavy, let me tell you Amerikanche (American boy) something, I think they are not heavy and dark enough.

In 2020, Alex had a Jewish friend who discovered an app for ghost detection.

He shared with him. Alexander was a historian and scientist, but Grandpa George was more intuitive and believed that his entire life, he had a constant connection with his grandfather Georgiy and St George as his spiritual guides in life.

"Well, the basement could do with a little dusting," George remarked.

"Nobody comes down here anymore," chuckled Alex. "This place is full of antiques."

"There's my father's old chair," George pointed towards an old armchair with a smile.

"Yes, grampa held on to it as a cherished treasure," Alex replied. "It was painted so many times that it has become a hotchpotch of colors."

One by one, Alex and George unloaded the boxes and divided the stuff into two large bags labeled 'Giveaways' and 'Reserve,' respectively. Alex had barely let me work; I had sat in a corner in front of my father's wooden chest that was covered in dust. It looked as if it belonged to seafaring pirates and had spent many years in the free-spun salty air.

As George opened it, he found many old family photographs. The photographs served as a window of the past, for the better and the worse, for the bitter and for the sweet.

Tears rolled down his cheek as he looked at the photographs capturing pure joy. There were memories of those old times, birthday candles, and friends galore. Yet, as much as the photographs made me happy, I could feel wisps of sadness caressing my soul, hinting towards the storms I had navigated and won. Each photograph had a story to tell; it reminded me of the carefree days. Then, all of a sudden, George's nostalgia hit a halt as he spotted a golden diary buried in the pile of photographs. George picked up the diary and blew off the dust that lay thickly like winter's first snow. As he skimmed through it, George was shocked. It was more than a 142-year-old memoir of his grandfather, the captain.

George suddenly had a flashback. He remembered himself as a 10-year-old boy clutching his father's arm as he begged the communist soldiers and state security and militia collaborators who were burning his books. As George realized that the memoir had survived along with correspondence and letters because it was hidden in his father's old torn doctor's leather bag, George hugged the diary. It was a precious heirloom of the family; it was the foundation of their family roots.

Finally, he discovered the history of his inheritance. Nothing missing!

Nothing lost! He crossed himself in the manner of the Orthodox and thanked St. George for his protection.

Then, as George had begun to feel as drained as a squashed lemon, George requested his brother, sons of cousins grandchildren to drive him back to his residence. As George sat in the car, he clung to the diary that he had discovered. George couldn't stop thinking how lucky he had proven to be by finding an *objet d'art*. At the same time, George was suffering from severe headaches and difficulty in breathing. It was most likely because he had forgotten to take his blood pressure medication again before the great discovery.

George couldn't wait to reach the house so that he could eat his pills.

After changing into his night suit, he got in his bed. After dinner, George realized he had avoided dwelling in the past when he lived in Chicago, USA. But, since George had arrived in Bulgaria, even looking at the ceiling above his head seemed interesting as it brought many memories. George was actively trying to reconnect with his past and the local environment. George stood up and walked towards the window with several thoughts running in his mind. From the ajar window, he saw a moonlit front porch. It reminded him of his parents, who spent several years sitting there anticipating their son's homecoming. Unfortunately, George couldn't even come back to attend their funerals. At that point in time, George was stigmatized. His grief was mixed with shame and anger. George feels it's true that death brings out the worst as families begin to fight. George's brother hadn't informed him about my parents' demise. He had deliberately hidden it from George because he knew that he would show up for the funeral and might even end up in prison.

To date, George can feel guilt running along with blood in his veins. It was a difficult time for George. As much as George had wanted to attend the funeral, the mitigating circumstances had made it completely impossible. He walked back towards his bed and pulled open the top drawer of my side table. George took out the diary and rested my back against the upholstered headboard of my bed. He was excited to read about my grandfather, Captain Georgiy Kakhovskiy. Five minutes later, as George was engrossed in reading the stories, Alex knocked at his door.

"Yes?" George answered.

"Gindpa, are you still awake?" Alexander asked, making his way inside the room.

"I am afraid, yes, I have been reading, Sasha," George replied.

"Reading what?" Alex asked, eyeing the diary.

"A memoir of your great grandfather," George chuckled.

"For real?" Alexander exclaimed. George nodded with a smile.

"Where did you find it?" Alexander asked.

"In the basement," George replied. "When you were unloading boxes, I had rummaged through some of my father's belongings only to stumble upon this diary. Remember, 'the Manuscripts Don't Burn' from Bulgakov's *The Master and Margarita.* My grandfather's Manuscript, diary, letters, army journals, and maps didn't burn in the front yard fire." George remembered his father's old leather doctor's small suitcase where he found the 142-*year-old* lost manuscript (and treasure) three hours ago."

"What does it say?" Alex asked, getting curious.

"It has stories of Captain Georgiy Kakhovskiy's son, who happens to have the same name as you, Alexander, who was forced to appear in front of the Bulgarian People's Court of Communist Justices in the city of Sofia," George answered, heaving a sigh.

"You mean your dad?" Alex asked, raising his eyebrow. Yes, my father, Alexander, is your namesake.

George nodded. His swollen, tired face with redness and bags under his eyes were warnings that he missed something already. His phone rang after midnight. The reminder was off. George took all his medications.

It was Maria from Chicago."Good day, George!"

It was 8 hours behind in America.

She was worried about the increased deaths in Europe due to COVID-19. George told her all about the great discovery in his life in the basement of the old house.

The great discovery in his life. It was the diary of George's Ukrainian grandpa, the captain, who was a military correspondent. But unfortunately, his manuscript was banned and rejected from being published in Tsarist Russia in 1889.

"The unknown reports from the Russian-Turkish Liberation War 1978 reveal an interesting documentary story from a time we don't know anything about. The working draft was presented in 1886 and 1889, but it never got published in the Russian press.

So far, there is no information that it was published in the Bulgarian language."

Alexander pulled out his cell phone, checked it on Google, and muttered, "I see."

"There is information about several monuments in Bulgaria for the Russian "Bratushki" liberators. Many Bulgarian songs have also been saved in the diary in praise of them. Still, as the manuscript was not inclined towards the military generals during Tsarist Russia and the USSR– the empire of evil–it was banned. George thinks that they are making history here. If we hadn't come here, we wouldn't have found it."

"My father came from a long line of royal generals and minor nobility of Kakhovka, Ukraine," George said after a short pause.

"He stood before the people's court and represented himself on his own. Who would think that once a 'bratushka' big brother and a liberator of imperial Russia would be considered a traitor before the people's government of the communist party?"

George could see Alexander wanted to learn more about his great-grandfather as he had comfortably seated himself on the chair and rested his legs on the ottomans. George continued to tell him how he had never known until he came across the diary that his father had to appear before a court to answer his love for poetry, which was considered a sin through the proletarian lens.

History is bound to remember the victims of the communist purge, which is remembered as the 'Bloody Thursday.' It was the day when the people's court, Bulgaria's new pro-Soviet courts, and the government began the mass execution of the bourgeois elite.

"In the first three months after September 9, 1944, nearly 3000 members of the elite were killed in Bulgaria," I said. "The goal was to clear the way for the uneducated and unscrupulous supporters of the Soviet regime."

George told his grandson how they were determined to isolate the educated, enterprising, capable, and successful representatives of the Bulgarian elites. It was the first and foremost goal of the so-called 'class struggle' waged by the communist regime in a country where the red terror of Lenin and Stalin was fiercely applicable.

George's father, Alexander, had stood firm and upright in the face of the massacre. Everyone in the neighborhood loved him. He was regarded as a people's doctor. After working all day long in the hospital, he would treat strangers at night without a cost. Even when George's father was suffering in the turmoil of communism, he taught George to replace his resentment with affection regardless of the situation. He didn't want George to become an extremist. But George, even as a child, was a sharpshooter in his mind. Be that as it may, George's father's personality can be regarded as an epitome of fortitude and melancholy.

At this point, George kept the diary beside his. He looked at his grandson, Alexander's, sunken expression.

Pasternak's muse: The real-life inspiration for 'Doctor Zhivago.'

Alexander and Emma had George, Dimtar, and Drago. As their plans were finalizing, Alexander and Emma met in the same traditional and humble church where their son, George, had met his comrades in his escape. As the two's nerves calmed as much as they could in a moment like the one they were in, a light shone in through the beautifully painted window. Either person in the couple could've sworn that the light projected an image of Christ's third phase of crucifixion onto the planked wooden floor of the building.

The World froze the second everyone saw the image on the floor. Light like that meant the end— everyone knew it. The state agent was planted–an informant from the inside. He told the police everything and crushed the dreams of all the potential immigrants.

The police threw open the large, heavy doors of the church.

People broke the windows in order to escape, only to run into the source of the light. Both Alexander and Emma were clever enough to know that running meant being chased or, worse, shot. So, the couple stood still and accepted their arrests. Soon enough, the two were in an internment camp.

Of course, as many militaries will do, Alexander was sent to do physical labor camp-type Gulag in a different part of the camp, and Emma was sent to the women's side. Neither saw the other again. Eventually, the despair set in from the loss of one another's love of their lives. Along with the hunger, the loss of hope and forced estrangement from loved ones took either person's hope, as it would anyone. Alexander took his own life six days before his wife, Emma, who had heard the news of her husband two days before doing so.

Nobody was supposed to know about the secret; a simple funeral was performed the next day with the closest relatives. Nobody informed George because he would travel back with the first plane to honor his father and later end up in communist prison for life. Nobody knew more details about the death of Alexander. After 2006, the secret state dossier record files were open to learning more about the life of Alexander and Emma in prison and their deaths. In the declassified prison records of the victims of Communism in Bulgaria, like Dr. Alexander and other political prisoners, many peoples' only dream was "I want to live in Freedom."

# Chapter 12:

## Final Revelations

Our spectators finished watching the story of Alex. They were devastated. George had known that his father and mother had passed, just not in the way that they did.

The two digested the whole story in silence. Alex had never seen things as intense as he had in this whole experience and didn't know how he could cope with it. George had seen things of such intensity as before but couldn't quite digest the whole experience because he couldn't dismiss it or cope how he usually did. The two felt trapped. They never fully understood the atrocity committed against the Communist victims.

Alexander rested his head for a moment on his grandpa's shoulder and closed his eyes gently. Take a short break, son! There is more to see.

This was too much information processed through his system. Take it easy and think about it if we have problems in America; these people live this unfortunate reality every day. Remember, Liberty, Freedom, Equality, and Justice are essential for a democratic society!

"I guess we went as far back as we could…" Alex started trembling without finishing. Stammering in his sentences.

"Mmm." George didn't feel like talking. He felt guilty for the whole situation- it was he who urged his family to attempt an escape. George figured that if he had never sent those letters, everything would've been okay— they would've just come using underground channels to come to America (or there was no other situation for them to leave this prison).

The World around George focused on something else— Nicky and Margarita— Alex's parents. As the scene composed itself, it felt like St. George was trying to cheer up our subjects.

The romance of the scene was clear. The couple embraced one another before the following scene appeared. The following scene was composed to show another beautiful and very pregnant wife. This one was of Margarita and Nicky; they were gleaming with excitement to be parents for the first time. Soon enough, the slideshow of scenes continued to show Alex running through the house and shouting in his childish and playful way. Next was Alex winning his first tennis tournament. The two felt the pride Alex had, and George thought that he could finally understand his grandson's passion. Alex continued playing tennis until late in high school, which was when he got a scholarship to play on the college team.

At university, our spectators watched Alex make a decision to change his major drastically. From his original choice of a prelaw course, which his parents had raised Alex to prepare for, he decided that he would study World history and political science at the prestigious Columbia University. Alex watched his future struggle through the rigid program he had chosen for himself.

Alex remembers the true love story between him and Jennifer, and later with Elizabeth, as well as their experiences with time travel.

Regarding Alex's car accident and out-of-body experience, the circumstances leading to the accident included drinking and driving. Alex's near-death experience and his encounter with a different dark realm. The emotional and psychological impact of the experience on Alex's life. For Alex and Jennifer's hallucinatory journey through time, their mutual decision to consume a "magic" mushroom cocktail containing hallucinogens - usually psilocybin and psilocin, resulted in shared hallucinations, transporting them to different historical eras as a result of the mind-altering substances. Experiencing vivid and immersive episodes in the past, blurring the boundaries between reality and illusion until Alex met a beautiful woman named Elizabeth at the library, where he was grinding away.

Alex married that woman and had two children with her. Somehow, the beauty of those moments was simply blurred with the beauty of his life. And then Alex realized something.

"This is my life!" he thought, "I'm watching my whole life flash before my eyes...."

A scripture from Psalms came to mind:

"Your eyes saw my unformed body; all the days ordained for me were written in your book before one of them came to be."

Alex neared panic. The boy no longer felt the presence of his grandfather near him. He lost connection. It was just like when he saw the vision of the hospital.

"Was this all just the lives of everyone flashing before my eyes before I passed?" For a young man, Alex had an unnaturally strong attitude of acceptance toward death. At that moment, he realized why. "I think I understand now. I think I get why the weird man that was my grandfather was that way; I think I know why my dad was that way, too."

Alex realized then, too, a feeling of guilt for disregarding his grandfather's culture as weird. "It wasn't weird... I was beautiful," Alex thought. Alex thought of the rude things that he said to his grandfather in his silly "New World" ways. Then, he thought of the even sillier things that he thought. Alex's vision darkened somehow even more than it already had.

"So here I go." Alex saw a light at the end of the tunnel and went towards it.

Suddenly, his grandson disappeared from his sight. George was left alone; he refused to return to his body—against St. George's advice. After visiting Heaven, he won't want to return to

Hell on Earth. He was looking for St. Peter at the pearly gates. But instead, he saw himself in a dark room of the nursing home in 2025. A voice came:

"Remember where you come from; do you still remember your family and country's history? One day, Alex will be called to be a historian. You will be part of his vocation."

George suddenly lost his precious memories. *Let's walk to the light.* He decided to go back; he left unfinished business down there. He had the memory of his ancestors, who were recording his family's past. His Flight into Eternity will end soon! He was looking for Alex and followed the light at the end of the tunnel!

For how many days does generational traveling— of reviewing lives—of living through their library of memories- do the two live? Yet—the two were only in the coma for 45 minutes before their death had been pronounced.

But they came to life again from the other side! From this heavenly library, a simple voice spoke— "Think about Captain Georgiy—and his diaries, military journal & correspondences."

"Look in the foundation of the house."

"What do you mean in the foundation?" He understood immediately: "Aha, you mean in the basement."

Just Imagine if you discovered a treasure chest in which were hidden old mysteries, revelations from heaven, secrets and answers to your family's most enduring, age-old questions, and the hidden keys that can enrich your life with wisdom, happiness, and success.

The voice was talking only in symbols: "What was the meaning? His Roots? His Fruits? Or, in the foundations?!"

George and Alex walked through an open portal— a dark corridor inside Columbia University's main building of the history department.

A large, tall Angel at the front (the other side of the room) asked about their names and looked into His big golden book to find them.

*Do they have a computer here?* Alex was thinking. The Angel smiled. He knew Alex's thoughts before he was able to ask questions. It's easy for you that way because the Historical Library is in your university on Earth.

The Angel checked out their names to see who was supposed to stay there (and, if so, where they may go) and who must return to Earth.

George and Alex were allowed to visit the Bulgarian Commonwealth territory in the Garden of Eden. Alex knew the History of Bulgaria.

"A country two times smaller than the United Kingdom and 4 times smaller than the state of Texas. What can you find here? A Paradise."

"When God created the Earth in six days, in the last one, he invited all the people and gave them a piece of his creation. He gave Germany to the Germans, India to the Indians, to all of them! But where was the Bulgarian? There were no tracks of it, and God gave everything to the others. The Bulgarian was late, and there was nothing left for him. God was angry and asked the Bulgarian where he had been. "Excuse me, God," answered the Bulgarian, "but I worked with all my children in the fields to collect some grain, some food. That's why I missed everything." God, because he is God, He knew everything, and He saw that the Bulgarian wasn't a liar. Because of the Bulgarian's honesty, God gave him a little piece of "paradise."

George liked the historical period of April's Uprising—The Renaissance period of Bulgarian history when, just a year later, there was the Russian-Turkish War in 1878. Everything there was created just for George's historical and intellectual pleasure and amusement. He loved this period of Bulgarian history.

Suddenly, he heard far away the" Bulgarian national anthem's" lyrics:

*"Dear Motherland*

*You are Heaven on Earth.*

*Your beauty, your loveliness*

*Ah, they are boundless."*

*In Bulgarian :*

*"Rodino, Mila Rodino,*

*ti si zemen ray!*

*Tvoyta hubost, tvoyta prelest,*

*ah, te nyamat kray"*

Heaven knew that.

George and Alex were met by a welcoming committee formed by his Ukrainian, Bulgarian, and Greek relatives. They took him to his grandpa's land— the property next to the Bulgarian-Greek borders on the bank of River Maritza. It was very similar to the Dnipro River passing in Kakhovka, Ukraine.

George and Alex describe their entering the higher dimension differently (usually, a person cannot find the right words) as the tunnel, entering the Valley of Death, or a very dark place (It takes everything you've got to get out of a dark place). A void— suddenly. He was sucked into the Matrix. George and Alex can't explain the experience, but it probably looked like how the baby leaves the womb and lands on this earth after a traumatic delivery from the mother's birth canal.

A similar thing happens in the spirit, which leaves the flesh body in the third dimension and goes to the higher fourth dimension. This is a totally different experience from any place that you've ever been in your life.

George remembers a lot of Bulgarian gatherings in the state of Illinois in Chicago, New York City, and Philadelphia, but then he visited the so-called "Bulgarian Heaven," which is a spiritual area of the Bulgarian National revival period. The people of the Balkans and Thracian valley roasted whole lambs and celebrated as though George and Alex were in the "Bulgarian Paradise."

Suddenly, George remembered a new vision: Interesting New Year's traditions. The atheist communists wouldn't allow the celebration of Orthodox Christmas/ Koleda.

So, though George's family would try otherwise, New Year's became a slight substitution. Very soon, under the chime of the clock, they would open the champagne, raise their glasses, and make a wish for good health and happiness!

All of George's close relatives were happy to meet him— even elderly relatives who had never seen him, and one girl who was sixteen years old came to him, welcoming George (he was 10 years old when she came about). The nameless girl didn't stop to embarrass and kiss him, and she was not able to introduce herself by the name—she was his biological sister, but he never met her before on Earth. George's Mother, Emma, never told him that she had a baby that died in her stomach. She had a miscarriage, but for God— nothing is lost; He keeps all these children under his care, and she was excited to meet the parents that she never got, but they were in a different place that she couldn't visit. St. George, as the servant of God, almighty, decided that it was time that George needed to be introduced to his Father in Heaven.

Angels were worshiping: "Heaven, and the Holy angels facing God Almighty." And, one called out to another and said, "Holy, Holy, Holy, is the LORD of hosts. The whole Earth is full of His glory."

Everyone from the Kakhovskiy clan and family lived together, and Captain Georgiy showed George the almost complete and massive mansion, which would one day belong to George. It sat next to his grandpa's mansion.

Did Jesus promise believers that, upon their deaths, they would receive mansions in heaven? George thought.

Jesus told His disciples, "In My Father's house are many mansions; if it were not so, I would have told you. I will go to prepare a place for you. And if I go and prepare the place for you,

I will come again and receive you to Myself; that where I am, there you may be also."

George and Alex met relatives they had seen for the very first time.

George was happy to meet his grandpa, Captain Georgiy, who called to him:

"Goshko (little Georgiy), what is going on? Where are you? Everyone kissed and embarrassed him as a little boy (George was at the age of 10 years old when his grandfather passed away).

Everyone was happy, and genuine love was pulsating around them. Telepathy was the method of conversation. Without words, they communicated with one another.

They heard another patriotic song :

*"Krai Bosfora! Shum se vdiga!*

*Near the Bosphorus, a noise is heard,*

*Swords and shields are shining.*

*Look, Simeon is coming,*

*He's calling his voivods.."*

The group was singing a March song about Tzar Simeon I the Great of Bulgaria marching at the gate of Constantinople...!

They used words to sing Bulgarian songs. Everyone was open, not afraid. There is nothing to hide. They were keeping healthy boundaries and smiling with genuine joy.

At this moment, George understood through telepathy that, before him, his mama had a miscarriage of her daughter, but God adopted her, and she was looking for her parents. The parents, unknowingly, were in a different part of heaven where they were more suitable. George asks why they do not hear?

"You can't meet them till they invite you," said Grandpa Georgiy. He explained to George what had happened and directed him on how to find them.

George was determined to find them both, even in Hell. Using an elevator next to him and going down floors, he stayed in place for Committed Suicide Squads:

George was picturing his father's big aristocratic brick houses at "Khan Asparuh" Street.

But in a formerly communist country like Sofia, Bulgaria, they looked a little different. Think of towering apartment blocks, prefabricated concrete panels, and loads of gray.

A place so ugly, entering the Sofia Center at the time was beautiful. Looking around at the ugly concrete buildings made from sovietski blocks / three- to a five-storied apartment building was a type of low-cost, concrete-paneled and soviet architecture full of graffiti, all covered with gray, depressing clouds.

From a distance, George could see his father's old house in the center of Sofia on "Khan Asparuh" street— ruined behind repairs.

Captain Georgiy came here many times to talk to his son Alexander, but he refused to talk. He only guided George. He believed that only he could talk to them to change their mind about the past. It's very dangerous that he may not return from this low energy sugging spiritual swamp.

George's old house in hell was destroyed beyond repair.

At one moment in time, just thinking, George was at his old house. This place was very confusing and strange. Suddenly, his mother, Emma, started to cry and scream. George couldn't recognize his mother. This was an ugly place, and he didn't know what had happened to their beautiful house, but he started to feel fear and guilt about his mother coming over him.

George said ecstatically and cheerily, "Hello, mama!"

"Who are you? I don't know you! My son is not home! Actually, I don't have a son; I lost him! I never saw my son again!" she was screaming.

Suddenly, his father came out from inside the house to see who was disturbing his wife.

He was listening to his favorite Joe Dassin song, *Et si tu n'existais pas, Dis-moi pourquoi j'existerais,* a French love song from his years in France in which the singer is asking himself how his life would be if his wife didn't exist. His father was drinking and crying for his lost youth, lost son, and the life he may have had in Paris. He was always furious, angry, depressed, and sad.

George couldn't recognize him. George's father had lost the strong figure that he used to have.

"What's happening? Who is this boy?"

"He is looking for our son," The mother replied in tears. George was sorrowful and depressed to see his lovely parents in this condition. It was the sorrow that George brought into their life because of his escape. He chose this moment to express his love to his mama and to his father—the love that the apostle Paul is talking about—the love who is gentle, the love that is patient, and the kind love.

George spoke to his mother:

"Thank you for everything you've done for me; your life was not in vain. You have grandkids and blessings. Your son is alive and very proud of you. God knows everything about us. He doesn't blame you but asks you to come to him. He believes in you, and he will bring you back to Himself."

George's mother and father existed in a nightmare prison in hell, like "The Walking Dead." From their prison on earth, they were moved to hell's version. Where their dead god of communism was. He was above everything, above all broken families, above the equal society. His parents hated their son George. He was declared to be a traitor! The Enemy of the People.

Everyone hated them because their son escaping the paradise of lies. Around the Old House, you can see the communist symbols: the red soviet flag sunk in a gray, depressing atmosphere. They were cut off from their family in Heaven and Earth, and there was a gap between them because they lost their son.

George had to sacrifice himself to become one of them to wake them up to learn the truth about God. Nobody in the West can understand that. That's way later; the communists even changed the history, rewriting everything that happened. So, nobody what their grandparents did.

Why is it that world hated the Nazi Germany, but they never went against the communist in Eastern Europe? America let them go.

After George left his parent's house, he met his school buddy Franko on the street. He was his neighbor, and George recognized him.

"No fucking way! Is that you, neighbor? Son of a bitch! How did you survive? You, American bastard!

After the border shooting, Franko was arrested, bitten, and thrown in prison; later, he committed suicide. He tried to be cheerful as a teenager but suddenly got depressed and started to cry.

"Why do I have to escape the border on this bloody Easter? It was a bit of bad luck. George felt the guilt of being the only one to survive and come back to visit his loved one."

"Who is this stranger outside?" his mother screamed from inside. My school best friend came to visit!" Be careful out there, Son. Someone ". may report you "Is this our neighbor's son, Georgiy, the traitor?"

George said, "Why are you afraid of death because you fear those stupid communists? Remember, God said: "I tell you, my friends, do not fear those who kill the body, and after that, can do no more."

"Not the saints who are his servants, but His Son Jesus, who bought all of us in our fallen nature with higher prices. Where are you? God is looking for you. Please respond to His voice."

George believed that demonic influence was very real in the life of his parents and that it created a threat to their spiritual well-being.

If my parents are in hell and I'm in heaven, how could I ever be happy? George thought. Is the death of a family member easier on an atheist because they don't believe in the afterlife?

How could a loving God not send everyone to heaven?

George continued in his thought, "Why should one who commits suicide go to hell? They died in the lord's loving grace!"

The mother wept. She heard George's voice, and even greater, she felt his love.

Something in her knew that her son had ventured into Hell to share his love and relieve her of her pain. The pain of Hell— the pain of losing her son.

"I still remember your help when I was a child," George continued, "Our most precious moments together. Please, papa, fight, remember your father, Captain Georgiy, and his afterlife story. You still exist, and you need to ask God for forgiveness for what you have done; God is good, and it is time to bring you to a better place above." George's father, just as George's mother, felt the love and intensity. George desired to bring his parents back more than anything in the world.

A new scene appears. Alex felt the presence of the demon spirit of his grand-uncle Vasiliy and his Bolshevik demons, Dominion. The veil was open, and George saw into the future. After one century— in the 1990s— Vasiliy was trying to escape from the lonely places in the wilderness because he had been cast out, but he saw that Vasiliy was coming back to turmoil with his nephew, Alex, in the Communist concentration prison and, during the 2018', he tried to influence and brainwash Alex's mind.

George saw another vision of his grandson Alex in the future. He was visiting Sofia, and his cousins, Ivan and Vasiliy—sons of Dimitar—were students at the US (University of Sofia). They secretly joined an underground Marxist group called "Young Socialists."

He met other socialists and anarchists who were part of Antifa and supported the movement "Occupy Wall Street." In NEW YORK CITY, they supported "Black Lives Matter," so he founded an honest socialist group that all believed in a Marxist Revolution.

According to Alex, the Socialist revolution is necessary today to overthrow the fascist government. Alex was at the Columbia University Campus, a fiery Democrat on the far left. He was excited to be part of the same underground group as his grandpa's uncle a revolutionary Bolshevik. Alex was so thankful to find people like his granduncle who were as open to ideas of Socialism as they were during the October Soviet Revolution, which succeeded in 1917.

He knew all three volumes of *Capital* by Marx and Engels to discuss the life of Leon Trotsky. Everything in his mind was for justice for workers' rights, of course. It was difficult for Alex to find a job. He was a so-called "freelancer," or an unemployed young man, but in the cafeteria, they all discussed Marx and Engels starting with coffee and finishing with beers and a lot of vodka.

Alex remembered that when he was doing his Columbia history dissertation, he traveled from Kyiv, Ukraine, to Moscow and St. Petersburg in Russia to search for Soviet History. Almost two years passed by, and he was working on his History Ph.D. Dissertation. The research was not going very well because he spent most of his time in the basement with the underground Marxist group, "Young Socialists," in the basement of University of Sofia (SU), whose main goal was to overthrow the democratically elected government of GERB party of Prime Minister Boyko Borisov.

Alex was arrested because of his involvement in anti-government activity. The press was all over the news on CNN that an American citizen like Alex was arrested in Bulgaria, saying that the Bulgarian police were violating the restrictions on the exercise of free speech rights to protest. It was exactly like his granduncle, the Bolshevik, Vasiliy during the Russian Socialist Revolution—1917 before they put him in jail in Siberia for anti-government propaganda.

The parallel lives of Georgiy and young Alex began to intertwine like threads in a grand tapestry. Alex, a young man in the year 2018, found himself captivated by the story of his grand granduncle, Vasiliy, and the turbulent era in which he lived. Vasiliy's journey from a carefree spirit to a staunch socialist/Bolshevik fascinated Alex, stirring his own beliefs and values.

Yet, in this tapestry of parallelism, a stark contrast emerged. Alex's youthful idealism clashed with George's deep-rooted love for tradition, ancestry, and conservative values.

Their perspectives collided, creating a dynamic tension that would shape their relationship.

Alex was the secret connection between the East and the West. This young girl Vera, Marxist Vera, the same name as his grandpa uncle Vasiliy's girlfriend, Vera (Viara means, in Bulgarian, Faith), fit with him at the first moment. It was ideological and emotional chemistry. Both saw the future at such a young age and imagined it as a "Utopian Paradise" where everyone would be equal. The Utopian Vision of the Future is one of the few places among college students where a communist can still dream.

To this day, every time Alex sees her in the group, he is energetically attracted to her. Her thin, tall body was like a ballerina. When she was walking or moving graciously, she put meaning in every movement she made.

Her large blue eyes were so expressive. Vera spoke proper English with a British accent definitely, her parents, as members of the Communist Party, were honorable graduates—so-called elite English Lycée (known as English Gymnasium abbreviation for Angliiska Gimnazia, the English Language School), which later, in the 1990s, was closed. Alex was so attentive to her needs. Every time Vera was talking in proper Shakespearean British, Alex was trying to tell her: "Don't worry, just relax."

"I understand English fluently, but she wanted to impress him. Alex felt so comfortable around her and wanted her to know that he understood her perfectly. One night, the group had just finished late. Both stayed together they wanted to go to the university coffee shop, but it was full of students, so they grabbed a cup of coffee and left. Vera felt frightened because she was living far away from the Sofia center. They took the last trolley, and after a two-hour ride alone in the night, they finally reached the last stop.

It was dark, and the old gray Socialist Soviet-type panels were hiding in the dark. There was not enough light on the street. Alex was surprised that Vera was living here at the end of the city limits, but he didn't ask because it was a mistake to ask her such an uncomfortable question.

Protestors in Bulgaria turned the volume up for government leaders to resign. Rallies were also held in Lovech, Haskovo, Plovdiv, Vratsa, Montana, Varna, Burgas, Kyustendil, and other cities.

Next year, Alex and Vera moved to New York City together from Sofia University.

What happened next was the dream of beautiful girls. Vera was called to a New York modeling gig for a "work and travel girls" job on three special months of work visa, paid off by George Soros' funds, which were paying for girls from diverse backgrounds like Eastern Europe.

"Thank you, George Soros," Alex said. The program was supposed to give a young girl like Vera the taste of America's entrepreneurship during the summer.

Vera's plan worked out successfully. She disappeared from Alex's life as quickly as she just appeared. She was seeking a luxurious lifestyle without having to work for it, trading her currency of youth and beauty for a wealthy millionaire husband.

On October 13, 1991, the Communist Party was forced to resign, and the first fair elections were held! Opposition forces were led by Zheliu Zhelev, a communist-era dissident who was first elected in 1989. He was the democratic president of the Bulgaria Union of Democratic Forces / SDS in Bulgarian Se De Se.

The Bulgarian Socialist Party (the new communist party's name) won. The intervention of State Security decisively deformed the development of Bulgaria's transition to democracy and, in practice, failed Bulgaria's chances of becoming a normal Eastern European country. The DS- Darzhavna sigurnost/State Security secret group of high and elite communists of the deep state formed a cabal group and took the power of the country's economy without thinking of the socialist revolution.

"The post-communist period never happened. It's time for a new Socialist Revolution," Alex was thinking. It looks like this demon still exists on Earth and is trying to get revenge on his brother's offspring.

The Return of the unclean spirit Vasiliy after one century. The final battle was between the brothers Kakhovskiy and Vasiliy, who became a red dracula the leader of the Soviet demons in Sofia, Bulgaria.

As legends tell it, Saint George was a red dragon slayer. The symbol that one day, Captain Georgy will be slain by the demon of his brother, Vasiliy. Soon, St. George will put him under his feet. Trust in God! Vasiliy sold his soul to the devil. He was the man who sold his soul to gain more power and control! So even after one century, Vasiliy's spirit (proud and arrogant—unforgiving towards his brother) had only grown. The Soviets sent him to work as the attaché spy and Soviet ambassador in Istanbul, Sofia, and later in Shanghai, China.

He has many women with whom he lived temporarily at places of service. His allegiance was to the Soviet Communist Party, not to his family or relatives.

As strong-willed, aggressive, and vindictive, even in their next life, he continued to attack Captain George's descendants. He joined the realm of darkness and became one of the fallen angels of Lucifer. The main idea is the generational fight between two brothers— one of good and one of evil.

The myth of Saint George slaying the dragon originated in stories all over Europe of his valiance and bravery. It was the Triumph of Good over evil through courage.

St George had to destroy the work of the Demon Vasiliy. It was in the war with his grandfather, the captain, against his manuscript, and his fight will remain in the memory here on earth and in the libraries of Heaven in George's memories.

George was called to be the restorer of his ancestors' bridge between generations, yet he would trust God and St. George to restore the generations in the Kakhovskiy clan.

Before meeting their long-dead relatives in the supernatural world of paradise, like Captain Georgiy in Heaven, they must fight against Dracula his brother Vasiliy, who is trying to harm Captain Georgiy (Descendants of his brother's generation).

When George approached the ruins of his old house, he was stopped by a red wall of demons.

He asked, "What is your name?"

"Legion! Because we are many!"

His motto was: "Demons of all lands, unite." The emotional and oppressed conditions of Alexander and Emma were due to the works of the demons.

Dr. Alexander, George's father, was a medical doctor like the famous Russian writers Anton Chekhov and Dr. Mikhail Bulgakov. He read *The Master and Margarita*, the gospel of Stalin, and the gospel of the Devil. Mikhail Bulgakov was the last aristocrat from the golden age living during Stalin's Atheistic Soviet Communism, which made it banned to write about "God and his son, Jesus' resurrection."

Many who defended the White Guard Army escaped through Sevastopol, Crimea, but Bulgakov, like Dr. Alexander, decided not to leave his country and escape to France to live in his motherland and serve the people during the Civil War. It was a good fortune that his unpublished manuscript was saved by his wife 25 years after his death. It was published as a forbidden book during the Stalin regime. The unexpurgated version was published there in 1973.

So, Dr. Alexander understood that his life's purpose was to be a doctor and serve the people.

He had similarities to the early younger life of Vladimir Nabokov and Mikhail Bulgakov. Mamachka the little mother

Margarita—always reminded me of her favorite book, *Lolita*, by Vladimir Nabokov.

Nabakov was a Russian-born American novelist. He wrote in both Russian and English, and his best works included *Lolita* (1955).

Alexander: "Over the course of five decades, the masterpiece vote has won out, more or less—but even two generations later, there is still a lot of debate."

After George's parents' house was confiscated, it was given to the KGB Colonel Vasiliy for free. The title of George's father's house was transferred officially to Colonel Vasiliy, who was a Soviet representative and ambassador in Sofia, Bulgaria.

George remembered his grandfather Georgiy, who was talking about the fifty years of jubilant learning that he received from his grandfather on his maternal side—Rabbi Jacob. After the Bolsheviks came, they took the property of Captain Georgiy's father, especially Vasiliy. He was not happy that his father gave everything to his brother, Captain Georgiy.

His grandfather from the paternal side, General Count Vasilly Kakhovskiy, the founder of Kakhovka village, who loved Georgiy, and Rabbi Jacob from the maternal side, who was from the Jewish community in Feodosia on Crimea who loved Vasiliy.

In Georgiy's genes, he can hear, " The Cossacks are coming!" straight out of some 19th-century nightmare.

In 1787, the Tsarina Catherine the Great personally founded with Prince Potemkin, her Commander-in-Chief of the Imperial Army - Yekaterinoslav , when Count General Vasiliy Kakhovskiy was appointed as governor on the territory of Modern Dnipro, in the Russian Empire who governed the city of Yekaterinoslav (the glory of Catherine).

After the Bolsheviks came, they took the property of Captain George's father, especially Vasiliy. He was not happy that his father gave everything to his brother, Captain Georgiy.

This made Vasiliy hate him more and more.

Grandpa used to describe envy as the most despicable of the cardinal sins. Envy is like a virus. It's known to travel through lies, gossip, and bad words.

On November 9th, 1989, Soviet communism fell. The Empire of Evil and the Berlin Wall fell. George celebrated the year of jubilance. Everything that Vasiliy stole illegally from his brother must be returned to the house of his son, Dr. Alexander, in Sofia. The property of Captain Georgiy's father, Alexander, in Kakhovka. All their land, houses, and treasure that was stolen must be given back to their rightful owners. This was the meaning of the "year of jubilee," celebrated long in ancient Israel.

There is a parable that tells of a man possessed by the devil who likened his life to a messy and dirty house. But when the evil spirit was cast out, George depicted the man's life as a clean and orderly house. After some time, the evil spirit returns to the man and finds him to be like a house: clean, well-swept, and orderly. The spirit enters the man and repossesses him along with seven other spirits.

The man is now more greatly controlled by the demons than before, and the later condition of the man becomes worse than the former.

The question—Why?

What led to the evil spirit's success? Was it because the house was swept and put in order? Then the passage says, "I will return to the house I left." When it arrives, it finds the house unoccupied, swept clean, and put in order.

This parable tells of a man possessed by the devil (occupied by Vasiliy the Demon), with Jesus likening his life to a messy and dirty house. But when the evil spirit was cast out, Jesus depicted the man's life as a clean and orderly house.

The offspring of Grandpa Captain Georgiy are coming back to claim their property since the communists lost their power.

The parallel passage provides additional insight: *When the spirit returned, it found the house not only clean and orderly but empty.*

In the future, George was planning to visit his father's old house in Sofia and Grandpa's old house in Ljubimetz.

Some elderly' relatives' neighbors still remember his grandpa Captain George's house well—another vision. So he showed him the place where the old house was demolished—some long relative who remembers his grandfather when the bulldozers came and leveled the house in one hour.

George's Grandpa/Batko (in Ukrainian, it means little father), with his white Tolstovka or traditional Russian shirt, came to stop them, but it was too late. Nothing could be done. They just evicted and confiscated his house and property like this without a trial of complaints. The communist party's decision was final! Nobody has the power to stop them! This was a direct order "from above" from KGB secret agent Colonel Vasiliy.

George felt the sting of guilt in his heart because his whole family suffered.

Baba Ivanka remembers the last days of Captain Georgiy (his grandpa). Often, he got lost, and the neighborhood children were looking for him.

When they ask him where you running to he always answers:

"I am going home to Kakhovka, Ukraine! His short steps decreased his walk, which affected his gait in his last days, the funny way of ambulating.

"The Alzheimer's disease and memory loss symptoms were not that familiar then. The changes in his walk were so-called Parkinsonian gait. "

clarified in medical terms the long-retired town doctor who knew George's father, Dr. Alexander - the people's physician who never came back from the forced labor concentration camp-type Soviet Gulag in Belene.

Suddenly, George was snapped back. He was not in heaven or hell but in space. Empty space. For a second, he worried for his parents and their souls, but he knew they were okay. He knew they were waiting for him and for his story to be finished. George was ready to be put in that divine library up there. George felt Alex's presence at the same time, but he knew that neither of them wished to speak of the existential horror they had just witnessed and fought.

The two saw a light in the abyss. There was just a feeling of warmth from the light that had appeared that said to follow it. As he reached the light, George saw a vision of the final chapter of his life.

The old man was sitting on the boat, going all around Lake Michigan in his rental rowboat. He was lowering his thin, wiry legs into the water. George loves spending time on the water; since he was 16, he has been boating and swimming in the water of River Maritza at the border of Bulgaria between Turkey and Greece.

George and Maria were approaching the late autumn of their days faster than anyone could imagine. George had endured several surgeries since the car accident— later losing the function of both his kidneys. Thanks to the donation of his middle brother, Dimitar, his life was extended. George's feet were always cold— even during warm weather. It was probably because of his poor blood circulation. But now, he took his favorite sweater— the same one that Maria gave him as a gift on his birthday. He was warmed by the sun. He stroked the sweater; it pleased him. George had already been sitting on the boat like this for five minutes, slowly moving the soles of his feet, now and then dangling them over the water and then lowering them into the waves, nearly lapping over the edge of the boat.

The waves and water were so quiet.

The sun had almost set on another fall, but there was still time to catch an autumn sunset (or sunrise) before winter was upon us.

Fortunately, there are plenty of spots on Chicago's North Shore where you can view the sky as it bursts with color. These were some of my favorite places to start or end the day. Maria loved the sunset of Chicago.

Today is Wednesday, March 1, 2023. George gets up in the morning and listens to the news.

The war in Russia and Ukraine continues. Town Kakhovka is in the hands of the Ukrainian Liberation Army.

Evidence was growing on Friday that there was an explosion at the Kakhovka Dam in southern Ukraine around the time that it collapsed, according to Ukraine and US intelligence reports.

Ukraine's security service said it had intercepted a telephone call proving a Russian "sabotage group" blew up the Kakhovka hydroelectric station and dam early on Tuesday in the Kherson region.

He sees President Biden on the news with his stammer and his rigid movement accompanied by the symptoms of early Alzheimer's disease and Parkinson's and understands that he has the same condition. Rigidity, slowness, gait impairment, and other disorders of movement accompany Alzheimer's disease and Parkinson's.

George is interested in the Russian-Ukrainian war, and Russian-American relations are so cold in the freezing war today.

George is taking care of Maria; she doesn't remember him at all in the other room.

The only thing that still kept him here on Earth was the unfinished manuscript of his crazy grandson Alex, who never called and never came to visit him. Finally, his unemployment is finished, and he frequently comes because Alex needs support and money so that he can finish his grandpa, Captain Georgiy's, memoir and support his family.

George is stuck in the nursing home. He wants to be outdoors and free. He wants to remember the water.

Why always the water? Why is time spent near water the secret of happiness? The sea and coastline, but also rivers, lakes, canals, waterfalls, and even fountains–are less well publicized, yet the science has been consistent for at least a decade: being by the water is good not only for your body but also your mind.

He remembered the boat over the years, which Maria had to go on Lake Michigan. Now, he is grievously stuck in the nursing home, but he still remembers the shores of Lake Michigan in his memories of the nursing home every morning for longer than this old brain can remember.

But I'm not one of those picky folks who need the most expensive caviar for every meal. Never have been. George stared at the food like they were a worthy opponent. I'll attempt to chew and swallow, and they'll try to kill me with a lack of flavor.

May the best man win. It's my birthday—the Big 93rd—which does nothing but remind me I have no one left.

I'm not proud of it, but I want to add two more relatives to that list of friends. Why else would he insist on a birthday visit? A glance at the clock tells me I'll be late for the appointment, but what do I care? You get to be my age, and people don't expect much out of you. I crush my pills up well—I only need one in the morning. Not one of those old-timers who have to take twenty pills a day. Guess I'll live another good day. My nurses will be happy about that, at least. I've been dressed since 6am because sleep doesn't come as easy as it did once upon a time. Seems backward if you ask me. A man my age should be able to sleep the day away if that's what he wants to do. Figure I've earned it.

With age, the afterlife becomes more attractive. George remembers how he felt after the car crash and his travel to the afterlife. In the vision, George saw himself sitting in a dark room in the nursing home; he lost all his memory and didn't know who he was in the past. George understands that he is the harbinger; he has to go back to earth, tell his family what is happening, and protect Alex's generation.

So many things are repeating in the US capital; on January 6th, the same thing happened in the capital building in Washington, DC.

Similar to the most significant event in history, the Russian socialist revolution and the stack of the Bolsheviks of Winter Palace in St. Petersburg, all this is coming back in the past.

George ignored his comfort in this much better place of Paradise and returned to Hell on Earth to suffer, once again, the pain and suffering, but also to protect his family and his grandson's future.

At the same time, a new scenario was developing. Nicky was praying in the same Lutheran hospital's small chapel downstairs with the Bible scripture, which was placed on the wall: "I set before you today— life."

He was praying for his father and son's lives. He was reading, and the scripture suddenly came alive, "Today, I have given you a choice between life and death, blessings and curses." Nicky prayed more intensely than he ever had.

"I felt as if I were sucked back into my body at one point," said George later on in an attempt to explain the feeling. "I was going through a completely black tunnel very, very quickly—a speed you cannot express because you just don't experience it." At the time of the prayer, Alex returned back.

The light was that of the brightly lit hospital room. The first thing that Alex saw was Nikolay and Margarita looming over him.

The shock and excitement that washed over the two's faces were unbelievable. "He's awake!!" Margarita nearly shrieked. The first thing Alex did was hug his father. The hug felt different. He knew the man now—beyond just a father, that is. The second thing Alex asked was: "Is Grandpa ok? Where is he?" Just as Alex forced those words out while adjusting to having a true physical body again, a doctor came into the room.

"George is awake."

Yet—they were only in the coma for 45 minutes before their clinical death was pronounced by the ER (emergency room) doctors. But they came to life again from the other side!

# Chapter 13:

# In the Hospital - A new flashback in time

Despite speedy recoveries, the two were held at the hospital for observation for a while longer than needed.

George thought, what was the location of a concentration camp where thousands of Bulgarian political prisoners were brutalized and killed from 1949 to 1953 - and in some cases, for years after that? Though it's officially known as Belene after the quiet Bulgarian village at the River Danube that sits 750 feet away on the mainland, old-timers here call it by another name: the Island of Death. *My father, Alexander Kakhovskiy, was sent here at the age of 40 and spent four years and three months interred at Belene after he tried to escape the Greek border (he suspected that his neighbor reported him to the authorities).*

Poems for Freedom, which was written from the Gulag/concentration camp prison in Belene.

Next to his were Grandpa Georgy's favorite books, War and Peace and Anna Karenina from Tolstoy, and his brother, George's uncle, Vasiliy's, favorite book of Dostoevsky: His most acclaimed novels include *Crime and Punishment* (1866), *The Idiot* (1869), *Demons* (1872), and *The Brothers Karamazov* (1880), and Bram Stoker's, *Dracula* (1897).

This was surprising for George because Jeremiah was telling them to look for his answers in the foundation of the old house (more precisely, in the basement).

"So," Alex began. The reality is—he didn't exactly know where to begin. Death had loomed over the two, and they knew everything they could about it. George and Alex both knew that there wasn't much to talk about.

George felt the same; he couldn't think of what to say. There were a million things, but no one thing could bring such an experience justice.

Eventually, the two got to talking, not about the experiences they shared but the ones that they didn't. After living each other's lives (even if for just a little bit), the two were attached—they understood one another.

Before Alex or George could realize it, the time had shifted from day to night.

When our duo realized the time and adjourned to bed, St. George still had work to do— he gave the two a vision. As George and Alex lay in bed, ready for sleep, they were granted a dream. In the dream, the two laid witnesses to a light of white and gold that could only be divine. Once the light cleared in the two eyes and they could see, a row of pure white pillars and marble shelves appeared. Though the remaining light seemed to give infinite clarity, neither Alex nor George could see an end to these shelves. Instinctively, the two walked forward down the row together. Neither could speak; despite the fact that there wasn't a hint of tiredness or confusion in both heads of our heroes, the idea of speaking in such a setting greatly overwhelmed either. On the shelves were uniform tomes—Grey in color, with a silver text as its title. The books spanned from the size of *The Manifesto*, a book George would rue for as long as he lived, to an edition of *Brothers Karamazov*, which, to George, might've been the greatest book ever written had he not been a Christian.

As the two continued, Alex's mind stopped wandering beyond the thought of, *where the hell are we*? As it focused more on its surroundings, Alex's only thoughts were of the titles of the books that he could read while he walked by them. As he read the titles in his head, another voice entered—it was George's. He was doing the same as Alex—reading the titles. As the two continued reading, a miracle happened; the two could hear each other.

"James Manson," broke George's voice into Alex's head.

"Ashima Noguchi," George heard Alex read. Within seconds of this link, the two realized that every book was a name. The two stopped to examine the book by "Maria Guchi." The name was printed in the usual silver lettering. In small print that could only be read when George examined it closer, "1967-2018." The lack of an echo from George's voice when he spoke these words aloud disturbed the two—it was like they were in a vacuum. Then, Alex shifted from the shelf, and it glided into his hand. They both had figured they were dreaming at this point, so the weight of this time surprised Alex when it felt as natural as it did. On the first page, the name, birthday, and place of birth (both in the country Italy and the geographic coordinates), as well as the place and date of death, were listed. Flipping through the pages, Ms. Quick's life story was told in excruciating detail and in as monotonous a voice as one could write in. The idea of this information scared Alex. He returned the book. George held no objection.

The two continued walking down the aisle almost robotically, George on the right and Alex on the left. While gazing at the never-ending list of names that appeared before George, he noticed something small at the foot of a book, "2004-2032." The person hadn't died yet. George was beyond confused, so he stopped to look into the novel. The book was the same as usual. The date that it said things had happened had just simply not come by yet. Once again, such personal information about one's life neither interested nor pleased our protagonists, so George replaced the book and carried on with Alex as they were.

After what seemed only to be a couple of minutes of walking, the two's gazes and personal thoughts were interrupted by a shaking of the earth, or whatever it may have been that the two were standing on. Alex and George turned around to witness the source of such a disturbance and found nothing. Literally nothing. Behind them, the shelves disappeared, only to leave an infinite white plane that neither our grandfather nor son could comprehend.

On the horizon of nothing, George and Alex, who were in the library of heaven, watched the librarian come and ask them what they wanted to see. He brought him to the section of his "founding fathers," where they saw a published hardcover book from his grandfather, Captain Georgiy Kakhovskiy, which he had never known on Earth that he had published. Who in Heaven would care to read the book on Earth?

This is the book from your family.

It's here for everybody to read on the earth.

Earth is the place you sow your seeds. Heaven is the place where you gather your harvest. George was confused; he was thinking in mixed languages— speaking English, Bulgarian, and Russian.

Without moving his lips, the librarian said, *don't worry, we don't use your voice here most of the time, and it doesn't matter what language you can use. Whatever language is comfortable for you. Here, we use telepatía to think without words.*

George found a book of poems from his father, Dr. Alexander, *Poems for Freedom,* which he wrote from the Gulag/concentration camp prison in Belene.

This was surprising for George because Jeremiah was telling them to look for his answers in the foundation of the old house (more precisely, in the basement). He gave them hints, clues, and guidance on how to find his grandpa's 142-year-old lost manuscript, and he would be able to write his memoir later in life.

After a long pause, the librarian explained that his relatives come here frequently to read the books of their offspring to pray for them and encourage them from the "balcony of heaven." George loved all that, but he was unhappy in the sense that he was expecting to see his parents in the first place, but they didn't respond to any of his invitations or acknowledge that he existed. No invitation.

He was not able to accept why everything is possible here in Heaven, but he could not see his parents.

Is it some kind of purgatory, like his wife Maria said, cleansing the soul of past sins? It is not in the Bible. But why does God punish like this? He doesn't punish people who turmoil themselves with self-affliction and judge themselves by no God. It's "Free Will!"

Everyone tries to help them but without success. Heaven chose you, George, to fulfill this mission, so George will bring them back. It will take time, but God gives everyone a chance. So, what can I do here to help them? Whatever you love to do, George. I can't fix cars down here as a job, but I can write my memoirs as a hobby.

George will be able to find his grandpa's 142-year-old lost manuscript, and he will be able to write his memoir later in life.

George: "How wonderful I feel here. I don't have to take medication for my blood pressure; my knee is bending perfectly."

I can bend and jump freely. George bent three times to demonstrate. No more headaches. His mind was working fluently. What happened with all my diseases on earth?

Once the duo looked away from their divine chaperone, they found that everything on the bookshelves was gone except for a copy of their stories. They then understood the meaning of the scripture, Psalm 139,

"You saw me before I was born. Every day of my life was recorded in your book. Every moment was laid out before a single day had passed."

George's mission was not finished. He remembered from his Sunday school that every life should be written in the "Books of Life" in Heaven before any soul is born on Earth. He recognized this as the history department that was described to him before.

So, our story's already been told. Alex thought.

"Yes." The voice boomed a short answer. "But that does not mean your choices are not your own. It simply shows that The Lord knows everything more than you might know yourself.

Since the conception of your soul, He has known you. He has known how you would be. And he loves you despite that fact. He loves you despite who you may or may not become."

Alex had a feeling of existential fear and exhaustion. He was reminded that he had a whole life to live and figure out. George, on the other hand, felt strong. He had lived his life and figured that it was about over. The fact that his story had even one more adventure gave the old man a strong feeling of vivacity. As the two let their understanding of the situation sink in, the immortal light of the library sank into near nothingness. The abyss neared the two, and they could feel their World disappear. A second later, Alex woke up.

On the desk near his hospital bed, he could see a green analog clock that read "2:03."

Alex sank into his bed and thought about the dream he had just witnessed. What is my root?

George lay in his bed at the same time and thought about his shared experience. *Where are my roots?* He thought. There was always a fear that he had abandoned his home when he left for success in America. George had always coped with this fear by explaining that it was "overtaken by the Reds," and he had no choice!

Did I leave my roots? George thought. Upon that concern, George realized the second part of Jeremiah's farewell: "Your roots are the anchor of such things."

*If I've lost my roots, what anchors me? What anchors my soul?* George had been a pious man since before he could remember, and because of that, his soul had been the thing that he took care of more than anything! The thought of his soul being incomplete, being unanchored, terrified the man. There has to be something I can do, he thought. I have to find my roots.

The two couldn't sleep for hours. They simply waited for the morning when they could visit each other. The visiting hours at George and Alex's hospital began at nine. That meant six hours that both had to wait until they could meet and begin to find their roots.

Morning came around. Each took it just one minute at a time until it did. The second their clocks reached 8:00 and set off their alarm, both protagonists cast their sheets aside, put on whatever they could find in the immediate vicinity, and rushed to the other's room. In the hallway on the second floor, the two met. They both saw each other and were surprised.

"My boy," George started, "I've had a dream."

"With Jeremiah," Alex finished the statement. It was at this moment that the two realized that what they had witnessed was the truth. There was no doubt about it—George and Alex must find their roots.

The days passed. George and Alex spent their days recovering and appreciating their loved ones. George and Alexander, though they didn't talk in person as much, stayed in touch. Alexander's love for history grew greater and greater the more lessons he received from his grandfather on the history of his people.

The winter weathered in, and the American Coronavirus only spread more and more. Soon enough, Thanksgiving came around. Alexander and George would see each other again.

The voices of the past: George heard the voice say, "Go to the roots to discover its branches!"

"At your place of Jubilee, you shall return to fix your foundations and find the place of Your Roots!" You shall go back and reclaim your inheritance from your founding father. You have to go back and reclaim the house of your ancestors!

In the place of your roots, you will discover the meaning of your family tree, which was uprooted not a long time ago! Your people shall rebuild the ancient ruins and will raise up the age-old foundations; you will be called the Repairer of Broken Foundations, Walls, and Roots St. George on Earth and St.

George in Heaven.

The servants of God Almighty were calling George and Alex for a new mission to the old world. They both knew that if they missed this lifetime opportunity to rediscover their past and find the right direction to the Future, they would never get it back. George was prompted to go back to take care of and reclaim his father's house. His property has to be claimed under the restitution law after 1990 (To restore property seized by the state during Communism). Surprisingly enough, George found out that in Sofia Municipality, "Sredets," his granduncle stole his father's house.

George has restored his Bulgarian citizenship. The last decision of the district court in "Sredets" refused to recognize the ownership right of the heirs. However, they have the right to appeal the restitution and do not have any rights. As long as it was Bulgarian property, according to the armistice and the peace treaty, it became the property of the USSR—as a reparation.

The fact that George had restored his Bulgarian citizenship has no bearing. At the time of the confiscation of the property, the owner was a Soviet citizen— this is the situation. After that, what the USSR did with the property was a separate issue. Most of the properties were donated to the Bulgarian fraternal people by a decision of the Congress of the Communists.

Party of the People's Republic in the 1950s. After the fall of the Berlin Wall in 1990, Vasiliy didn't have a family—only two daughters from two different wives didn't demand home ownership.

Vasiliy transferred the title of the house to himself. George had never heard about his indecencies. They also didn't have a family and children. After one century, Vasiliy's demon wandered the dry places in the wilderness. The demon of Vasiliy came back here to claim the house. Not only its roots but the branches in the fruits of the next generation—Alex. It is clear that he still exists and is trying to influence his brother's offspring.

George was thinking, "Really, I want to travel back in time to fix some of my mistakes. That is if there was a way. And I want to find and spend more time with his Pap before he passes away. Please, God, help me!" May God give him the power to do it.

He understood the mission from his grandpa Georgiy and his 142-year-old unpublished book.

"My military journals from Bulgaria 1877-1878" For all both saw there, downloads from the Library of Heaven. He knew inside that a book was born in his soul and soon would be out there, available for the World and all of his offspring/descendants. George felt a heavy blanket of his old bag of bones and flesh over him.

The heaviness pulled him down.

What is this? Brain death or hallucinations.

Back in the hospital bed, George tried to move his right arm, but it was heavier than stone. He was in his bed next to his grandson. This dead person in the patient's bed became. He just arrived from the other side with his afterlife travel experience. He was not alone. His grandfather Georgiy did it before when he was mortally wounded during the War of 1878. He was not sure if St. George was helping him or his grandpa or God to navigate his life down on Earth. There was nothing that he could do. The doctor said that only rest would help him gain his power back.

George and Alex appeared to be crazy, talking to dead relatives and hearing voices. It's a mental dysfunction due to a lack of oxygen to the brain!

Hallucinations are where you hear, see, smell, taste, or feel things that appear to be real but only exist in your mind.

Doctors suggested medical help for George and Alex after the coma. They believed that they had hallucinations. Is this a pathological or supernatural experience?

Or God's miracles? Who helped him? The prayer of his father, Nicky, in the hospital chapel or the medications? It was difficult to deal with the disbelief of the Doctors, "Keep your religious experience for yourself." Alex and George kept quiet in the hospital. They shared only in the family so many questions, dreams, hallucinations, or real awakenings. The last time before he woke, he was looking at *"the river of water of life, bright as crystal, proceeding out of the throne of God."* George was quick to look at the crystal lake. Suddenly, on his face, he saw the beginning of his father Alexander, grandpa Captain Georgiy, and all his "founding fathers" or grandparents in front of Khan Kubrat (the founder of Bulgaria), who sent his son, Khan Asparuh, next to Shem and Japheth, the face of Noah, the beginning of Adam in God's Image and last, the face of Yahweh, the Creator of All.

At last, he was home, exhausted, and immediately fell into a trance and slept with one open question in his mind: "Why did it have to be tennis?"

How can we believe that an unexpected car crash can open the door to the future?

Alex sees his own grandfather, still alive in 2022, learning about his family heritage through DNA testing and making the somewhat dangerous decision to return to his roots despite the ongoing COVID pandemic and the geopolitical crises sparked by the Russian invasion of Ukraine.

The story ends with Alex and George leaving the spiritual space to wake up in the hospital, having survived their car accident.

The two can reflect on the hidden parallel lines between past, present, and future and remark on their newfound respect for each other.

In the higher dimension, they both saw things very vaguely, "This time of imperfection we see in a mirror dimly a blurred reflection, a riddle, an enigma, but then, when the time of perfection comes, we will see reality face to face…" according to the heavenly visions.

"Fairways, I moved into my old house on Khan Asparuh Street."

In Sofia in Bermuda's Triangle "portal" of the future...

George was lying in bed and reading when Alex knocked on the door and asked what it was he was reading. "It's the diary of my Ukrainian grandpa, who was a war correspondent. Unfortunately, his manuscript was banned from being published in Russia in 1889. The unknown reports from the Russian-Turkish Liberation War 1978 reveal an interesting documentary story from a time we don't know anything about."

After a long cleaning of the old house, George was very tired and called a taxi to bring him to his brother's house. He was exhausted that day.

Last night, after the great ancestor's discovery, it sounded as if something had fallen down, followed by footsteps crossing the room and stopping midway. George looked at an appearance that seemed to be illuminated by the moonlight. It was his Grandpa Georgiy–Captain Kakhovskiy–paying him a midnight visit. He was glad in an old army uniform and carried his memoir under his arm. He looked towards George and, with a sense of pride, said,

"Finally! Finally, someone from my descent has discovered my 142-year-old unpublished manuscript. It is the happiest day of my life."

As George heard him declare his happiness triumphantly, he couldn't tell when he drifted off to the world of slumber.

Saint George became the dragon-slaying hero. The symbol that one day Captain Georgiy would slay the demon of his brother, Vasiliy, his constant fearsome enemy.

Soon, St. George will put Vasiliy under his feet— Trust in God!

George always used his military icon of St. George, who always slammed Dracula (the demon Vasiliy) in his life.

"What the enemy intends for evil, God will use for good!"

George heard a noise in the back of the room, like something had fallen down. Later, he heard steps crossing the room that stopped in the middle and looked at him. Illuminated and happy by the moon, George saw his Grandpa Georgiy, Captain Kakhovskiy, in his army uniform.

George was happy to check all events on his to-do list in Bulgaria. Thousands of pictures, documents, videos, and audio recordings with relatives and ordinary people who they met in Bulgaria. Alexander was very happy finally to catch up with Elizabeth, his wife, after the crazy last days traveling in Bulgaria.

Maria, on the other hand, halfway around the World, felt happier that both of them were safe and in good spirits.

But deep inside, she was mad. She could not understand in her mind what in the World the need was to travel in such a dangerous time of the pandemic of 2020.

George already knew that she would not forgive him for a long time for his irresponsible deeds. All that to write a book about people he didn't know and never met. Total waste of time and risk, so she will be alone and worried all day long after checking the number of deaths from COVID-19 in Eastern Europe.

George definitely violated their marriage covenant, and she will make sure that he feels the pain in the future.

George was so happy in his imaginary World of nostalgia that he already started the first chapter in his mind today of his memoirs.

He accomplished too much.

But the most important thing was to bond with his grandson, Alex.

He and Maria secretly pray for their firstborn grandson to find a Bulgarian girl and have Bulgarian children, but his parents free him from these traditional National obligations and give him the freedom to find a smart girl like Ellie, the love of Alex's life.

George and Alexander, according to the vision to look for their "Ancestor's Roots," memorialized this trip so much that they will have time to discuss it in days to come.

George is teaching him that if you get the opportunity to open a door in your life, you need to jump by faith and never look back. Never regret it later—you will understand why.

Alexander didn't want to come to Europe, but because of his grandpa, he did it. He was happy to be there.

One "emergency visit" for the funeral of his brother, Dimitar, opened a new World of dormant memory, like Divine Appointments that followed everyone wherever they went.

Suddenly, the name of George's brother, Drago, came up on his cell phone. What a surprise since they saw each other for the last time when he left Ljubimetz. Drago decided to break the fragile ice of his long, freezing silence. George was able to restore the relationship with his last sibling, who was still alive. Life is not that long to hold him responsible for the past of their family. Drago was curious to find out if George discovered more relatives with the same surname. They have long and warm brotherly conversations for times they never talk about all these years.

Life is too short not to continue their relationship!

Drago asked about their common relatives in Kakhovka, Ukraine, Feodosia, and Russian Crimea. The visit to the historical museum was about their family's founding father, General Kakhovskiy, who founded the small townships of Kakhovka and Lubimovka in Ukraine on the River Dnepro. Drago connected with his long-relatives families. In February 2022, Russia invaded and occupied parts of Ukraine in a major escalation of the Russo-Ukrainian War, which began in 2014.

Even after the Russian-Ukrainian war broke out, he traveled to the Romanian border and rescued his relatives with his van as refugees ran for their lives at his house in Bulgaria and took care of them.

Freedom is crucial for life. Its loss is the beginning of the next extinction. "We didn't pass it to our children in the bloodstream. It must be fought for, protected, and handed on for them to do the same or one day, we will spend our sunset years telling our children and our children's children what it was once like in the United States, where men were free."

—Ronald Reagan.

Those who do not learn his family history are doomed to repeat it in the next generation!

Really, is that right?

History shows time and time again that both those who know and those who don't learn from history are doomed to repeat it.

# Chapter 14:

# Returning Home

George and Alex were beyond overjoyed. They had accomplished a wonderful trip across Eastern Europe and were now returning on a flight to Chicago.

The flight was delayed by an hour.

George scoffed, "Even after the hours we had to spend in the security line, we still are too early!"

Alex and George remembered the horrible, invasive security. While trying to go through, both groaned while removing their shoes, and George was "selected" for a random search, though Alex was certain that it was due to his accent and criticism of the system.

As an elderly with disabilities, George was allowed to fly on airplanes that are required to do so free of charge. But he decided to travel like everyone else. He was chosen for the search.

The search included questions that George was certain that they couldn't ask.

"Where are you traveling to?"

"Chicago," George relented, knowing that, constitutional or not, he wasn't free to go until he told them what they wanted to know.

"What are you bringing with you?" The agent asked George. He knew that if he lied, there could be harsh consequences, but something was telling him that if he told them about the manuscript, it would not bode well.

Instead, George said. "A few books, my phone." He tried to sound as passive as possible while talking to the agent, who stood too close to him and seemed to be trying to appear taller than he was, as though he was trying to intimidate the old man.

"Your ticket says that you're flying to London, not Chicago," the agent, whose face looked both tired and snarky, said.

"Well, it's a layover." George looked tired. He knew that the agent was aware of how layovers worked and that he could likely see on his ticket where he would end up.

UK allows US security checks on passengers before transatlantic travel.

The Department of Homeland Security already has staff working at several European airports who issue "advice" on which passengers should not be allowed to travel to the US.

If the UK and US are increasing security at airports, why not secure the U.S.-Mexican border as well?

Why are people still coming into the United States through airports if the border is closed?

"Mhm." The agent grunted affirmatively, but as though it was just a common lie that people told each other.

George was watching the CNN report next to him on the TV monitor: "Migrants break past the human wall, vehicle barriers in Juárez, Mexico to get to El Paso, U.S on the side of Rio Grande," and another one: "Hundreds of migrants cross the Rio Grande nightly: 'We all came with dreams.'"

"Mass of Migrants Crosses Rio Grande, Enters U.S. Illegally as Border Crisis Worsens"

George remembered his life behind the Iron Curtain.

Today, many young people like Alex ask,

"Is it true that Bulgarians before 1990 were forbidden to leave the country?"  and "Did they really kill people trying to escape Bulgaria at the border?"

"Freedom is certainly become more and more of a fight," George said after recalling the security check. Vasiliy the demon would fight for the freedom of people no matter where it was— as long as there was an opportunity.

After the time it took for the two to remember the security, their conversation was interrupted by the boarding call.

Alex and George sat on the plane. It was the closest to an empty flight that Alex had ever seen, and the two talked more about freedom on their way to London.

During the layover in London, George and Alex had some time to wait. They stretched their legs after the flight, and George's knee felt especially stiff after sitting for so long. George was never one to sit for long. Alex was 6'2". When is tall considered to be "too tall?" Sometimes, fitting into an airplane seat is a challenge, and I can't imagine how much taller people would cope with this flight experience.

George was a worker, not someone who spent their day doing nothing in bed or at a desk. The only time that he would sit for an extended time was when he was reading or writing, and even then, he would take a walk to think. As old age approached, the walks became more and more difficult, but nothing could keep George down.

Alex looked around. London was the center of much culture and innovation, though it was just as well a victim of "new world" thought that plagued many cities. The two walked around and talked about the beauty of the city.

"It's like New York, but different." He observed.

George laughed. "Well, you know New York is about four hundred years old, but London is nearing two thousand!"

Alex remembered hearing the fact in his undergraduate world history class but only now had it set in.

"It's older than America!"

George nodded, "And since its beginning, it's been a center of thought and art since the beginning! It's always been the home of free thinkers like John Stuart Mill, who developed the idea of liberty and a free economy! George Bernard Shaw and the Fabian Society founded the London School of Economics in 1895.

"Today, the society functions primarily as a think tank and is one of twenty socialist societies affiliated with the labor party," mentioned Alex.

"Wow!" Alex forgot about all the theories that came out of London.

"Well, don't forget that he was an atheist and believed that religion was impossible!"

Alex laughed. "It's funny how many of these thinkers tend to be short-sighted on things that are beyond man!"

"Just like Faust!" Faust was a fictional scientist who sold his sold to the devil after wanting to know everything. George knew that the lesson of his story was that some things are just beyond science or man's understanding—especially matters of the divine.

Alex nodded. They talked more about Mill, Faust, and the search for knowledge before they started flying to New York.

As they landed in New York, Alex was reminded of George's younger self. He saw the alleys between the skyscrapers and thought about the people who may be living in them— how his grandpa, for a short moment in time, was one of those people and how he would likely never experience something close to that position in life thanks to George and the family that he started.

When they landed at JFK airport in Queens, Alex and George got out of the airport as quickly as possible. Though they had a full five hours until the final flight to Chicago, they knew that there wasn't enough time to explore even a fraction of the city that George had once called home.

After a day of traveling, the two were hungry, so the first thing that they did was grab a hot dog from a cart— one of the classic symbols of NYC. The man smiled. George smiled back and asked a question that shocked Alex: Where are you from?

The man seemed happy that the question was asked, "Iran!" Persians are not Arabs, and they don't speak Arabic — they speak Farsi.

The Iranian men are also more than happy to speak up about freedom because they fled Iran's 1979 revolution.

The two talked about the experience of American emigration and how George had just visited his homeland before they walked off with their lunch, holding his iconic NYC Greek deli coffee cup. "We are happy to serve you."

"Why did you ask that?!" Alex was embarrassed.

"Why wouldn't I?" George seemed to know what Alex was thinking but asked the question to further the conversation that they were having.

"It's rude! People don't like to be asked that! Especially with the current situation with Iran!"

George chuckled. "We don't like to be asked that when it's used to act like we don't belong here! Besides that, why wouldn't we want to talk about our home? It's a part of my heart!"

When George used the word "we," Alex remembered that his grandfather wasn't born in America; he was an emigrant, just like the man at the cart!

They talked to a man at a bodega (New York corner store) next. He was Puerto Rican, and the man behind them was "fresh off the boat" from Russia! Another Slav!

After talking at the store, the two rushed to get through security (which, thank goodness, was less of a hassle than the people on the way to London).

Meanwhile, Alexander headed towards Blue Smoke on the Road, located in Terminal # 2, to grab a bite to eat.

The same place where Victor  asks, "Amelia, would you like an eat-to-bite?" Bite to eat? Cantaloni?

Tom Hanks's performance in Steven Spielberg's "The Terminal" Tom Hanks did actually learn to speak Bulgarian for his role as Viktor Navorski in the film "The Terminal."

Yeah, Alex remembers the Krakozhian citizen Viktor who just wants to go home, just like his grandpa during the Cold -War Era.

Unfortunately, his home no longer exists due to the outbreak of civil war within his country.

As a result, his passport is deemed invalid and Viktor is stuck in New York's JFK Airport until further notice. Navorski is a man who travels thousands of kilometers to keep a promise for his father and his quest to fulfill one of his dad's dreams. Similar to Grandpa George.

George was growing tired when his phone began to ring. George took it out and smiled as I saw his wife's name flashing on it.

"Hello, Maria," George greeted his love.

"Darling, have you reached J.F.K.?" she asked. "Did you take your medicine?"

"I am doing it right now,"

George said.

"Are you observing social distancing? Make sure to wear your mask all the time," instructed Maria.

"Don't worry, Maria," George assured her.

George's wife was always in panic mode. After all, it was a very dangerous time to be traveling to Bulgaria and back.

"I told you to postpone it," complained Maria.

"I am alright," George replied, "a man can die but once."

George learns to block all thoughts of fear of one's death. He remembers William Shakespeare and Julius Caesar in the back of his mind:

"A coward dies a thousand times before his death, but the valiant taste of death but once. It seems to me most strange that men should fear, seeing that death, a necessary end, will come when it will come."

"Don't worry Maria, I am not alone. My guardian angel Alexander is with me. Soon we will be home."

# Chapter 15:

# Home at Last

As the plane took off on its way to Chicago, George and Alex were full of energy.

"Freedom," Alex said in thought. "Freedom seems to be the theme of this trip."

George smiled. He felt his grandson finally got it. Since he was young, freedom had always been George's biggest concern, be it freedom attained through wealth, freedom from mistreatment as an immigrant, or freedom from the once tyrannical government that was Communist Bulgaria.

"Yes, my boy! Freedom is everything. That's why I came here! The land of the free

Alex thought.

He had experienced many of his grandfather's memories in their spiritual journey, and now that he was putting the pieces together, he saw that freedom was all that his grandfather ever wanted.

"What do you think freedom is worth?" George asked. He was curious. He didn't envy Alex for this fact, but he knew that freedom wasn't scarce in the young man's life.

"Everything," Alex said in the convictive way that young people speak.

"Everything!"

"If your life was at stake under a tyrannical government, you would die to be free?"

Alex then realized what everything meant.

He paused for a moment.

"I don't know what freedom's worth."

"Is freedom worth the blood that gets spilled?" George asked. "Is it worth the death of the oppressors?"

Alex thought about those who killed their oppressors to be "free," like in the French Revolution, where the lower classes beheaded the aristocrats.

The Declaration of Independence, adopted by the Continental Congress on July 4, 1776, the 13 American colonies severed their political connections to Great Britain. The Declaration summarized the colonists' motivations for seeking independence. By declaring themselves an independent nation, the American colonists were able to confirm an official alliance with the Government of France and obtain French assistance in the war against Great Britain. The colonists fought the British because they wanted to be free from Britain.

"Maybe…" Alex was being more careful with his words. "But I think that 'freedom' is more than just the freedom of a specific group. I once heard that the oppression of one is the oppression of all, and that really stuck with me. I think that if one group of people is subjugated, then it threatens a standard of oppression for everyone else! The fight for freedom is something that should never be devalued."

George smiled. He was proud of how his grandson was navigating such a difficult topic.

"What do you think our greatest fight for freedom is now?" George asked.

Alex immediately thought of the recent claims of election interference and censorship but remembered hearing of countries where free speech was banned wholly, as well as Christianity, something that was essential to his life and identity.

"I think that people around the world are being restricted from believing their own God," Alex said. The answer felt right to him, and he remembered how the Communist regime banned Christianity and all Christian artifacts. "And I think I'm confident in my answer. Freedom is worth everything."

George smiled again, and he couldn't help but agree.

What was freedom for George?

He had never spoken about it before in front of the family, his son or grandson. He wanted to travel to Bulgaria with Alexander so that he could open the floodgates of their ancestral history. How did he survive the bloody cross-border shooting between Greece & Bulgaria?

"Could I ask you a question?" asked Alex, pushing the luggage cart toward the taxi pick-up area.

"Of course," George replied, sanitizing his hand.

"How did you manage to flee Bulgaria? I mean, as I have read and heard, the law and order situation was in its worst form," answered Alex.

I don't remember you talking about this experience.

The old man looked into his eyes as if they were projecting the video of his escape that day. It was Sunday night, like today, but the Resurrection Day of Easter!

"On foot, running, jumping for the most part," He replied with a frail smile.

"After we decided to escape on our own as young high school students at 16th, I was not alone in charge of making decisions," George continued. "Hence, while running away, I thought the safest thing to do was to crawl through the snow until I reached the river Maritza."

He paused as Alex ordered the Uber taxi service through the concessionaire of Chicago Airport from the arrival hall.

They were told to wait for a while as the service tried to arrange a ride for them.

The pair sat themselves down on a cold metallic bench; they were thankful for the central heating at the airport as it was snowing outside. There is no doubt about it that winter in Chicago could be quite tough, yet the beauty always made one fall in love with the city that George wanted to make his home.

"After escaping the cross-border shooting, I reached the river, I stopped crawling and started running as fast as I could,"

I continued my story as Alexander brought us coffee. "If my memories serve me correctly, the river was a hundred meters wide. I assumed the border ran down its middle, which meant I would have to crawl another hundred meters or so to make it over to the Greek side. I took a few deep breaths and started inching my way forward again, hoping that the next time I stopped for a break, I would be in Greece."

"Did you manage to reach the river Maritza without getting detected?" asked Alexander.

George nodded, taking a sip of the coffee. He loved the rich French Vanilla flavor with creamy oat milk.

"The fact that I wasn't caught had energized me," George chuckled. "I kept going, thinking that I had to cover another hundred meters or so before I could rest. I kept crawling and entered the frozen river where the night temperature kept dropping."

"Half of my body was above the ground," He said, indicating towards his waist. "But, I had to stay low to avoid getting spotted. So, I kept my head down by taking quick glances behind me and noticing that I was about twenty meters from the Maritza River bank."

On the border zone, the soldiers were shooting without warning. The most important thing was not to panic.

The emergency squad of border soldiers with ferocious dogs were already investigating some other refugees, so he had time to escape by swimming across the river Maritza— "The River of Death."

At the age of 16, George was in the best physical shape in his life to run, bike, and swim. That's why he was the best high school champion in the Haskovo district for that year.

Alexander was listening to his grandfather quite diligently instead of staring at his iPhone. He wasn't interrupting or misunderstanding George. For the first time in his life, he had felt understood. He wanted to thank Alex for being such a good listener and filling his heart with joy. Grandpa shared this with his grandson for the first time,

"I began to smile because, within a few minutes, I knew I would be safe on the water," George narrated. "I quickly begin to think about the things I would do when I reach the other side. The first was the victory dance."

"The victory dance?" laughed Alexander.

"Yes! Do you think I don't know how to dance?"

"The only time I had seen you dancing was with Aunty Yordanka in her wedding video," sniggered Alexander.

"That was a waltz! The victory dance is a little different," George assured him.

Celebration of a victory with a dance, shuffle, with happy body movement. It is most commonly used in sports.

I had done it for the first time when I won a district athletic competition back in my high school days."

"Wow! You are full of surprises," commented Alexander.

George laughed and continued, "I kept crawling until I was thirty meters away, then forty, then fifty, and then sixty. At one point, I stopped seeing the bank that too because of the moonlight as it was dark. I saw the forest that went all the way down to the river, and I wondered if it was the same spot where I had waited for the fog to clear a long time ago. I figured that I'd reached the halfway point by now, and I got up and started running with my body hunching forward."

"I was lucky if you ask me,

Alexander," George paused.

"Why do you say so? I think you were courageous!" replied Alexander, drinking coffee.

"I guess because there were not too many Bulgarian border guards to shoot. The Greek border guards yelled at me to stop me,"

George answered. "And then, before I knew it, I was running along the tree line. I had made it. I had actually crossed the border. But it was a little bit early to celebrate. Hence, I kept running without turning around until I reached the barbed wire fence. A few minutes later, I was on the ground with my face towards the sky. I was crying instead of doing a victory dance."

George felt goosebumps on the back of his neck due to an emotionally intense experience. It had been years, yet he was still moved by it as if the events had taken place yesterday.

"Against all odds, I had managed to escape the most oppressive regime in Eastern Europe. It was a country where soldiers patrolled the borders to prevent their compatriots from escaping instead of preventing outsiders from entering," he added. "I was free at last. I was happy that I would be able to tell the world about my ordeal. I would be able to talk about the life of Paradise behind the Berlin Wall."

"Sir, your taxi is here," announced the dispatcher with an Indian accent.

Alexander and George quickly gathered their belongings and made their way to the taxi. All the way, George recalled the way he had walked towards the lights of the first Greek village he saw after crossing the wires. He had noticed that he held a small soldier's icon in his hand, and he quickly hid it in his inner pocket. It was windy; the gusts of winds were carrying the new forecasts of a blizzard.

As George saw me completely exhausted, he kept digging to push myself forward. He guessed it had taken him a total of fifteen minutes to reach the first Greek village, and as soon as he arrived, he was panting like a marathon runner who had just crossed the finishing line. He was dizzy and hungry. He used every bit of his strength to walk up to the first house he saw and knocked on the door. He thinks he must have knocked a dozen times before he passed out. Hence, he ended up sleeping in a barn with the animals. George didn't know his skin itched from a dozen hay pricks while the strong smell of animals assaulted his nose until he woke up the next day.

As the driver took their luggage, he stared around with respect and admiration. Within a couple of moments, tears began to roll down his cheek as his pain at last condensed into a deluge of rain. George quickly wiped them with the corner of the sleeve. He had always thought that regardless of the time he chose to return, his mother and father would always be sitting on the front porch waiting for him as they had for several years. But unfortunately, he couldn't even come back to attend their funerals after many years. However, the guilt that had remained inside him made him a better person, less rotten, and healthier. I saw so many deaths of my friends in front of my eyes. I still remember that!

"God saved me from death so many times because he has plans for me to fulfill my life's purpose.

God protected my life, so today I can tell my grandson about His goodness & blessings."

Thank God for Captain Georgiy in Heaven,

And St George they always must fight against the dark monster the Demon of his brother Vasiliy. Who is trying to harm Captain Georgiy's Descendants of his brother's generation?

Remember, the curse of Vasilly was broken. George survive. God protected him.

The executions of the Kakhovskiy Family occurred after Vasiliy was banished from his father's estate in 1916. He placed a curse on his parents and brothers and vowed that Vasiliy would not die until every member of his Georgiy Kakhovskiy immediate family was dead. But St George, by the power of God, broke this curse.

Thank God today they are alive and well.

The two were silent for a while until they began talking again about the trip that they had just been on.

"The manuscript," Alex said suddenly, remembering the piece of history that was carefully packed into their luggage.

"Oh yes!" George said, almost too loudly for the plane.

The two talked about the house that was cleaned out before its sale. George was tempted to take everything that had any relation to the old Bulgaria. Though it was terrible, it was how I was raised, and it's my home. Alex remembered George saying that phrase and being shocked at his grandfather's complexity. At first, he thought it was a kind of Stockholm Syndrome, but soon realized that everyone will be nostalgic for their childhood, no matter the horrors committed there.

The three talked about their love of the country more, how Alex felt a special connection to his extended and long-lost family, and how George felt complete as he talked to his other countrymen.

As the two landed, they knew that something had changed in them. Alex felt like less of an American and finally felt like labeling himself as a Bulgarian or something of the sort. George, on the other hand, realized how much he missed his home and his wife and knew that, though he was from Bulgaria, America was his home.

Finally, Alex knew what freedom was worth, and he knew to fear and fight what may take it away. The new generation of those destined to battle against Vasiliy the Demon and his temptations was born.

Alex had no questions. He understood what had happened so far; he just needed to think. Alex had heard all of these stories about immigrants, their poverty, and their struggles at the southern border with Mexico, but he had never really applied these things to his grandfather. He had also never witnessed it firsthand. This was a forbidden topic of his conversation till now when they reached the taxi drop-off.

After a minute of silence. Alex had a question: "Where are you escaping?"

"To the West! To America where Freedom lived," George answered simply. He knew it was a bad answer, but this was his American dream.

First of all, the group passed the border with Bulgaria and Greece and crossed the River Maritza— actually, the bloody event happened on this Eastern Orthodox Easter on April 30th, 1948.

What saved me from the midnight shootout? George remembers an old lucky pocket version of the Bible— a gift from his grandfather, which he kept in the left pocket of his jacket with a Bullet stopped exactly on Psalm 91:7 on the sentence: "A thousand may fall at your side, ten thousand at your right hand, but it will not come near you."

Also helped him was his old Russian army bronze icon of St. George the Conqueror (with GK/"ГК" engraved initials in the Cyrillic alphabet), the very same one he had inherited from his grandfather (and namesake) Captain Georgiy Kakhovskiy.

George remembers that he found in his treasury box, back in his office, a 400-year-old single silver ruble and an antique 1880 silver coin (20 kopeks) from Emperor Alexander II (Tsar Liberator) of the Russian Empire, a gift from his grandfather, the captain.

These were valuable antique coins and his key to the front door of his house on "Tsar Liberator" street that, at the last minute, he took with him before he escaped the border. The magic of his child's imagination was that every time he turned the key in case of a time of need, something new would happen the next day. Between the icon of St. George and the silver ruble, it was a combination that opened the door to a magical, supernatural power of opportunity for him. He believes that his grandpa and Saint George will always be there for him. Those were relics for him —

something that you can see— you can touch something real, something material from the past and from across the Ocean.

His grandfather, like most elders in the Old Country, held onto relics like these under the belief that Sveti Georgiy Pobedonosets (St. George the Conqueror) was always watching over them and their elders. Was his own grandfather sitting next to his saintly namesake up there in Heaven and looking down on him just then?

George rubbed his chin and seeped from his coffee, and he ran his other hand across the St. George icon. In his mind, George also had a small thought floating in the background— one that his grandfather once passed into the next life, had created a magic portal in the spirit world, leaving his soldier icon as a point of faith that lingered on Earth for people like George to hold onto and maintain their connection to the past and the World that they had come from. He had, after all, been clutching that icon when he was able to escape safely to the other side of the Maritsa River on the Bulgarian-Greek border by some miracle that he had never fully understood. He had kept the icon as he had survived so many more hardships during his "new" life in the USA.

He kept all these Holly relics in his small pocket all this time for traveling safety & protection.

So this was the moment when, after arriving home in Chicago, George Will gave them to Alex to keep them & protect them for the next generation.

When they arrived at the O'Hare International Airport in Chicago, George was immersed in the surge of his feelings coming from Bulgaria when he heard chuckling. George quickly locked at his grandson, to whose presence he had become oblivious. Alex turned around his phone, and George saw everyone's faces on the screen. He was unaware that his whole family was watching his reaction as he exited the plane being poignant.

"Maria! Nicky! Rita! Mary! Georgie!" George exclaimed, being caught off-guard. "Alexander, you were on a video call throughout."

"And Ellen!" replied Ellen as Alex panned the camera.

"My darling!" George said with a wide grin.

"Grandpa, watching you fathom a moment was such a treat," said Georgie. "I am not even kidding."

George laughed as his face glowed.

"Congratulations on being successful in getting Alex with you back to the USA," jested Mary.

"How was the flight, Dad?" asked Nicky.

"Did you take your medicines?" asked Maria.

"Can you guys talk one by one?" Margarita helplessly tried to discipline everyone. "By the way, you are glowing, George!"

"It's because of Bulgaria, Mom," replied Maria.

"No, Mom, I want to ask about London," said Ellen, snatching the phone.

"Grandpa, do you have to wear the mask throughout the flight? I am curious!" interrupted Georgie Jr.

"Can I talk to your grandpa in peace?"

"Guys! Guys!" yelled Alexander with a grin. "Cut us some slack. We are still at the airport."

George laughed and said a silent prayer for his family. He is blessed in countless ways, and the greatest blessing is a loving family.

I'll call you guys later," George said, bidding goodbye. "We have to catch a taxi for ourselves."

"But…" protested the family.

"No, Buttt! Goodbye," said Alexander as he dropped a line.

Alexander and George exchanged looks and shook their heads.

"Welcome Back at Home Sweet Home"!

# Chapter 16:

# In a Near Future

Where does a country begin? Alex sighed.

*The airport or at the border?* Alex thought, "It only seems to become worse and worse every time I visit it."

Alex clearly remembers the story of his grandpa's illegal "Border crossing." At the so-called "River of Death" on River Maritza. On this Bloody Easter of 1948, many Bulgarians, who were dissatisfied with the new oppressive Communist regime, massively fled across the border of Turkey and Greece. Escaping to the West—Especially to America!

"The idea," he continued in his head, "The idea that as time goes on, things always get better is such a myth. If you want things to get better, you must work for it! Right here in 2025 is a prime example!"

Alex published his great-great-grandfather, Captain Gerogiy's, memoir about a year ago. The resurrection of a hundred-and-forty-two-year-old lost manuscript from 1878, which gave Alex great merit as a historian, had become quite popular.

At JFK Airport, Alex was holding his brand new hardcover copy of his grand-grandpa, Captain Georgiy's *Memoirs, military journals & letters from Bulgaria* from the Russian-Turkish War of 1878.

Alex made a promise and pledge at his grandpa's memorial grave tomb in Ljubimetz. He had a plastic bag with soil from the cemetery there that one day he would pour into his grandpa's grave in his Ukrainian Cemetery in Chicago to reunite him with the Motherland.

Alex stopped thinking to himself so much and focused on the ordeal. He was in the middle of JFK airport, trying to get home before Thanksgiving. In front of Alex was a large, sad, gray terminal. The screen read: *Ticket failed to load.*

Alex arrived in another New York—one totally different from what he remembered in his childhood.

Alex scoffed. "It started with those ridiculous self-checkout lines, and now it's come to this!" For the past few years, jobs have been slowly being replaced with machines and artificial intelligence. At first, it was little things for little jobs that people didn't seem to care about. In 2019, grocery stores started replacing the checkout lanes with computers, which killed millions of jobs!

Next, it was fast food in 2022. All the restaurants began replacing people at the counter with little kiosks, and before anyone knew it, nobody could find a job in fast food! A million more jobs are gone!

"And now this," Alex thought. In the past few months, the process of automation sped up exponentially. Once companies realized how much money they saved by simply not having to pay anyone, they axed entire branches and even entire companies (save one or two people who would watch after the robots)!

Alex felt especially lonely when he realized that on this entire adventure in the airport, he didn't need to speak to a single person! People were all around him, but they wouldn't talk!

"What has this world gone to?" Alex thought again, "Look at how artificial intelligence is changing our future!"

These next-gen solutions increase security but also amplify the airport experience for travelers all year round. Global airports are increasingly relying on AI technology as a solution to elevate their safety measures and overall passenger journey. Through machine learning, these smart solutions will eliminate any margin for error, strengthen capabilities, and mitigate risks.

Alex was still trying to navigate the interface.

He kept pondering again and again: "It's time for everyone to read or reread *Brave New World*." It was recommended by his grandpa a long time ago. What a masterpiece…one of the most prophetic dystopian works of the 20th century.

People seemed to prefer texting and sending posts from social media over real, face-to-face interaction. Sure, people would talk, but you would have to Facetime or Skype them before anything else.

"It's absurd," Alex kept thinking, "that people will go through all of these hoops to imitate real-life interaction, but all they have to do is look up from their stupid phones and meet someone!" The machine kept failing. Every time Alex thought about something, it seemed like the terminal was harder to use. "It's like they're allergic to thought."

Eventually, Alex got to his ticket, which read Nov. 29. "What?" this time, Alex spoke aloud. "I ordered it for the 26th! I'll miss Thanksgiving!" Alex clicked through the terminal to get a refund, which the machine eventually forfeited to him after loading 20 different pages.

"It's like a test of my will," Alex thought. He got the refund and then went about ordering a new ticket.

The only plane ticket available from NEW YORK CITY to Chicago had two layovers because Alex had to reorder the ticket the day before one of the biggest travel days of the year.

"Whatever," Alex thought, "I just want to go home and see my wife."

Eventually, the screen loaded for the ticket, which read, JFK—O'Hare, 2 Layovers, $7,325.

"Seven thousand dollars?!" Alex almost yelled this, but after thinking about how weak the dollar was becoming, the inflation seemed to line up for a fair price.

Since all of the people lost their jobs to automation, everyone expected a massive economic recession, but instead, President Biden administered handouts to everyone who had lost their jobs, which meant that the people had plenty of money for spending! This, as well as the unbelievable national debt that was accrued, caused explosive inflation, making the US Dollar less and less valuable every day.

Alex bought the ticket and went to sit down. He looked up at the myriad of television screens that seemed to be facing him. The information media has become the biggest job in America. It seemed to Alex that almost everybody he met worked for the media in some way.

On the only TV screen that wasn't streaming the news, there was a list of the flights and their arrival times. Every single flight that was going to East Asia had the word "CANCELED" in red letters next to it.

"Chinese leader Xi Jinping arrived in Moscow on Monday for a three-day visit to Russia, as the two nations appear to be growing closer amid Russia's yearlong war on neighboring Ukraine. "

"Russian fighter jet forces down US drone over the Black Sea!" What is going on with America's supremacy?

"Who knows what is coming? Russia and China have a common interest in weakening U.S. dominance of the World order!"

On Twitter, it said:

*"The US Navy said its guided-missile destroyer, the USS Milius, sailed through waters claimed by Beijing in the South China Sea in a 'freedom of navigation.'"*

"Oh yeah, Alex thought, "China's threats." For the past few years, China has been building military and economic power, and Chairman Xin Ping finally decided that it was time to strike; the country blocked all of its exports to America and had been threatening to invade.

"Back up the enemy of the US! He remembered the "Little Boy" in Hiroshima and Nagasaki seventy-eight years ago!"

"Ironically," Alex said to himself in a dark, sarcastic tone, "the scarcity that was caused by the lack of China's exports might be the only thing stopping America from going down a full-on spending spree-fueled spiral of inflation!" Alex could only think to be facetious and look at the bright side in such a dark time.

Alex sat down at a nearby bench and pulled a book out of his bag, The Master and Margarita, by Bulgakov. Alex liked how the book made tongue-in-cheek remarks about the authoritarian state. As he started reading, Alex caught glances and scoffs almost constantly. Everyone in the airport seemed to almost take offense at the man reading.

Nobody misses that old book in today's digital World!

Eventually, Alex had enough of the unwanted attention, so he decided to look around again.

The first thing that came into Alex's view was a newsstand. "So that's something they don't mind seeing someone read," he thought. The most popular magazine at the stand was Time Magazine. It was the "Man of the Year" edition. On the cover of the magazine was a bald man with a slight smile and a strongly pressed suit—Vladamir Putin.

The news has been focusing on Russia instead of China for the past couple of years. Putin had denied any interference in the election of 2016, which landed President Donald Trump in office. He said that it was made up by Democrats as an excuse for running a terrible campaign.

The sight of Putin reminded Alex of Russia's history with America—all the way back to the beginning of their interactions— the Civil War.

"Nobody remembers this," Alex thought, "but France and England were supporting the traitorous South in the war, and nobody wanted to help the North! Oh, how the money overcame the ethics. They wanted to hide it, but France and England supported the slavers. At the same time, the Russians landed in New York one fateful evening with the sole intention of saving the great American unity!"

Alex continued telling the story to himself. "It was a cold September night. Just a slight chill in the air. The Royal Russian fleet landed in Manhattan. Alex remembered reading an excerpt from the commander of the US Navy after the Civil War had ended and the North won, 'God bless the Russians,' The commander said."

"And in the Grand Duke Alexis Music Hall," Alex continued thinking, "The children sang the national anthem!

'Shadowed so long by the storm cloud of danger, thou whom the prayers of an empire defend, welcome, thrice welcome! But not as a stranger—come to the nation that calls thee its friend! Bleak are our shores with the blasts of December, Fettered and chill is the rivulet's flow, throbbing and warm are the hearts that remember who was our friend when the world was our foe.

Look on the lips that are smiling to greet thee. See the fresh flowers that people have strewn. Count them thy sisters and brothers that meet thee; Guest of the Nation, her heart is thine own! Fires of the North, in eternal communion, Blend your broad flashes with the evening's bright star!

God bless the Empire that loves the Great Union. Strength to her people! Long life to the Tzar!'

The children's choir must've been amazing! Oh, how I'd love to witness such a thing!" Alex almost seemed nostalgic about the event.

Russia was the only country to extend direct military support to the Lincoln government during the fall of 1863. One is in New York, and the other is in San Francisco.

But after Russia became the USSR, the Cold War began.

A ding came from Alex's phone, "What does it want now?" Alex thought as though the phone was a whining baby that he was suddenly tasked with taking care of. After checking the notification, he saw that his flight was ready.

"All right," Alex sighed, "Let's do this again."

The "this" that Alex was referring to was twofold. First was homeland security. Second was the actual flight that he was fighting with the computer to get on at one moment.

Homeland security, after the "robot revolution," as Alex liked to call it, had only gotten worse and worse.

Alex stood up and walked to the security area. The airport was bleak and tiring. The soft colors that looked like they were trying to be soft on the eyes instead looked drab and gross. The only art that was on the walls was simple and had soft colors. "Art is being brutally murdered," Alex thought as he walked along the airport, "and I have to bear witness."

When he was getting close to the security area, Alex could tell. How? The line. The line from the security computers stretched forever. "Somebody on staff should probably notice and fix this. That is if there is anyone on staff in this place!"

The line moved forward, and Alex joined the back. For about the next twenty minutes, Alex slowly inched further and further until he eventually reached the terminal.

At the international customs check-in, the terminal asked Alex where he was going, as though he hadn't just told it, and then asked him: Business or pleasure?

"Does it matter?" Alex thought to himself. Little did he know, that was just the beginning.

First Name:

Last Name:

Alex obliged and entered his name into the terminal.

Place of birth:

Alex didn't understand the reason that the terminal asked these things, but he followed directions and entered the information. He had tried to fight it on the flight to Bulgaria, and the people behind him became hostile–they didn't want to have to wait any longer. Besides, Alex's spirit had already been broken by the whole ordeal of the airport anyway. The computer terminal always seemed to have an error with him; people always scowled when he read—as if it's some sort of sin to read a physical book—and television screens pointed at him in every direction while all blaring their own audio. Sometimes, the TVs gave Alex such a headache that he would have to go to the bathroom and sit in silence for a moment.

One time, Alex's bathroom peace was broken by a man at the urinal who was browsing through TikTok. "What in the World could be so important on that ridiculous app?!" Alex felt like screaming. TikTok didn't even hide the fact that they stole people's information anymore.

"Information age, all right," Alex thought, "our information. Being taken from us without even giving us, the owners, any say in it!" This brought Alex back to the terminal.

Height:

Body Weight:

[If you are not sure of your body weight, give your best estimate.]

[If you lie, you will be prosecuted]

Alex wanted to take the heaviest thing that he could find and smash the computer to bits.

But security cameras were all around him. Of course, Big Brother is watching.

Behind him, Alex could hear the person before him in line sigh because he was taking a couple of seconds to answer it. This was the first time that Alex felt like he understood someone in the airport.

"I get it. I was impatient, too, when the person in front of me took a little longer than they needed to. Maybe that's why this is here, so we all get annoyed at each other, not the stupid machine that caused all of this."

When he finished filling out everything on the screen, Alex's next action was prompted: Please put all belongings on the conveyer belt and stand still in the marked area for a scan.

Alex placed his duffel bag and backpack on the conveyor belt, which fed into the X-ray. He stepped forward onto a gray rubber platform, put his arms flat by his side, and watched the heavy machinery whir around him in order to complete the full-body scan.

Once the machine stopped, a plastic barrier opened in front of Alex.

He stepped forward, took his bag, and got ready to board the plane.

"Big brother is watching you," Alex thought in reference to the evil all-seeing dictatorship that ruled the World of 1984 by George Orwell. In a more serious tone, Alex muttered the word "Apparatchik," remembering the World apparatus.

It was okay. Everything changed since the recent pandemic, but the information he learned from *Brave New World* is the same feeling of fear of control of information regarding banking. All your accounts and social credit are in one national app. Alex understood that the World changed so much lately. His app saw all his parameters of body functioning, social and credit scores, pick energy, spending power, and everything you need to know about him.

"You can run, but you can't hide."

Welcome to today's digital age of apparatchik.

An Apparatchik was a member of the Bulgarian Communist Party that would spy on people to make sure that they weren't disobeying Communist law. Disobedience would range from plotting to rebel to wanting to play the piano on Christmas.

Two hours in flashback flight to Chicago in separation, George was reading his memoirs.

The new memories of George.

Five years ago, it was approaching Thanksgiving Day. He started the first chapter of his memoir. He wished that his son,

Nicky, Margarita, and all the grandchildren would be in the kitchen of his son's house. Maria and Margarita would cook the turkey together.

George loved Chicago. He can't compare it with Florida, but he is stuck in this nursing home and in the care of Maria.

A blaring beep jumped George awake.

"Ay–ay–ay–ayia! What machine?" For his whole life, George had no trouble getting out of bed before 6 am, but recently, he decided that it would be nice to have an example of that, as he called it in his head, "insipid alarm clock!"

George rose out of bed, still thinking about Lake Michigan and the wonderful summers that he spent there. Before looking at the calendar on his kitchen table, George said in his head, "Why always have to be the water?" Many times that he spent near water–the secret of happiness, the sea, and coastline, but also rivers, lakes, canals, waterfalls, and even fountains–are less well publicized, yet the science has been consistent for at least a decade: Being by the water is good not only for your body but your mind, too.

George would ask Alex to take him to the Lakeshore in his wheelchair for a couple of hours since the weather was nice.

All his precious memories are around the water.

In 2015, George remembered the boat sailing over the years. Both with Maria, and to go to Lake Michigan. Now, when he is stuck in this dumb nursing home, he still remembers the shores of Lake Michigan.

"Guess I'll live another good day. My nurse–A smiling Alabama girl with Southern charm—will be happy about that, at least. I've been dressed since 6:00 am."

The previous health aids didn't respect George, but recently, a Ukrainian Home Attendant came; she was very nice. She was the only one able to make George happy and relaxed. There was a different vibe.

She could listen to him. It so happened that she was from Kakhovka, Ukraine, and George heard a lot of conversations about Classic Russian literature of the Ukrainians like Anton Chekov, Nikolay Gogol, Mikhail Bulgakov, and the poetry of Pushkin and Anna Akhmatova. George felt some kind of history about his grandpa, Captain Giorgiy, and the poetry of Pushkin. Anna (the home attendant) was able to recite the poetry, which opened his heart to memory and joy. She was a God-sent, a young lady who was cooking for him the best Ukrainian dishes—a warm and caring lady that made him so happy.

She reminds him of the story "Pnin" of Vladimir Nabakov in imitation by Anna Akhmatova:

"Ya nadella temnoye plat'ye I monashki ya skromniy: Iz slonovoy kosti raspyat'ye Nad kholodnoy postel'yu moyey. No ogni nebyvalykh orgiy Prozhigayut moye zabyt'ye, I shepchu ya imya Georgiy - Zolotoye imya tvoye!"

The Russian poetry of Akhmatova, translated into English, reads: "I put on a dark dress and nuns. I'm more modest: Ivory crucifix above my cold bed. But the fires of unprecedented orgies Burn my oblivion, and I whisper the name George -your golden name!"

Last year, George was traveling to places in Eastern Europe and to some god-forgotten cemeteries to look for some long-dead people whom he never met and whom he knew only from old pictures. Maria was unhappy having to stay home and was always worrying about George's health.

He was always too busy for her. Adding some drama George didn't have a fear of anyone except Maria because her father was connected to her extended family in Little Italy in Manhattan—connected to the Mafia.

The Italian saying, "La Famiglia e Tutto," translated means: "The Family is Everything." That's the truth.

Maria's parents came from Calabria, at the toe of the boot of Italy. Every time she has pain in her foot, it reminds her of her place of ancestry in Calabria.

She traveled many times to Italy to rediscover her Italian roots.

"November 27th, Thanksgiving." George checked the calendar and saw that he was, in fact, correct about the date. He congratulated himself in his head. George refused to let himself lose track of the days. "If I lose my memory," George thought to himself, "who would take care of Maria?!

Some stranger? Not a chance in hell!"

Maria, George's wife, was suffering from Alzheimer's disease, which made her husband her caretaker—a job that George took on without complaint.

"For better or for worse, for richer, for poorer, in sickness and in health, to love and to cherish; from this day forward until death do us part. Love never fails." It is emotionally difficult to watch your spouse suffer–and at times, it may seem like your life has been reduced to nursing homes and hospital appointments."

It was a ring. George picked up his phone. This may be the only time that George was actually happy to pick up the little glass rectangle that seemed to own him more than he owned it.

He unlocked the phone. "Unlocked," George chuckled at the thought, "the only people that I don't want to get into this thing own it!" And George dialed his grandson

The two talked on the phone for a while before Alex arrived at his house. Shortly before they arrived, George was thinking, "It seems like I'm all alone. Thank the Lord that Alex is coming this Thanksgiving." A small nagging voice told George that it was only so that his grandson could secure his inheritance, but George ignored it.

Nicky, George's son, hadn't visited him in what felt like years!

George was thinking about his son's relationship through the years.

George decided to return to the places all over again to the moments where he had failed. He was among the "Dad guilt epidemic" and was thinking of all of the ways to overcome the feeling that he was a bad parent.

"My father may not have been perfect, but he did what he was best at: Being my dad. But I was just a bad father and a terrible son!"

Personally, George had twice attempted to untie this knot, first with his father and much later with his own son Nicky.

His favorite German novelist, Franz Kafka, reveals this about his father in "Letter to My Father."

"What was always incomprehensible to me was your total lack of feeling for the suffering and shame you could inflict on me with your words and judgments."

It was the psychology behind a strained father-son relationship similar to George and Nicky's relationship frozen in the past.

There's this cultural expectation that once you reach the legal age of an adult, then you should be moving out of the family home and providing for yourself.

Westerners have very big egos (to contain all that individuality), so it can feel cramped pretty quickly when there are too many adults in a limited space.

George wanted to be with his son, but he suddenly remembered this particular conversation long ago when Nicky was in college:

"Every look from you, Dad, makes me crazy. I feel that you do not approve of anything I do. I make my marks! Changing my major is disappointing for you and Mum. I feel guilty that I was not born into the right family. Why are you disappointed in everything I do!"

George replies:

"That is not true, my son! I'm sorry, Nicky if I offended you. I hope and pray for the best for you and your sister in your life!"

Independence is a part of the American psyche that remains with people throughout their lives. George and Nicky were the product of two different generations.

But Nicky answers every time: "I don't deliver according to your expectations. All this hurts me a lot. It hurts me, Daddy. Do you understand? You don't see me, Daddy, or everything I do!"

George took his own necklace of St. George, the Conqueror, and gave it to Nicky for good luck and protection to help in moments of need. It was to give him guidance in life. I always pray for the best for you and our family. I believe Saint George will be very near to help you out in any situation."

George was angry and left alone at this lonely nursing home. He was probably paying for his past sins...

When he escaped, he left his father and mother alone. Nicky was doing the same to him.

"What Goes Around... Comes Around."

Eventually, a knocking came from the door.

When George opened the door, the chaos of two young children erupted in the house.

"Pop, pop!" The two yelled in unison, though it was hard to tell, considering the incredible amount of noise that the two together were able to emit.

"Hello, George Jr. Hello, beautiful Mary! Hello, dear grandchildren," George said cheerily while the two children hugged his legs. Alex hurried in with a side dish while Elizabeth held the other. Alex hugged his grandfather while Elizabeth stood in the line to do the same.

The two ushered the children into another room to play while Elizabeth helped fix dinner. Before they visited, she was shopping in the supermarket.

Alex got George his favorite Bulgarian food. Many times, he complained about the nursing home and the terrible, tasteless food that they gave him.

He was depressed and had no appetite or joy for nothing. All his medications made him vomit and caused him heartburn; the whole body is protesting. Why is he still alive here on earth?

Alex got him his favorite food from the Bulgarian-Mediterranean store, but he responded as usual: "I'm old; I don't need anything. My soul is sorrowful, and I wish to die soon. Soon, I will die, and I will be forgotten. Everything I did was in vain. Maria doesn't remember me. I am here alone. My son, the Floridian from Miami, only calls and never comes to visit."

The big bird was in the oven. George still kept all of Maria's old turkey recipes. He likes the idea that all his children and grandchildren can be around him in the last days of the last chapter of his life.

After four hours of cooking, it was story time. He started to read from his book of memoirs to his grand-grandkids from the middle of the first chapter.

In 2020, the Kakhovskiy family was all together for Thanksgiving Day: Nicky, Margarita, Alex's sisters, Mary and Ellen, and little George Jr.

"Wow, honey! You have outshined yourself," said Nicky while looking at Roasted Turkey, Mashed Potatoes, Green beans, Casserole, Cranberry Sauce, and an expensive bottle of Pinot Grigio.

"What do we do before we dig in?" asked Margarita

George shows the grandchildren the framed portrait of their grandparents, Nicky and Margarita, next to him.

They were not all present today, but George loved to read about his happy memories with a leading smile.

"Say grace!" replied Mary, rolling her eyes, which made George give a soft but hearty laugh.

They all held hands, and Margarita started the prayer: "Oh Lord, with humble hearts, we pray for Thy blessings. On this

Thanksgiving, where grateful folk say words of grace, we thank you for your blessings–the food we eat and the people we greet. We pray Thy love will bless our hearts, our homes, and our feasts. Amen."

"Amen," uttered everyone in the chorus.

George's lips mumbled by heart the prayer of "Our Father in Heaven" and crossed himself to the manner of the Eastern Orthodox, kissing his crucifix and St. George's the Conqueror and old icon talisman of remembrance from his grandpa...

"Let's dig in," shouted George Jr. excitedly.

"What is the thing you guys like the most about Thanksgiving?" George asked him while pouring himself a glass of wine. "Duh," said Nicky, "Of course, food."

"That's surprising," George replied. "Why?" asked Alexander, who was listening to their conversation quite diligently.

"For me, it's not about the turkey or the stuffing or the mashed potatoes. These are delicious," George said as Margarita nodded at him. "Don't get me wrong, Margarita, Thanksgiving would not be the same without the food, but it is more about connecting as a family," Georg continued, "I was listening to Margarita as she said grace. She was right. We have to be thankful for everything – food, house, money, successful career, social status, and security. But, is it everything?"

"Dad, I know where it is going," said Nicky, shaking his head. "Yes, we know the drill," said Alexander with a grin.

"There are many people who have everything, yet they feel unsatisfied and empty from within."

"Isn't it, right?" George asked while digging his fork into a juicy piece of turkey.

"It could be," answered Mary, "but isn't that what the American dream is about?"

"No, Mary," replied Alexander confidently. "The American dream is the belief that people can acquire success regardless of their social class and race. That's what I like about the US. The country's values restore our faith that climbing the social ladder is a reality."

George chuckled, "For me, it is just a rat race."

"And why do you think it is wrong, Grandpa?" asked Alexander, gearing up for a debate, "Aren't we supposed to accomplish our goals?"

"I didn't say that, Alexander," George replied, "I am just worried about our obsession with the American Dream. Constant stress!" A silence descended as they had once again failed to understand George's critical point of view. George had often felt alone in this land of dreams. Perhaps because his dream never aligned with the ongoing pursuit of so-called exclusivity.

The American dream, to me, seems like a race. A race that I have been trying to understand since I landed in the US, George thought at that moment.

He always asked himself, why are the people running without even knowing their destination? Why are they tiring themselves unnecessarily? Life is not supposed to be only a race. There would be days when George would fight off my urge to tell his son and grandsons, who have assimilated according to the American cultural values, that they do not have to try so hard. They do not have to win anything. There is no competition. He wants them to stop. He wants them to realize that they are enough as they are. Easy said since George had retired a long time ago since he sold his auto shop repair business, "Nicky's."

It was easy to talk since he didn't need to get stressed over running the business. "Whenever someone mentions the 'American Dream' in front of me..."

This is a long story. I came to NEW YORK CITY in the 1950s.

In 2025, do Americans still believe in "the American Dream?" George was silent, wondering how tired he was after reading for so long. He was sad that he wanted his family, maybe on his last Thanksgiving, to be together with his son, Nicky, and daughter-in-law Margarita, Mary, Ellen, and George Jr., like in 2020.

At least his grandchildren and Alex's children were happy for someone to read their interesting stories.

He loves snuggling into the blanket Maria gave him as a gift when reading his memory stories—*that* he likes! It gives George space to think, and he likes having some alone time delving into another fantasy World back in Europe, away from the noise of day and life in general. Sometimes, George can imagine himself in the position of a main character, and it's nice that he can think of alternate endings and their thoughts when he's alone with a book.

Eventually, dinner was served. Elizabeth, being the saint that she was, walked Maria to the table and guided her through everything that was going on. George loved his wife to the ends of the earth, but it was nice to let someone else take care of her for a moment. "As long as it's someone that I can trust," he thought.

Alex pulled out the turkey from the oven and began carving it while talking to his grandfather across the room.

"And guess what it said, Grandpa?"

"What did it say, Alex?" George shot back.

"Enter your weight here!"

"Bah!" George exclaimed."Apparatus Apparatchik!"

"That is exactly what I said!" Alex exclaimed back. "It's like they're trying to know every single thing about every citizen!"

The two enjoyed how much this seemed to matter to one another. When Alex brought up the subject with his wife, she brushed it off as an air-safety thing. And George's wife, Maria, couldn't have too deep of conversations for too long without getting very tired.

"So," Alex began, "how've you been?"

"I've been fine." George, even in his old age, saw himself as a strong man, and he didn't like the idea of complaining about the end of his well-lived life. "I've been having the same dream about Lake Michigan. Nothing really happens; I just enjoy the place."

"I miss Lake Michigan too," Alex said. His grandfather didn't say it, but Alex could tell that he longed to go back. "I remember those summers were amazing." Alex stared off in recollection of the good times that he had on that lake.

"Oh yeah. And Jennifer?" George asked in a surprisingly facetious tone.

Alex chuckled. Ten years ago, he would have been peeved at the comment, but it was so long ago that Alex almost felt like he was laughing at a different person.

"Oh, what a nightmare that was!" Jennifer was Alex's summer girlfriend while he stayed at Lake Michigan. Before the summer ended, Alex found out that Jennifer was a socialist who liked to drink underage and smoke marijuana. When Alex became ready to accept her for these issues, she cheated on him.

What a girl?!

The two looked at Elizabeth. It seemed like now was the time to reminisce over poor Alex's relationships.

"And then along came Elizabeth," George said simply, staring across the room at Alex's wife. Elizabeth, at this time, was trying to talk with Maria.

"Oh yeah," Alex said. He seemed perfectly content while he lovingly gazed at his wife.

Alex and Elizabeth met each other in the Columbia Library while looking for the same book. It was Kasmet! Eventually, the two decided to start dating after getting along for a while, and then, eventually, the two fell in love and tied the knot.

Alex saw the historical ancestor's gift that he received from his grandparents on his wife's left hand. It was the engagement ring of Captain Georgiy Kakhovskiy, which he had given to his wife Anastasia, George's Greek grandma. This ring was from the time of the first imperial wedding to take place in Russia since the Russian October Socialist Revolution in 1917.

Alex and Ellie both graduated from Columbia University. Alex has a PH.D. in world history and political science. Elizabeth, in the major of Slavic Study, Russian Literature, and Art History.

Her family loves to visit Christie's auction house, the Russian Fine Arts Department, and Sotheby's, where they bid on Russian royal jewelry.

Elizabeth, Alex's wife, had an internship and was later accepted to work for one of the major galleries and auction houses, Sotheby's Russian Art Department (also in Christie's Magnificent Jewels auction in New York City).

Elizabeth was hired because of her parents' connections and grand interest in Tzar Peter the Great and Tzarina Catherine the Great. The new Russian oligarchs remembered that Lenin & Stalin sold all the Tzar Romanoff's jewelry for money.

Soviet Russia was ready to turn her crown jewels into American plows, tractors, and machinery, but today, the oligarchs want to buy them and bring them back to the museums in Moscow to be on display so everyone can see them where they belong.

Sotheby's and Christie's have both revealed to the Art Newspaper that they are canceling their upcoming London auctions of Russian art due to Russia's war on Ukraine. The auctions, typically held in June, had been favorites of Russian collectors and oligarchs.

Many times, Elizabeth received so many compliments, and her boss asked her about her engagement ring and her last name. Was she born in the US, or did her parents come from Russia, the previous USSR, or the Soviet Union? "Kakhovskiy is my husband's surname, and my wedding ring is a special gift from his grandfather from the Russian empire."

Her supervisor had the impression that she was the spoiled daughter of one of the Russian oligarchs, many of whose slavic names ending in suffixes "ski/sky/skiy", like Berezovsky, Khodorkovsky, or Medovsky, and who were valuable clients at the auctions.

Elizabeth possesses the original protestant puritan work ethic from British ancestry, which she had connections to working as a Christie's auction employee coming from her rich British old-money family from her maternal side; sure, her ancestors came from the Mayflower to the colonies a long time ago.

Alex was a third-generation immigrant. He gave Ellie his grandfather Captain Georgiy's priceless wedding ring, which made her more interested in Russian culture, so she studied Russian history.

Alex's family coming to America is not rich in ancestry jewelry and real estate like her grandfather (from the paternal side) Sir Lord Charles Williams, who was the "Last Pasha" defending the British crown's interests at the gate of Constantinople/ Istanbul against the Royal Russian army in 1878.

Whenever Alex goes over this love story in his head, he feels frustrated that there's no easy way to explain it; even with the love of his life, it wasn't easy! They had fights! With the good times, there were many bad ones.

"You know," Alex lowered his voice and was preparing to change topics into something much more serious.

"Ever since that out-of-body experience, I've been thinking about that red demon, Vasiliy."

"Mmm," George grunted in understanding. "He'll fall under the heel of our patron saint."

"Well," Alex continued, thinking aloud, "Do you remember the final part of the book of the prophet Daniel when he described the fall of Babylon?"

George did remember. His past few months in isolation had let him take proper time to study the scripture. "The Western empire peacefully surrendered to the East?"

"Yes!" Alex was excited someone was finally connecting with him on these concepts.

"This spy balloon in 2023 was shot down! The government reduced trade! And now–they're showing their military power to the point that no airline is daring to fly even remotely near them."

"It really does seem... like we are already peacefully surrendering to this king of the east," George said pensively. Part of him was glad that this wasn't his time.

"It almost reminds me of the fall of the Roman Empire from Grandpa Georgiy's diary!"

George shook his head, "that combined with the technology-advanced surveillance state of 1984."

"And a little bit of the hatred for learning from Fahrenheit 451," Alex said, remembering how everyone was so focused on mindless entertainment while glaring at him like the book that he was reading was an assault on their way of life after having a good time of Thanksgiving in freezing Chicago's nursing home.

Alex went off home to work in New York the next day.

The young man looked down at the skyscraper. Alex loved his office. From the view down from his office, Alex felt like he was on an island that could weather the waves of this modern absurdity.

Alex exhaled softly and looked at his watch. He couldn't stop thinking about his grandfather and the fateful out-of-body experience that he lived through with George. It was his lunch hour, so Alex decided that he would take a trip up to Brighton Beach to eat at a diner that he and his grandfather both loved.

The Brighton Beach station was located over Brighton Beach Avenue between Brighton 5th Street and Brighton 7th Street in Brighton Beach, Brooklyn. The station is always served by the Q & B train.

"My boss won't mind if I take a long lunch," Alex thought. His boss was the head of the company, so there was no problem if he wanted to let something slide.

Alexander took the train down to Brighton Beach, and it bore absolutely no resemblance to the place that he once loved.

Russian flags come down in New York's Little Odessa: Putin has turned it into a fascist symbol.

The New York neighborhood of Brighton Beach, home to a large ex-Soviet diaspora, opted to remove its plastic "Taste of Russia" sign.

For years, the sign for Taste of Russia, a grocery store in Brooklyn's Russian-speaking immigrant community of Brighton Beach, featured the distinctive domes of St. Basil's Cathedral in Red Square. But soon after Russian troops invaded Ukraine on the 24th of February, the owners of the shop took the sign down. In the window, they hung a large blue and yellow Ukrainian flag.

'Nobody supports this war,' here down on the Brighton Beach boardwalk, some anti-war Russians. In 30 years, Russians will no longer be allowed in Brighton.

Brighton Beach is changing from ex-Soviets and the Russian-Jewish population to a Latinos and Pakistani-Muslim majority.

For one, the diner was closed. Permanently. Instead, it was a shop named "Holy Pupusas."

"Ridiculous," Alex said to himself while looking around for other Russian or eastern-European-owned restaurants. It was at this moment that Alex fully looked around and realized what he was looking at. Not only were the once-new buildings of Brighton Beach worn by decades of business, but they weren't what Alex knew at all. There were still Russians and Ukrainians in Brighton Beach. But it was shifting towards the South American and Middle Eastern immigrants.

Alex kept walking. Eventually, he settled on a place and held the door for a woman wearing a black burqa from head to toe while pushing a stroller into the restaurant. He had a saddening lunch and decided that it was time to go back to work.

George was watching a Joe Rogan Experience clip. Rogan was arguing with a guest speaker on his show about whether President Joe Biden was developing dementia before seeing a new report.

Biden's disapproval hits new high as voters give him bad grades on the economy, a new CNBC/Change poll says, but believe that he must lead America again.

Later in October of that same year, a billboard was put up in Fayette County, Pennsylvania, which made the same claim, though it spelled dementia incorrectly.

"Biden's dementia is worsening; he is not fit," the billboard said.

Newsweek asked for comment but received no comment. Trump has decomposed a lot in the past couple of years. He is getting older.

Biden is eighty and has had two brain surgeries along the way, which affected his brain function. Aging is also affecting his brain. His minions tell him what to say—which is a common sign of a dangerous oligarchy.

George from the old school didn't understand what was happening with American youth today. He was worried about George Jr, who was involved in woke culture madness on the college campuses.

George said: "The only thing wokeness has to offer in exchange is to brainwash bright young minds." Since George was raised in a propaganda regime, he knows they like you to believe that you are victims, to believe that what you must do to improve the World is to complain, to protest, to throw soup on expensive paintings in museums, and so when you see somebody who is an adult talking to young people and being straight with them and saying,

"Look, if you care about certain issues in the World, if you care about climate change or racial injustice, whining and complaining is not going to fix that problem. We need young people to step up and actually work and build and create and invite new stuff..."

George thought that wokeness was Putin's weapon. Russia and China capitalize on the West's moral and political confusion.

It's getting even worse with President Biden's response to Hamas's terrorist attacks against Israel and Russia's ongoing brutal war with Ukraine. Also President Biden insists US can back two wars at the same time in Israel and Ukraine and be remembered as " a war president"

Decline is no longer a choice for the fading USA as China rises to power.

China is rapidly closing the gap on the US on the economic and military fronts as its geopolitical influence grows.

"Is this the last days of America and the end of the West as a superpower?"

This is surely just one more sign of the apocalypse. Or, at least,  the end of Western civilization. Alexander the Great conquered the known world at the age of twenty-five! What's your excuse, Alex?

Alexander the Great was known as cunning, ambitious, charismatic, and ruthless. His  13-year reign as king changed the course of world history!

"Macedonians today believe they are the rightful descendants of Alexander the Great. When do they speak Bulgarian and not speak the ancient language? It doesn't make sense. I'm not being a nationalist, and I'm simply looking for the truth."

During most of the period between the 7th and 14th centuries, the territory of today's North Macedonia was part of Bulgaria. In this period, there was no ethnic concept of "Macedonian," and there were no attempts to form a separate state of "Macedonia" from Bulgaria.

In the period from the 14th to the 19th century, the territory of almost the entire Balkan peninsula was under Ottoman slavery, including the territories of today's countries, Bulgaria and North Macedonia.

Only some Slav-Macedonian (North Macedonian) ultranationalists claim that Alexander was a Slav, while other Slav-

Macedonian ultranationalists only claim that he was not a Greek. Both are wrong, of course, because, as we know, the Slavs arrived in the Balkans in the 6th and 7th centuries AD, that's 1000 years after the demise of the ancient Greek kingdom of Macedonia, and because ancient Macedonians actually identified themselves as Greeks!

In 342 BC, Plovdiv was conquered by Philip II of Macedon, the father of Alexander the Great, who renamed it Philippopolis or "the city of Philip" in his own honor. Later, it was reconquered by the Thracians, who called it Pulpudeva (today, Plovdiv is Bulgaria's second-largest city).

Alexander the Great's legacy is both far-reaching and profound. First, his father was able to unite the Greek city-states, and Alexander destroyed the Persian Empire forever. More importantly, Alexander's conquests spread Greek culture, also known as

Hellenism, across his empire.

George remembers that history is the Battle of Thermopylae, hundreds of miles from his grand grandma, Anastasia's birthplace in Greece. Grandma Anastasia was proud of Ancient Greece as the cradle of Western civilization with a legacy that echoes through time as their profound contributions to philosophy, democracy, and culture. She always talks about her lost Greek inheritance later in her life. She hates the evil Turks who stole her national heritage, like Hagia Sofia in Constantinople, parts of Macedonia, Thracia, and part of Crete, the Island in the Mediterranean Sea.

A rear-guard action by Spartan King, Leonidas, and 300 hand-picked men. He chose only warriors who already had sons to carry on the family name as he knew everyone would die in battle. He and his small band repelled thousands of Persians at Thermopylae down the "hot gates," a mountain pass too narrow for much of anything but an ox cart.

In a word, class-cists, the culture over, should rejoice at the chance to correct the caricature till you all play on wokeness. The western civilization is falling down. We need our "the 300" moment and what you will do about it.

"Trump declares that progressives are getting crazy."

"All the Barbarians arrived at the gate. The West is under a severe attack within itself. The Romans destroyed their republic in Partisan warfare. Why don't you think we can do it too?"

"Because of Government corruption and political instability, the arrival of the Huns, the migration of the Barbarian tribes, and Donald Trump's unleashing of an armed mob on the Capitol to overturn an election on January 6, 2021, was a stark warning of the fragility of democracy," Alex thought.

Grandpa George felt like he understood Biden very well. The stuttering and rigid movement. George has the same condition sometimes when he walks and speaks.

George continued browsing the news. He read a report that the US-Russian war is frigid. The US-Russian ambassador compared the relations between the two to an "ice age," and he expressed that the risk of the two clashings was unbelievably high.

"Bah! Who cares about American politics," George said. He had long ago lost trust in the US politicians that, time and time again, promised that they would keep people safe. George had things to do beyond listening to mindless news. George completed his morning routine, took his medicine, and took care of his wonderful Maria, who was in the next room.

On the other hand, George was always having a conversation with his uninvited guest: On the other hand, George was always having a conversation with his uninvited guest: His relative's great-great uncle, who became a demon. The two were alone in their nursing home. Maria didn't remember George, but he would never forget her. Alex was always too busy to call or visit George. He seemed to have forgotten George's sole bucket list item of finishing up his book. George might be the only remaining primary source on which Alex could complete the book of memoirs. It was supposed to begin long ago and then go through four generations of family before arriving at the new Americans.

"A living document," George thought. "A living document of the Kakhovskiy family history! How wonderful would that be? I want this legacy, but I don't have much time!"

When he's stressed, George will remember the water. He loves the water—it seems to connect all things.

He remembered the water of the river Maritza, which he would swim against to become strong as a boy. That same water helped George escape into a new World of hope!

He remembered the lapping waters on the edge of Brighton Beach that a young George would watch every day as he went home from his first job as a car mechanic. George, even to this day, could swear that the light and soothing waves on that beach were a promise from God that everything was going to be okay.

Finally, the waters of Lake Michigan. The lake was so vast that it was larger than Bulgaria's Black Sea. George still remembers seeing Lake Michigan for the first time and being shocked that Americans would call such a thing a "Lake."

George kept thinking while relaxing in his chair. He recalled the journal that he kept with him while he traveled all across Europe, from the gates of Constantinople to the gates of Sevastopol to the gate of Varna. *"All the gates,"* George said to himself, laughing. George felt pride in the different places in which he connected the different parts of his family's history throughout Europe.

In the Nursing Home, George felt the demon spirit of his granduncle, Vasiliy's dark and evil presence, the same way that he felt him when he was sixteen years old. He had a terrible night and terrible dreams about the Devil as a bloody snake who disturbed his dreams. His grandparents started to teach him the Bible about Saint George, who was his protector at this age, just before he escaped the border.

This was the time when George began to stop believing in God, since he denounced in praying that God exists, and George was so angry with God because he didn't save his grandfather, Captain Georgiy when George believed that God would save him. And now, he felt the same evil presence of Vasiliy. This constant fear of evil followed him in his life. He believed that the World is not governed by a good God but by an evil god. Every time his family had to escape to unknown places, every time they had to be refugees, every time they had to build up life again and again when George arrived in America, the evil was there.

Even today in America, religion is for the old people, the stupid, the dumb, the uneducated. Like him, it was the opium of the masses back in communist Bulgaria.

George still remembers the book *The Master and Margarita,* his father's favorite book by Mikhail Bulgakov.

His father lost his son, George, who escaped the border. He was in constant pain and started taking morphine. He was addicted, and many times in his life, he didn't see hope for the future. For him, the World was governed by an evil god.

He blamed God, who didn't help him.

This morning, George seemed to blame God for his life and circumstances again.

George felt his dark, heavy presence.

"Are you ready? today will be your last day." Vasiliy asked George, like a devil on his shoulder. "Mha ha ha ha ha!"

"Are you still here to trouble me early in the morning?" responded George.

"I don't want to be here, but from the end of the Earth, you are calling me; your anger, everything you do attracts me to be here. You are calling me constantly! It's not my fault I am here!"

George knew about the tricks of Vasiliy the demon, the power of death, sickness, and disease that he was carrying. "The disease was in my body, and its attacks against my health were constant. And each time, it weakened my defenses against it, and it was worse than before."

"The sickness took its toll on me, and I lost my desire to fight to live. And I asked the Lord to take me home and give up the ghost. I was dying before my appointed time."

But George knew that he was more than a conqueror, including a victory over Vasiliy, death, and sickness.

George knew how to walk in the victory of his Lord and his patron, St George, to fulfill his earthly destiny & mission.

The last few weeks of George's life were full of physical and emotional changes. Near death is approaching.

This was a time when his relatives and friends felt they were waiting with a sense of anticipation. You may feel like you've 'had enough.' Thoughts and feelings like this are normal and very common among family members and people providing care.

"Did you know Alex remembers his grandpa's story: "An oyster that has not been wounded in any way does not produce pearls? A pearl is a healed wound. Pearls are a product of pain, the result of a foreign or unwanted substance entering the oyster, such as a parasite or a grain of sand."

"The inside of an oyster shell is a shiny substance called 'nacre.' When a grain of sand enters, the nacre cells go to work and cover the grain of sand with layers and more layers to protect the defenseless body of the oyster. As a result, a beautiful pearl is formed! The more pearls, the more valuable... God never allows pain without a purpose."

It takes many years of pressure, stress, good times, and bad times before you can achieve the honor of being a "diamond."

Anything in life that is worth having takes time, pressure, and work.

Unlike coal, though, we don't want to wait.

A diamond is a piece of coal that is stuck to the job.

What if your greatest help to others comes out of your greatest hurt or your deepest wounds?

Amen for all the sacrifices, hardships, and challenges George dealt with, faith, hope, and perseverance. At the end of all these, you will come out shining and precious like pearls, hardened but beautiful and priceless.

Today was that final day.

The veil was removed. George met his long-passed-away ancestors' welcoming committee. All of George's relatives were happy to meet George. Even the elderly relatives who never saw him came to him, welcoming, embracing, and kissing George.

Finally, George crossed over. On earth, he was a survivor! He survived as a premature baby. He survived the Cold War. He survived Communism and oppression in Bulgaria! He survived the bloody massacre at the border of Greece. He survived an immigrant life in NEW YORK CITY. He lived to see the fall of the Berlin Wall. He survived to see the rise and fall of Pax

Americana. He started to worry about his offspring in America, who didn't have a place to escape should China become *the* world superpower.

Last night, he had a dream. "One more day!" He was told. George was given his last twenty-four hours to say goodbye to his loved ones.

Before, when George was younger, he was proud and would say that he was complete, but something was missing in his life. What was that? Even his plot in the Ukrainian cemetery was purchased, and the memorial stone ordered—a black granite monument in the shape of an arrow with gold-painted letters of both his and Maria's full names. He didn't want to be a burden on the family, even though he had life insurance to take care of times like these.

George was a survivor of near-death experiences and shared 'afterlife' stories, but this time, he was staying forever.

"There were some presences there. There were some ladies... I didn't know them at the time... They were so loving and so wonderful, and I just didn't want to come back... I didn't see any pictures of them until I was an adult, but then I said, 'Oh, yeah.'... They were my great-grandmother Anastasia and mother Emma, who had died years ago."

George was welcoming, too.

Alex was sitting next to Grandpa. He didn't understand what was going on but still held his hand in prayer.

"When my time comes, dear Lord, please just make it easy and quick."

It is George's last request.

"He saw strange visions and long-time passed away relatives who he knew from the old album pictures. From far away, George saw his grandpa, Captain Georgiy, with his old uniform, approaching him with excitement and joy. Behind him walked his father, Dr. Alexander, Emma, and his brother Dimitar, who said a warm hello.

He saw his younger sister walking behind his mother, Emma, who had died when his mother miscarried at three months. He could see that his sister's soul was happy because his parents gave her a name, Anastasia, and she could rejoin the family, and God added to his family.

George's mission to hell was not in vain. In heaven, nothing was missing. No one can snatch his parents out of his Father's hand."

George heard he was full of love and joy entering Paradise. He heard that God fulfilled all his prayers and heart's desires on His right. When you don't understand what God is doing in your life as a child, you do not know the work of God, who makes everything in your life perfect. George's books and prayers help parents to understand and come to their senses and faith so they can spend an eternity with him.

Far away, he was able to see the dark figure of his grand uncle, Vasiliy, trying to mount the family.

As legends tell it, Saint George was a red dragon-slayer.

It was the symbol that one day, Captain Georgiy would slay the demon of his brother, Vasiliy, as his constant fearsome enemy.

Soon, St. George will put him under his feet. Trust in God!

Alex didn't understand what was going on, but he felt peace all around.

But after days of confusion, breathing, and seeing strange angels in the room, the family gathered to say a final goodbye to their beloved grandpa.

Alex heard George's favorite Vangelis Soundtrack of 1492: "The Conquest of Paradise," in his heart when they both entered Paradise during their visit to Heaven in the unexpected crash car accident in 2008.

After a long and eventful life, George ends up in this cursed nursing home. Looks like this is the last stop in his life. Not only did George witness some of the most important events of the twentieth and twenty-first centuries, but he also had a larger-than-life story to tell.

His life story started from the beginning.

George did witness some of the most important moments of the twentieth and twenty-first centuries, but he also had a larger-than-life story to tell. He remembers he was born in 1932, five years before 1937, the beginning of World War II (WWII), as were many from the "Silent Generation.

George was able to share his life's memoirs from the end to the beginning in his last chapter, "The End of All Things," about his emigrant experience when he was a big 93-year-old in the last days of the last chapter of his life on November 27, 2025, amidst his birthday and thanksgiving celebration in the freezing Chicago nursing home. He had the company of his grandson, Alex, grand-daughter-in-law, Elizabeth, and the great-grandkids, Georgie Jr. and Marry, who visited from NEW YORK CITY, along with a few elderly Bulgarian friends who were much younger than George but still had respect for him because of what he did for the Bulgarian community. George didn't have too many true friends, except that ex-pat from his village who would speak his Southern Bulgarian dialect, "Real friends, who you can trust, not like these cold Americans." George believed that he would come at the last moment of his life to close his eyes for eternity.

Not everyone gets to say goodbye to the people they love before they die. Seize the chance if one seems to present itself, so you never have to wish you had told them something. Tell the person you love them and what you have loved about them. You might share special memories, activities, or places you remember.

Consider saying these things:

I love you. I am sorry for any difficulties I have caused you. I forgive you for any hurt I perceive you to have caused me. Thank you." There is more joy in heaven over one person who repents on earth.

Eternally on the right side was St. George, who slammed Vasiliy the dragon, who stayed on his left all the time.

But thanks to the God of Peace, he will crush Satan at his time and put that old snake under his feet shortly. Remember, you can always overcome Evil with Good.

What George waited to hear after his entire life: "Well done, good and faithful servant" when he will arrive in heaven.

Finally, George heard this: "WELCOME home, son!"

The End.

# Conclusion

Letter from a grandfather on his last day in the nursing home:

"Dear fortunate next generation," George wrote, "On my 93rd birthday, November 27th, 2025, I want to thank God, and I wanted to bless all my grandchildren with these words of encouragement!"

"Follow the call of your heart! When moving forward in life, you must believe in something greater than you must to discover your true destiny. Even if you happen to find yourself in a dark place, don't be afraid. Even if life leads you into darkness, God will light the path before you through His Word. He will direct your steps day by day."

Remember, you are part of the Spirit of God, you have a soul, and you have been stuck in a body that can only be in one place at a time. Don't forget you are here only temporarily; your time on Earth is limited. Therefore, use it wisely, and don't waste it doing stupid things or being dramatized in somebody else's life. Listening to other people's opinions will always drown the call of your inner voice! I don't recommend any key to your success, but I know from my own experience that the key to failure is to try to please everybody else around you. You must discover your gift, which is deep inside of you and which will inspire you along the way.

Your work by which you'll make a living will be a significant part of your daily life, but even more important will be the work that you love to do out of your deepest desires, not just because you are compelled to do it. If you have not discovered it yet, don't settle for anything. Follow the "little voice" of your heart as God already lives there, gently knocking on the door of your soul.

In life, you are going to have both ups and downs. Some people say that our earthly life is a happy abode covered with flowers, while others justly assert that it is a dirty and disgusting place. But no matter how nasty it could be, life will only put you down on your knees if you would allow that to happen. Most people don't stand up firmly for themselves, giving up without a fight, even before a trial has started knocking on their door.

On the other hand, do you have the slightest idea how powerful your human spirit is? There is nothing more substantial on this planet than your spirit. In fact, it is practically indestructible. Of course, any person can feel on top of the world when all things are perfect in his life—if he happens to have good health, a lot of money in the bank, and a happy family. In situations like this, anybody can have a positive attitude and be a believer. The faith of any person can be substantial under such ideal circumstances. But the real test of growth, of spiritual and emotional maturity, comes at a time when life has delivered you a knockout blow.

You will need the courage to be able to stand up on your feet and continue forward. You need to be a man to come back after another knockout blow. You will need the utmost manliness to stand up after the defeat and start all over again.

You are given a chance to do something more. Otherwise, the worst thing that could happen to you is to remain as mediocre as many others. This is not a joke! Fear destroys dreams! Fear destroys even our last hope for life! Fear strikes down people on a sickbed for a long time! Fear will age you prematurely! Fear will rob you of the opportunity to live a real life. Certain things are dormant and waiting inside of you, and deep down, you know well that you can do them. After all, your feelings or job do not determine who you are.

But despite everything, behind any failure lies a promise for a new beginning. Many people are not where they should be in their lives because they have been "arrested" by powerful negative feelings.

"How do you feel?"

"I feel very depressed today! I don't feel like getting up and going to work this morning."

Is there a person in the World who feels excited about

waking up?

It's appalling to keep saying day after day "no" to your dreams, and that is because of persistent procrastination, the fear of the unknown, or the lame excuses. Maybe that's the reason why you hold them back from being accomplished for a whole year or a couple of years, or even for longer, because of this one day when you didn't feel like getting up on time.

"I don't feel well today! I'm not ready to do anything!"

Never allow your feelings to control you! Even though we have been created as emotional beings, we must begin to discipline our emotions. Unless we train them and bring them into submission to our will, they will do with us whatever they please. If you want something that badly, you will have to pursue your dreams and train your emotions to work for you, not you for them. It is not that easy for a person to be transformed in the blink of an eye. A firm decision and a long time are needed to break the bad habit and replace it with a good one. Had it been so easy, then everybody would be doing it without a problem. But if you are seriously intent on living out every moment of your life in a real way, you will have to show who the boss is in your life.

I will not let any circumstance or difficulty destroy me. However, I have been knocked down only temporarily. I will do everything I can to get up on my feet again, I will shake the dust off me, and I will continue forward, much stronger than before. I will come back stronger from my defeat!

Our mistakes are the teachers who teach us not to fall into the same trap again and again when passing near it. You must declare to the whole World what you believe, that you are standing firmly on the principles of the Word of God, and that God's healing belongs to you according to His promises of abundant life. Based on the Bible's principles, declare to your family that you have taken full responsibility for your life. It's up to you to decide how you are going to continue living from now on.

You are the one who should take full responsibility for your decisions and live your life as if today were your last day here on Earth. Even in your hurried daily routine, always make time for God because He will always be there for you to guide you. Live your life with inspiration every day, even if you will need to push yourself a little. The last chapter of your life has not been written yet. How much does what happened to you yesterday matter? What matters is what you are going to do about it today. Your dream will come true because there are no impossible things! Through Jesus Christ, you are more than a conqueror, and you can cope with any difficulty in your life because He gives you the power to overcome any challenge, whatever it might be!

*Remember:*

*Never give up!*

The End.

# About the Author

Kiril Kristoff is a physical therapist and acupuncturist by trade and a "healer" by calling. Mr. Kristoff has a postgraduate degree in Oriental Medicine from the Tri-State College of Acupuncture in New York City, as well as an undergraduate degree in Physical Therapy.

Kiril's memoirs were first published in his native language of Bulgarian, and are now available in the updated English version with the help of his son.

Kiril lived the first twenty-seven years of his life in his homeland, Bulgaria, before spending the past thirty in the United

States. For his first years, Kiril and his family lived in Brighton Beach in South Brooklyn, New York. The first half of this time in America was spent pursuing the "American Dream" in New York. The latter half was spent living in suburban New Jersey with his wife, two daughters, and his son.

Kiril has written memoirs: "In Search of the Roots, At the Crossroads of Life: A Testimony of Faithfulness to God," and "The Memoirs of My Father's Son, The Journey to Freedom."

He is a member of the Bulgarian Writers League in America.